Rave reader reviews for *RUSH*

'Very well written, and the relationship between our protagonist and her love interest was captivating . . . I would definitely recommend'

'A compulsive read that was hard to put down'

'It was fire. So loved this'

'Totally absorbed in the world of Lena and Nico'

'I love how this story celebrates relationships that buoy women emotionally without breaking their spirit'

'Couldn't stop reading'

'I enjoyed this one . . . I absolutely would read more from this author'

'I devoured this book over the course of two days . . . an absolute pageturner'

Saskia Roy is an award-winning writer and journalist. She has written for *The New York Times*, *The Guardian*, *The Times* and the BBC, but cut her teeth writing about sex and relationships for a monthly glossy magazine. Saskia started reading Jackie Collins far too early, and has been a Formula 1 fan for over twenty years. She has been stunned by the sport's soaring popularity following Netflix's *Drive to Survive* and brings together her two passions in *Rush*.

For more information visit saskiaroy.co.uk and follow her on Instagram and X at @saskiaroybooks

Rush

SASKIA ROY

ONE PLACE. MANY STORIES

HQ
An imprint of HarperCollins*Publishers* Ltd
1 London Bridge Street
London SE1 9GF

www.harpercollins.co.uk

HarperCollins*Publishers*
Macken House, 39/40 Mayor Street Upper,
Dublin 1, D01 C9W8, Ireland

This edition 2024

24 25 26 27 28 LBC 6 5 4 3 2
First published in Great Britain by
HQ, an imprint of HarperCollins*Publishers* Ltd 2024

ISBN: 978-0-00-865613-3

This book is set in 10.7/15.5 pt. Sabon by Type-it AS, Norway

Printed and Bound in the United States

For Jackie. Thank you for the good times.

Content warnings

This story contains explicit sexual content,
morally grey characters, coercive behaviour, and
topics that may be sensitive to some readers.

Chapter 1

Lena Aden pulled the wet clump of mail from her tiny postbox. She sorted through soggy leaflets and pizza menus, peeling them apart to check in between. LA really didn't know how to deal with rain. That's one thing that could be said for her hometown of London: a perpetually drizzly place that didn't lose its mind in a rainstorm. LA in comparison felt damp and moody, tilted off its natural groove.

She discarded the leaflets in a cardboard box that lay in one corner of the foyer. A heavy cream envelope escaped her grip and fell to the muddy floor. Her heart skittered when she saw the logo: three elegant letters in blue, spelling out the name of the top screenwriting agency in Hollywood, WME. She picked it up gingerly and quietly chided herself for getting so excited. It was going to be bad news. Of *course* it was. These neat squares of rejection arrived on a regular basis, but still she dared to dream. If that wasn't allowed in this city, well, then there'd be no one left in LA. She slid a finger beneath the seal and opened it carefully. This could be the moment that changed her life and she wanted to remember the details. She touched the paper inside: thick, and heavy with quality. Surely they wouldn't waste it on a rejection?

That was the problem with trying to make it here. Like a lovelorn suitor, you read outsize meaning into tiny detail: *'he looked at me after that punchline, so I must be the one he likes'*, or *'he added a kiss emoji so surely that means he's interested'*. Lena pulled out the letter and allowed herself to envision the words: *we loved your script, we loved your script, we loved your script*. Maybe 'manifesting' could magic the response she so desperately needed.

She held her breath and read it: 'Though there was much to admire we unfortunately didn't feel strongly enough to be able to offer representation at this time. Due to the volume of pitches we receive, we cannot give individual feedback.'

The air shrank in her lungs, thinned by disappointment. You had to be resilient to make it in this city, but every rejection hurt. Every time she was told that she wasn't quite good enough, it tightened something inside her: an anxiety that told her, *you said five years. You said five years and then you'd leave.* When she had moved to LA at the age of twenty-five, she had vowed that she wouldn't spend her thirtieth birthday in her crappy flat. If she hadn't made it by then, she'd reasoned, she would return to the UK with her tail between her legs and do the law conversion course that awaited her there. Her deadline was five months away – and it wasn't merely theoretical. Lena had a place at the prestigious LSE, but her scholarship was only available to those under thirty. If things didn't change here soon, she would have to give up and go back. The thought of her mother's disdain at all these wasted years and the quiet smugness of all her old friends lined her stomach with dread. She ripped up the letter and threw it in the bin, then stared at it morosely, paralysed by this feeling.

'Lena,' called a voice behind her.

She turned to find her housemate in the foyer, shaking the rain from her hair. 'Hey. What are you doing here? Aren't you meant to be on a job?'

Johanna tutted. 'The photographer didn't turn up, the fucking cokehead, so we were sent home. We're not even getting paid for fuck's sake.'

'Oh shit. I'm sorry.'

Johanna waved it off. She sidled up to Lena and grabbed her arm chummily. 'So! I've got a thing tonight. Will you come?'

Lena sighed. Johanna, a model, was sent frequent invitations to events and parties. She would arrive home each evening and offer them to Lena like a fistful of daisies: a film premiere, charity gala, or launch of a luxury handbag. Tonight, it was a 'Come as You Are' party for Gucci, most likely at some bland white mansion overlooking the hills. Being seen was part of Johanna's job and she often cajoled Lena into accompanying her – at least until she found someone else she knew.

'I can't. I have to be at the Aston.'

Johanna pursed her lips. Though twenty-seven, she still looked like a teenage girl – a fact that kept her in work despite being practically geriatric in the fashion industry. 'Come *on*,' she said. 'You've got a whole team there. Just bail and come with me.'

'I'm not going to do that.'

'Well, what time do you finish?' she asked petulantly.

Lena checked her watch to make sure she wouldn't be late. 'I work six 'til eight. You *know* this.'

'Okay, well, forget the Gucci thing. How about this party at Tag Heuer? It starts at eight but won't get going 'til ten at the least?'

Lena hesitated. 'We've been out a lot lately.'

'Isn't that why you moved to LA?' said Johanna, with such excessive drama, one might think her an actress. Lena envied her for all the things that Lena was not: fun, spontaneous, carefree. People spoke of misspent youths, but Lena had had an *unspent* youth, too busy upholding the strict moral code of her conservative upbringing. LA was meant to be an antidote so when Johanna said those words, it felt like a correction: a reminder of why she had come out here five years ago, leaving an ailing career as a freelance writer to try her hand at the stage and screen. Everyone had told her that LA was different; not as classist as London where her English degree from a mid-tier uni was treated with disdain.

'Well?' Johanna pressed.

Lena threw up her hands. 'Fine,' she relented.

'Oh, yippee!' Johanna dipped into a mock English accent and clapped daintily.

Lena rolled her eyes. 'So I'll see you back here at eight fifteen?'

'Yes, we'll need time to sort . . .' She waved at Lena's outfit – an old pair of jeans and loose grey vest. 'Whatever this is.'

'Okay,' Lena said gamely and turned to go.

'Oh and one more thing,' Johanna called just as Lena reached the threshold.

She turned, propping open the door with an elbow. 'Yes?'

'There will be lots of eligible bachelors there so we need to turn up the smoke show.'

Lena shook her head, but then laughed as the door swung shut behind her.

*

The Aston Theatre was a crumbling old building that looked like it was on the wrong coast – all New York redbrick and curved iron balconies. The year 1922 was printed in smoky black letters above the panelled door, announcing the theatre a hundred years old. A dark stain ran along the piping and the pediment above a window was chipped. It desperately needed renovation, but Aston was a community theatre and funding for the arts was fiercely contended. Film and literature had been a lifeline for so many when the world stopped for two years, but art was still regarded a luxury; a thing posh kids did in lieu of law, medicine, accountancy. This wasn't entirely wrong, of course. The arts were filled with boys and girls whose dads ran so-and-so bank or so-and-so conglomerate. Lena, in comparison, had come from poverty and it sickened her to think that the thing she loved most in the world – to write – was likely to keep her there. She and Johanna could slide into their executive Ubers dressed in complimentary haute couture and pretend that they lived the high life, but they went back home to a flat that was dark and cramped. She was so tired of living like that, so determined to make something happen. She couldn't go on like this. She knew it was all too easy for five years to turn into ten, or fifteen, and before she knew it, she would be one of those seventy-year-old women prancing around in community theatre, her frustrated ambitions as loud and obvious as the zany bracelets that clinked on her wrist. No, these five months was it for her – her last chance saloon.

She pulled open the door to the theatre and was hit with the smell of sawdust and bergamot. She walked into the writers' room, really a glorified broom cupboard. It felt close and humid after the surprise springtime rain.

'Okay, settle this for us, Lena,' said Ahmed, a twenty-four-year-old hipster whose beard was often mistaken for religious. 'Best fictional detective. Sherlock Holmes or Poirot?'

Lena scoffed. 'Wrong and wrong. It's obviously Columbo.'

Gloria clicked her fingers. 'How did we forget Columbo?' A forty-something import from Miami, she had leathery skin that lined when she spoke.

'I reckon it's Holmes,' said Ahmed.

Gloria clucked derisively and the two of them began to bicker as Lena set up her laptop. They waited for Brianna, the leader of their ragtag group. Formally, they each had roles – Brianna, the director; Ahmed, the audiovisuals; Lena, the writer; and Gloria, the set and costume designer – but they all pitched in by necessity. Their funding was scant and they each took home a nominal wage with little margin for extra staff.

Brianna strode in and sat at the head of the table. She was in her late fifties and had the mien of a serious auteur: pinched mouth and frequent scowl. Ahmed and Gloria often aped her secretly, but they all had an abiding respect for her. She was sharp and incisive, and unafraid to check egos when needed. Today, she seemed especially tense.

'Okay, kids, I have some news.' She squared the edges of the script in front of her. 'I'm afraid to say that we've lost our Mogford funding.' Her formal tone slipped a little, revealing unease beneath. 'They've had a couple of awful years and are cutting back on charitable activities.'

Lena felt a spike of anxiety. The Aston was already teetering on the edge of oblivion. To lose their biggest funder would surely send them tumbling.

Brianna cleared her throat. 'Now obviously, this isn't good for the theatre, but we have options. We're going to seek emergency funding, but that's not guaranteed. So . . .' She took an audible breath, bolstering herself. 'We have got to give *Please Understand* everything we've got. If it doesn't turn a profit, we're going to be in real trouble.'

Lena bristled. *Please Understand* was her first full-length stage show. To put it under so much pressure felt unduly daunting. The play was a two-hander with a yet-to-be-cast eleven-year-old girl who acts as a translator for her immigrant father who cannot speak English. The girl, an aspiring footballer called Hana, helps her dad at a hospital appointment and its attendant challenges. She is both proud of her role and cowed by it, shrinking visibly when she can't understand a word like *cyst*. Hana speaks to the audience about the fears and frustrations of navigating systems like the NHS and HMRC, in a language her dad can't understand. The play was an homage to the East London of Lena's childhood and the people with whom she grew up. It was the best thing she had written, but to task it with saving the theatre felt like certain failure.

Brianna rapped the table with her knuckles. 'But let's not let that distract us,' she said. 'We've got a job to do so let's do it.' She motioned at the script and turned to a scene in which Hana clashes with some bailiffs.

The team worked diligently, but their camaraderie had a forced quality as if they themselves were reading off a script. Midway through the evening, after her third cup of coffee, Brianna shook her head as if losing an argument with herself.

'I think we have a problem, kids.' She tapped the script. 'It's bugged me all throughout and I think we need to fix it. Right now, our girl, Hana, is talking to the audience in English and the idea is that her dad can't understand her – but why can't he see the audience? It feels too contrived. Can we find a way to do this more naturally?'

Ahmed frowned. 'But actors break the fourth wall all the time.'

'Yes, but as a *break* from the action. Here, it happens *in parallel* to the action, so why doesn't the dad notice?'

Lena instantly saw the problem. Something about the structure had bothered her too and Brianna had just pinpointed the issue. For the next hour, they worked on the problem to no avail. Just as they approached the end of the session, Lena had an idea.

'What if Hana is talking *to* her dad?'

Brianna frowned. 'But he can't understand her.'

'That's fine. Maybe he's trying to, or maybe he's humouring her. Maybe he thinks she's being playful or silly – but really she's expressing all these frustrations that she can't be honest about and so is speaking to him in English so she doesn't hurt him. She does an adult job and has to think about these adult things.'

Brianna considered this, then broke into a rare grin. 'That could work. It's so simple but elegant.' She laughed a little, surprised by the solution. 'That's actually a brilliant idea.'

Lena beamed, warmed by the praise. There were days – so many days – when she doubted if she was actually good. When you had tried so hard and for so long with only rejection to show for it, it was hard not to blame yourself. These small seeds of praise were just enough sustenance.

'I think we're gonna do it, kids.' Brianna's spirits lifted. 'I think we're gonna save this grand old place.'

Lena felt a thrum of hope. Maybe this would be her ticket to the big time. She had come to LA to do big things. With five months of runway left, maybe she was finally on her way.

*

Johanna smoothed her dress, a burnt-orange sheath that skimmed her frame and made her blonde hair seem fiery. Usually, Lena felt ungainly next to her waif-like housemate, but today she felt feminine; maybe even sexy. The two of them had prodded her body into one of Johanna's sample sizes and though it had initially seemed impossible, it somehow fit her perfectly. The racing-green silk was liquid on her skin. Cut-out panels at the waist exposed her light brown tone and the asymmetrical neckline showed off her shoulder and collarbone. Her dark hair was in a loose chignon while Johanna's practised hand had made her features more pronounced: her eyes seemed bigger, her delicate cheekbones sharper, her subtle brows darker. Lena marvelled at what an expensive dress and good heels could do. Maybe tonight she could hold her own after all.

'Are we going to be late?' asked Lena, checking her watch. 'It's already nine thirty.'

'Relax. This party will go on all night.' Johanna snaked an arm around Lena's waist. 'You look fucking stunning.'

Lena rolled her eyes. 'Yeah, until I stand next to you and your model mates.'

'Fuck off with your false modesty.'

Lena accepted this with a diffident nod and leaned into her friend. 'Thank you for bringing me along.' She often griped about these outings, but without Johanna, she could have easily slipped into loneliness. It was a hazard in LA. Everyone seemed to have more friends than you and, with them, a better time.

Johanna ordered an Uber and they gingerly descended the stairs. The elevator was out of commission as usual. Outside, Lena was hit with humidity, the surprise rain long steamed off the pavement. As they waited for their ride, two men paused nearby. They were both about six feet tall, athletic, and sweaty as if they'd just left a basketball court.

'Evening, ladies,' said one of them, the more muscular of the two.

Johanna smiled. 'Evening, boys,' she said with a hint of amusement.

The men bristled with possibility. Lena knew how easily

Johanna did this, but was still amazed by the effect of a mere two words from her lips.

'Where are you off to?'

'A party,' Johanna answered, still smiling. That was the thing about her. She was fun and forthright; none of this coy *wouldn't you like to know*, or playing it cool and aloof. She was open about the fact that she liked the attention.

The second man looked at Lena. 'I'm Jake and this is Ben,' he said. The slight catch in his voice made her smile instinctively and she saw him react to it. Maybe she had it too, whatever *it* was. Only, she couldn't turn it on at will. Lena's conservative upbringing meant she was always too rigid and wary for the push and pull of effortless flirting.

'Where's the party at?' asked Ben.

'In the hills. It's an industry thing.'

'Can we come?'

Johanna laughed – a playful, teenage sound. 'I'm afraid not, boys, but I hope you enjoy your evening.'

'Can I get your number?' asked Ben.

Johanna considered this. 'Tell you what: give me yours and we'll see where that takes us.' As the two of them flirted, Jake turned back to Lena.

'See, he's beaten me to the punch so now if I ask for your number, I'll look like I'm just copying him.'

Lena held up a palm. 'Oh, I'm sorry, I'm just passing through.'

'How long are you here for? I'd love to show you around.'

'Oh, that's okay,' she said evasively.

Jake gave her a sheepish look. 'It was worth a try, but I guess a girl like you wouldn't even spit on a guy like me.'

'No, I would,' said Lena. 'I'd spit on you.'

The other two happened to fall silent at the very same moment and looked over curiously. She read the message on Johanna's face. *Girl, you need to seriously work on your game.*

Their Uber beeped, cutting into the conversation.

'Call me maybe,' Ben said to Johanna. She gave him an arresting smile and slid into the Uber. Lena raised an awkward hand at Jake.

He puckered his lips in regret. 'Have a nice night.'

Lena got in the car and the door caught on her seatbelt the first time round. She pulled it free and tried again, and the Uber rushed away.

'"I'd spit on you"?' said Johanna. 'Please tell me that was kinky talk.'

Lena gave a sardonic laugh. 'Ha, I wish.'

Johanna studied her. 'Do you?'

Lena lifted a shoulder, non-committal.

Johanna leaned forward to catch her eye. 'Because you often make those quips, but from where I'm sitting, you could have whatever you wish when it comes to guys like Jake.'

'I was only joking.'

'But were you?' Johanna pressed her. 'Lena, you came to LA to make it big and have fun, and I hate to say this but it seems like you're not doing either. I know the screenwriting stuff is hard – really fucking hard – but having fun is not.'

'You don't get it.'

'So explain it to me. You always say "you don't get it" and no, I don't 'cause thank fuck my parents were hippies who told me to fuck whoever I want, so explain it to me.'

Lena swallowed. 'Growing up in my family was sort of like . . . indoctrination. It gets so deep and ingrained. I try – I *really try* – to relax and have fun, but it's not something as facile as my mother's voice in my head but *my* belief – my *own* deep belief – that if I let a guy take what he wants, then he won't respect me. Then *I* won't respect me.'

'So you're slut-shaming yourself?'

Lena exhaled. 'Yeah, I guess I am.' She expected Johanna to be glib; to tell her she needed to get laid, but instead she gripped her hand fiercely.

'Lena, you have limited time in which to have fun and then, bam, it's over. You've got to get over this mediaeval bullshit.'

Lena nodded. 'You're right,' she said, but could she really shrug off years of conditioning in pursuit of *fun*?

'Of course I'm fucking right.' Johanna kissed Lena's cheek, then gently rubbed off the lipstick. They settled into a companionable quiet as the car snaked through the LA night and ascended into the hills.

*

A loud splash cut through the music as a man leapt fully clothed into the pool. Lena watched with false amusement, trying to seem at ease. Johanna had been commandeered by her fashion colleagues, leaving Lena alone. She told herself to network but instead hovered on the periphery. She was wary of unwittingly accosting somebody famous and looking like a groupie. She drained her cocktail and headed back to the bar, a sleek white slab of plastic planted in the massive garden.

She asked for another mojito, shouting to make herself heard above the thumping bassline. It was heavy and insistent and thrummed through her very skull. Glass in hand, she retreated from the bar, back to the safety of a wall. Soon, as with any of these parties, a middle-aged man approached her. He planted his hands on either side of her, boxing Lena inside. Though nearly thirty, she still hadn't learnt the fine art of telling a man to fuck off. She politely entertained him while slugging down her drink. When her glass was finally empty, she held it up like a weapon.

'I'm just going to get a top-up,' she said, ducking under his arm and hurrying away before he could offer to join her. She deposited the glass on a passing tray and went inside to hunt for a bathroom. She climbed a white marble staircase and slunk along the corridor, not entirely certain that guests were welcome up here. She noticed an open door that led out to a balcony. It faced away from the party, onto a manicured rose garden instead of the Hollywood Hills. She slipped through the door and into the balmy night, drinking in relief. Here, the party was muted: not a growling beast but gentle and domestic. A cloud of mites danced around the fairy lights in the otherwise empty garden. She leaned forward to watch them and let herself relax.

Something shifted in her periphery, making her startle. The shadow there clarified into the shape of a man. He had loosened his tie and had the edgy, angry energy of someone who loathed wearing a suit. Their eyes met and she registered . . . contempt?

'I'm sorry,' she said by instinct. 'I can leave.'

'It's fine,' he said with the barest lift of a shoulder.

She tried to discern his accent. American with a distinct European bent, but she couldn't pinpoint where. She studied him for a moment for he seemed somehow familiar. 'Have we met?' she asked.

A smile curled the corner of his lips, but it wasn't warm. There was a mocking in it. 'I don't think so,' he said. His gaze dropped to the exposed skin of her waist, but then he looked away, leisurely, almost bored.

It rankled her, but she didn't show it. She turned away too, feigning nonchalance, but her skin felt strangely prickly. She let the silence steep, determined not to work to put them both at ease.

He rubbed a hand across his face. 'God, I fucking hate these things.'

She was surprised by his candour. 'They can be a bit much,' she said, cringing at her own banality. She stole another glance at him. There was something familiar in his face: the stubble, the dark hair, the strong jaw and aggressive energy. She squinted, trying hard to place him. Then, it hit her: he was Nico Laurent, a Formula One driver – last year's world champion and heir apparent to the great Lewis Hamilton. It clicked into place. No wonder he was so arrogant.

He saw that she recognised him and half shrugged. *So what if I am?* Lena held eye contact to show him she wasn't flustered, but when his gaze intensified, she felt her skin blush red. A smile was on his lips – more genuine now. He was enjoying her discomfort. Lena wanted desperately to wipe her upper lip. She could feel the sweat collecting there. Instead, she leaned against the balcony and watched the dancing mites. She could feel Nico staring at her, but refused to look his way. After a beat, she sensed him shift closer to her. The nearness of him made her unsteady and she gripped the lip of the balcony. He waited and when still she didn't look at him, he stepped into the space behind her. His presence hummed like a magnetic field and Lena stayed very still, attuned to his every move. She could feel the heat of him, achingly close to her. With his chest against her back, he traced a single knuckle along the open seam of her dress, barely brushing her skin. His touch made her rigid. He added a second knuckle, the twin strokes eliciting little catches in her breath. He leaned in closer in a heady mix of cigar and whisky and slid his hand beneath the seam. He pressed the slightest tip of his finger into the dip of her navel. Lena's body reacted, preening beneath his touch. Faintly, her conscience protested. She couldn't let him do this. Did he think she would relent mere minutes after meeting him?

His voice was low and blew wisps of her hair loose. 'If you want me to stop, say *red*.'

He traced a path across her stomach and down between her legs. Lena tensed but a little moan escaped her lips. Lightly, he brushed his thumb over the flimsy sheen of her underwear. Lena pressed against it, feeling herself grow wet. Nico made a sound in her ear – a low growl, like a warning. He closed one arm around her waist, locking her in place. The power in his grip made her shiver. He pressed his body against her, firm and insistent, and she could feel from the tension in his chest that he was trying to restrain himself. Lena moved against his fingers, needing more from him. He stroked her, not yet skin on skin, until she began to quiver – and then, cruelly, he withdrew. Lena moaned in displeasure and turned to him searchingly. He kissed her then – a long, slow kiss that made her unsteady. She felt his hard-on and pressed against it. Nico groaned and searched for ways to get at her skin. But when he found the zip at the back of her dress, Lena pulled away from him.

'Wait,' she said. She wanted somewhere more discreet. He unzipped the dress and tugged it off her shoulder. He yanked it down and revealed her bra. Her nipples were clearly visible through the sheer black material and Nico exhaled at the sight of them. He moved the fabric aside and took her bare breast in his mouth. The pleasure was instant and immense. Lena felt weightless, tipsy with disbelief. When Nico pulled back, Lena's senses resurfaced briefly. 'Wait,' she told him. She tried to hold him at a distance, but he gripped her hands and pinned them behind her, easily circling her wrists with his fingers. His mouth on her skin grew hungry, teeth bared in want. Lena twisted away from him. 'Nico, wait.'

His body tensed and he pulled back briefly to look her in the eye. 'Listen. Say *red* if you want me to stop.'

Lena's breath was quick and shallow. She took a moment to steady herself, then nodded.

'Say the word,' Nico instructed. 'Tell me what you'll say.'

Lena trembled. 'I'll say *red*.'

Nico studied her closely. 'You're okay?'

'Yes.'

On hearing that word, his clarity faded again, giving way to a baser instinct. He bent and took her nipple in his mouth, her hands still pinned in one of his. There was aggression in his touch, but knowing that the word was there – *red* – Lena let him take control. He wrenched her dress down and they both heard it rip. The sound ignited something inside him and he grabbed her hair in his fist, tugging to the point of pain. When he didn't ease, she tried to pull away but he restrained her easily. He unzipped himself and Lena realised that he meant to fuck her right there on the balcony.

'Nico, wait.'

'I can't wait,' he said, low and urgent.

His need for her was intoxicating and Lena struggled against him, adding more heat to it. When he couldn't restrain her, he lifted her up onto the balcony wall – a two-storey drop behind her. Lena instinctually grabbed at him. He smiled, satisfied, and tipped her backwards to spark her panic. She cried out and clasped at his shirt. He pushed up her dress and when he put his fingers between her legs, Lena was soaking wet. He brought his fingers to his lips and licked them, making her quiver. She clung to him, her body keening with desire, all the more acute combined with her fear. Nico manoeuvred himself against her and, after an extraordinary moment of stillness, pushed his way inside her. He tipped her back so that she wouldn't – couldn't – resist; would cling to him instead. He moved inside her and Lena felt possessed by him, utterly in his control, and not just because of where he had her but what she was willing to let him do to her: completely strip her of self-control. She submitted and let her body take over. She arched against him, crying out as he moved inside her. She felt the pressure build and just as she was on the cusp of coming,

Nico pulled away. Lena cried out in disbelief. She was keyed up and desperately needed release. Nico pressed the tip of his cock against her, not entering her, but rubbing it against her, making her tremble. The sensation was too much to take and she bowed against him, letting herself cave. He rubbed harder and her juices soaked his cock until, finally, blissfully, and with something akin to delirium, she came: an explosion that filled her sight with starbursts. Nico made a deep, shuddering sound and pushed inside her again. This time, he was rough, clawing the nape of her neck and thrusting deep as her body was rocked back and forth. She felt another orgasm build and moved to his faster, frenetic rhythm. His groans were buried in her neck until, finally, he came with a guttural roar. She felt him deep inside her. His arms circled her to the point of pain and, in that moment, his power was so absolute, it felt like a form of worship.

And, then, his body relaxed, the adrenaline rushing out of it. He folded against her, his head pressed against her neck. His panting slowed to a patter and the warmth of his body radiated into hers. She held him and when he finally pulled away, she was left strangely bereft. He zipped up and leaned his head on the balcony wall, folding his arms for a cushion. His chest rose and fell and she watched him carefully. He began to laugh – a sound of release, of relief, of freedom.

Straightening, he bent his head towards the night sky and laughed with abandon. Lena waited for him to look at her. He righted his jacket and, for one awful moment, she thought he would leave without even acknowledging her. He pocketed his tie and looked across at her. Lena felt acutely self-conscious, her body on display. He approached her and gently cupped the back of her neck, then leaned forward and kissed her. The aggression had left him and the kiss was soft, tender, stunning. She met his ice-blue eyes and instinctively held her breath. He brushed back a panel of her hair, now loose from its chignon, and leaned in close to her ear, his breath hot in the curl of it.

'Thank you,' he said. Briefly, he rested his head on her shoulder. A smile, not unkind, was on his lips as he turned and walked away, stepping through the double doors and back to the party downstairs.

Lena stared at his wake, stunned by a rush of emotion: shock that he had left, the sting of wounded pride, but also a sense of elation, of being thoroughly exorcised of something, of being gifted something else – freedom, lightness, even glee.

Lena's legs began to shake and she buckled to the floor. There, she sat and caught her breath, the night springy and light around her. It took her a long time to gather herself: to refasten her bra, to pull her dress back up, to calm the race of her heart. She saw that the rip in her dress had made the slit deeper but not noticeably so. She raked her hands through her hair and gathered it into a bun, using a moonlit pane of glass as a guide. It was only when she looked composed that she felt the urge to cry – as if her body knew that she could be in either physical or mental disarray, but not both at the same time. She blinked rapidly, waiting for the knot in her throat to ease. When it did, she ventured back into the house and slipped into a bathroom off the upper corridor.

There, she cleaned and inspected herself. She stared into the mirror. She had fucked Nico Laurent. Or, more accurately,

Nico Laurent had fucked her – not by force, but a few shades close to it; magenta to its red. She held that knowledge like a stone, inspected it for sharp edges, and found it flat and smooth. The truth was that she had wanted it. She wanted him. She wanted to be fucked by him. And now that she *had*, she wanted it again.

So *this* is how it felt, she marvelled. To want something – to want *someone* – so intensely, that it blacked out conscious thought. There, stood in front of the mirror, she threw back her head and echoed Nico's laughter: a bright, careless sound that almost made her teary with joy.

When the laughter abated, she checked herself one final time and slipped into the corridor. She returned downstairs and scanned the room for Nico. When an acquaintance gripped her elbow, she gracefully eluded him and moved across the room, searching for Nico's athletic frame. She rehearsed what she would say to him. *Can we . . . ? Do you want to . . . ? I need to . . . Please . . .*

Half an hour later, it became clear that Nico had left the party. Lena's elation gave way to something else: a dark and heavy ennui. She stood to one side, guzzling champagne to wash down her disappointment. A hand brushed her shoulder and she wheeled round, certain it would be him. Instead, she found Johanna.

'Lena, where've you been? I've been looking for you!' Johanna was about to scold her, but something shifted in her face. 'Are you . . . okay?'

Lena smiled brightly. 'Yeah.'

Johanna studied her. 'Did something happen?'

Lena lifted a shoulder. 'I wish,' she said with a laugh.

Johanna's frown evaporated, shifted easily back into camaraderie. 'Listen, I'm going home with Harry.' She held up a hand pre-emptively. 'I know, I know, but it's purely a business arrangement.'

Normally, Lena would protest. Johanna's ex, Harry, treated her like trash, but, tonight, she didn't have the energy to argue. 'Fine.'

Johanna raised a brow in surprise. 'You'll be okay getting home?'

'Yes.'

'Great.' Johanna pecked her cheek. 'See you tomorrow.'

Lena watched her friend disappear into the crowd. She scanned the room one final time and then left with resignation to wait for her cab. Suddenly cold, she shivered in the night air.

A white Prius pulled up and the driver asked, 'Lena?'

'Yes.' She slipped inside.

'How's your evening been?'

'Good, thanks.'

The driver sensed her mood and fell quiet. He steered her out of the long driveway. As he sped up, she noticed a lone figure at the edge of the rose garden, gazing into the darkness. She recognised him immediately and almost urged the driver to stop. She imagined running across the gravel. *Can we . . . ? Do you want to . . . ? I need to . . . Please . . .* Instead, she watched his silhouette grow smaller and then finally disappear.

Chapter 2

The sun was on her eyelids, warm and tingling, almost painful. She roused a little and realised that she hadn't drawn her blinds. Light filtered into the small, square bedroom and splintered across the rough wooden floorboards. She must have drunk more than she had planned last night. A memory clarified in her mind and she jolted wide awake, sitting up ramrod straight.

She had fucked Nico Laurent last night. She had fucked Formula One world champion *Nico Laurent*. Minutes after meeting him. Her stomach fluttered and it came to her in a heady rush: the feel of his skin on hers, the muscles rippling beneath his sleeves, the ferocity beneath the surface. His strength and insistence, the sound of him losing control.

Lena clamped her hands over her mouth – and, then, she began to laugh. It had actually happened. To *her*. She shook her head and fell back on her pillow. She grabbed fistfuls of her sheets and yelled in delight. It was the first time in her life that she'd had a one-night stand. She felt something wild and electric in the base of her gut: a sense of possibility, of promise. Is this who Lena could be? A woman who didn't worry about the consequences? Who wasn't weighed down with pre-emptive shame? A woman who was impetuous, thoughtless, carefree? She held the promise like a delicate flower, reluctant to look too closely lest it break the spell.

She stepped out of bed and headed to the kitchen where coffee was already brewing. Johanna was on the couch, scrolling through her iPad.

Lena squinted at her. 'I thought you were staying at Harry's?'

'So did I.' Johanna set down the tablet. 'He called me an Uber afterwards.'

Lena groaned. 'Fuck. Are you all right?'

Johanna rolled her eyes. 'Yeah, I'm fine. He's an asshole but he's worth it.' She stuck her tongue between the V of two fingers.

Lena cringed but laughed. 'You're incorrigible.'

'If *incorrigible* means someone who came five times last night, then yes I am!'

Lena poured herself a coffee and settled on a stool. She locked eyes with Johanna. 'In that case, I'm halfway incorrigible too.'

It took Johanna a moment to catch her meaning, and then her eyes grew wide. 'No fucking way.'

'Yes fucking way,' said Lena. The frisson of rebellion felt good.

Johanna leapt off the couch and joined her at the breakfast bar. 'Who!' she demanded.

Lena puckered her lips with discretion.

'Come on! Tell me!'

Lena took a sip of coffee and slowly set it down.

'Come on!' Johanna urged.

Lena tried to swallow her smile, to play it cool, but laughter burst out. 'Okay, so you'll likely know him – or at least *of* him,' she said.

Johanna danced with impatience. 'Tell me! No, wait, don't tell me. Let me guess.' Johanna was well used to her friends sleeping with famous men and knew how to be discreet. 'Tell me it was Jon Hamm.'

Lena laughed. 'No.'

'Timothée Chalamet?'

'No! Isn't he like nineteen years old?'

'Nineteen years of pure fat-free goodness.'

Lena laughed.

'Oh god, not Shia LaBeouf?'

'No. It was a sports guy.'

Johanna's eyes rounded. 'Not Nico Laurent?'

Lena smiled coyly.

'Oh my god! He's only the most eligible bachelor in the whole fucking world!' Johanna cried out with glee. 'How the fuck did you swing that one? He's notoriously reclusive.'

'It just happened.'

Johanna narrowed her eyes. 'What? You slipped, fell and landed on his dick? I want details!'

Lena basked in the attention. All her most interesting anecdotes came from other people and now it was finally *her* raising cries of outrage. 'Okay, so I went upstairs to take a breather,' she started. 'I ended up on a balcony off the back of the house. I didn't know anyone was up there, but then saw something move in the dark.' Lena recounted the night, deliberately holding back details until Johanna begged for them. She revelled in the story, pulling it on like a rare fur coat.

Johanna's eyes grew wide as she listened, alternating between shock and cheer. 'Oh my god, what a night,' she said when Lena finished. She cocked her head to one side. 'And you had fun?'

'It was incredible.'

'Okay, good.' Johanna let her breath out. 'For a sec, it sounded like you were getting MeToo'd.'

MeToo'd – the language women used to deal with brutality; to gild red-hot rage with something cool and manageable. But last night wasn't that. Nico had given her a way to halt him – *red* – but she had wanted for one moment to be someone else; someone who took pleasure where it was offered and wasn't ashamed about giving it in return.

'No,' said Lena. 'Nothing like that.'

'Okay, so how did it end?'

'He gave me this stunning kiss and left. I fixed myself up and came back down.'

Johanna delighted in this. 'Do you want to see him again?'

Lena considered this. 'I mean, I wouldn't say no.' She was tempted to reflect Johanna's gesture back to her – tongue between two fingers – but couldn't bring herself to do it. 'It's probably best to leave it as a one-night thing,' she added.

'Okay, well, let me know if you change your mind. I'm sure my agency could hook us up.'

The thought raised a thrum in Lena's chest, but she tamped it down. 'No, that's okay. Not everything has to be a long-term thing.'

Johanna broke into a happy grin. 'Welcome to LA, Lena.'

She laughed. 'Thank you. It's good to finally be here.'

*

The following week had a strange opiate quality. Lena felt light and calm. The world hadn't caved in, the fires of hell hadn't risen up to claim her and, most significantly, she felt at peace with how quickly Nico had made her submit. The knowledge of that night felt like a magic cloak, furnishing her with confidence – maybe even sensuality – she'd never had before. She strode down the streets with an air of assurance that made others pause and watch her. She basked in it, a secret smile on her lips, imagining that anyone watching would wish to be privy to it.

As the weekend approached, however, this newfound vigour turned sour. Lena became distracted in script meetings, snappy with Johanna, impatient with the LA heat. When she had first arrived, she had loved that about this city – the ever-reliable sun – but the seasons never changing elongated time, creating the sensation that nothing was moving. In truth, it wasn't the weather at all, but something more concerning. Lena *knew* she wasn't supposed to do this. She wasn't supposed to obsess, but she couldn't lie to herself. She desperately wanted to see Nico again. She wanted his cool-eyed gaze on her, and to see it bleed into lust. She wanted to make him lose control, just as he had done with her. The memory of him was a compulsion; a wound she couldn't stop touching.

On Friday morning, she ambled into the kitchen, still casual in her sleepwear: a Desmond & Dempsey cami and shorts that Johanna had discarded, saying it was too big for her.

'Morning.' Lena dropped onto the sofa, affectedly non-chalant.

Johanna was checking her teeth for lipstick in the full-length floor mirror. 'Hey.'

'What are you up to today?'

'I've got a meeting with a casting director and then I'm pretty much free.'

'And this weekend?'

'I'm not up to much. Why? Do you wanna do something?'

'Maybe.' Lena traced the arm of the sofa. 'You know how you said that your agency can sort out tickets to things?'

'Yeah.' Johanna carefully hooped an earring in.

'Does that include sporting events?'

'Sure.'

'Like maybe the Miami Grand Prix?'

Johanna met her eyes in the mirror. 'You sneaky little fox,' she said with a grin.

Lena groaned and stuffed her face into a cushion. 'I know, I know.'

Johanna finished with the earrings and came and sat next to Lena. 'Okay, listen to me.' She pulled away the cushion. 'If this is purely a physical thing, I'll do it, but if there's a modicum of you that thinks you're going to marry Nico Laurent and have his babies and live happily ever after, then you've got another thing coming. Men like him are something more than alpha, okay? They exist on a different plane and they're all about excess, do you understand? So you look me in the eye and tell me you won't get caught up in him and I'll go ahead and make the call.'

Lena felt chastened for she *had* imagined what it would be like to be Nico Laurent's girlfriend. To walk into a party with him or dine with him in a restaurant and feel everyone's eyes on them. But Lena was an adult and she knew the difference between fantasy and reality. The most she hoped for was to see him again; to put herself in his orbit and see if he would come to her. She met Johanna's waiting gaze.

'I won't get caught up in him,' she said. 'I promise.'

Johanna studied her. 'Then consider it done.'

'As easy as that?'

'Honey, I'm a model. There are two things we do: look good in clothes and look good at parties, so, yes, it's as easy as that.'

Lena flushed with gratitude. 'Thank you, Jo.'

'It's nothing.'

Lena folded her hands in her lap and tried to tamp down her glee. Her mind raced ahead, already planning her outfits for race day, after-party and first date, the things she would do to Nico, and the things she would let him do to her.

*

The lights winked off, then on, then off again. Lena paused in the dark hallway, waiting to see if they would come back to life. When they didn't, she reached out and traced the pockmarked wallpaper along the hall to the writers' room. She found the doorknob and twisted it open.

'I see the lights have gone again,' she said.

Ahmed nodded in a brief commiseration, then turned back to Gloria. 'You are *so* basic,' he told her.

'And you're a pretentious hipster,' she replied.

'What is it now?' Lena took a seat opposite them.

Ahmed tutted in distaste. 'I asked Gloria the number one director she'd like to work with and she said Damien Chazelle.'

'What's wrong with Damien Chazelle?'

Ahmed shivered in a showy manner. 'He's so cynical.'

Lena drew back. 'Cynical? He's the very opposite of cynical.'

'Oh, come on. Don't tell me you fell for his *La La* syrupy bullshit?'

Lena arched a brow. 'I think that you're being the cynic, Ahmed.'

'Oh my god, you *did* fall for it,' he cried with outrage.

'Okay, so who's *your* number one then?' she asked.

'Michel Gondry.'

Lena scoffed. 'You're so predictable.'

'Okay, Ms Arbiter of All Things Good, who would *you* choose?'

Lena considered the question. A dozen directors came to her, chiefly Noah Baumbach, but she said, 'Christopher Nolan.'

Ahmed groaned. 'As if *that's* not predictable.'

Lena shrugged. For her, Nolan struck the perfect balance between critical and commercial appeal. 'His films get seen, all right?' she said defensively.

'And that's the most important thing, is it?' asked Ahmed. 'Mass appeal?'

'Well, what's the point of making anything if no one sees it?'

'You get to be proud of yourself. That's what. Working on those big commercial vehicles would leave you cold.'

'Then I'll light a fire with fifty-dollar bills,' quipped Lena.

Ahmed didn't laugh. 'Seriously though. Would you rather take a paycheque than do work you're proud of?'

Lena knew the answer he was angling for. She was meant to wax lyrical about artistic integrity, to romanticise a life of penury, to suffer for her art – but she wasn't so naive. 'Look, Ahmed,' she started, but didn't have a chance to finish before Brianna strode in with a perfunctory knock.

'This is the final room,' she said to the man next to her. He was tall and wiry and wore rimless glasses above a beaky nose. 'Sorry to disturb you,' she said to the team. 'I'm just showing around this gentleman from Keller Stone.'

Lena felt a charge in the air. Keller Stone was a corporate developer that had recently come under fire for buying up historic buildings – theatres, libraries, courthouses – and redeveloping them into luxury flats.

'What's going on?' she asked.

Brianna offered a wan smile. 'Nothing to worry about.'

The man cast a glance around the room. 'Does it always smell like this?' he asked.

'Like what?' said Brianna.

'Dusty,' he replied. He made a coarse sound at the back of his throat as if coughing up a fur ball.

'Yes,' said Brianna with a hint of petulance.

'Hm,' he said, unimpressed. 'Okay, well, I've seen enough.'

He offered his hand to Brianna who surveyed it coldly before accepting. 'We'll be in touch,' he said and left without acknowledging the rest of the team.

'What's going on?' Lena repeated.

Brianna sat at the table and drew a hand over her face. 'Our landlord is thinking of selling the building.'

'What?' they cried in unison.

'Yes. They wrote to me last month with a rent hike, but I pleaded them back down. The next thing I know, I get a call about a viewing.'

'They can't do this,' said Ahmed. 'They'll get murdered on social media.'

Brianna laughed harshly. 'They don't care about Twitter, kid. Look at how they gutted the Frobisher Building.'

'But they can't force us out, can they?' asked Lena.

'We're in arrears,' said Brianna grimly. 'If our next show tanks, we'll be out on our asses.'

Lena felt a knot in her stomach. Their next show was *Please Understand*. She looked across at Brianna and with more bravado than she felt, said, 'Well, then, let's give them a hell of a show.'

Brianna smiled but Lena read unease there. After a hundred years in business, would the Aston meet its demise under Lena's script? She couldn't let that happen. It was do or die, and she had to do everything possible to keep them all afloat.

*

Johanna glanced sidelong at Lena as their Uber turned onto Lincoln Boulevard en route to LAX. She drummed her fingers on the seat between them, then fiddled with the pleats of her skirt. Eventually, she lost her patience.

'What is up with you?' she asked, her tone snippy.

Lena looked across at her. 'Nothing.'

'You've barely said a word all morning. Have you changed your mind about Miami?'

'No. It's not that.' Lena grimaced. 'It's work. The Aston's in trouble.' She recounted yesterday's visit from Keller Stone and the uncertain future of the theatre, but Johanna was typically glib.

'You'll have other opportunities.'

'But the Aston won't.'

Johanna sighed. 'Look, I know you're bummed out, but this weekend is meant to be *fun*. Some racing, some cocktails, some . . . cock.' She grinned devilishly.

Lena smiled despite herself. The driver caught her eye in the mirror and she felt her cheeks flush. 'You're right,' she said, grateful that Johanna could bully her out of a bad mood. Besides, Lena owed her a good time. Johanna had wrangled them box seats at the grand prix and that was no easy feat. 'Let's fuck shit up,' she said.

They both laughed at how formal this sounded in her English accent, but it rallied them nonetheless. They arrived at the airport and Lena felt her stomach flutter. The thought of seeing Nico again made her light-headed. They boarded the flight and Johanna turned left towards business class while Lena turned right. Johanna's agency had managed to book her a job in Miami, which meant that the client, Cartier, had paid for her business-class flights. Lena felt a pang of inferiority. How she longed to be similarly courted – a symptom no doubt of growing up poor. Her family hadn't been *can't-put-food-on-the-table* poor but *can't-buy-sanitary-wear* poor. When period poverty became a cause célèbre, Lena had given an interview to an activist cum author about her experiences and it was all she could do not to bawl. She remembered the shame of those early years: stuffing her underwear with kitchen towel that her father bought by bulk from the cash and carry on Williamson Road. When the government announced free sanitary wear for all, Lena had locked herself in the toilets at work and cried – with relief that other girls wouldn't suffer like her but also sorrow for her younger self and everything she had gone through. Though more secure now, Lena was tired of making those choices: taking the bus instead of an Uber, buying substandard groceries, using knock-off AirPods because she couldn't justify spending two hundred dollars. She still felt like she was failing that little girl who had never known stability. It was this thought that played on her mind as she leaned back in her seat and fell into a fitful sleep.

Soon after landing, they headed to the Ritz. Cartier had booked a night there for Johanna, and Lena was able to share her room. *The millionaire lifestyle on a shoestring*, she thought wryly as they were shown upstairs. Johanna tipped the bellhop smoothly – something that Lena, as a Brit, had never been able to master. She looked around the room. The road to riches, it seemed, was paved with soft furnishings: heavy brocade curtains and wingback chairs in cream velvet. In the distance was the bright blue ribbon of the Atlantic Ocean. Lena walked out to the balcony and felt her body relax.

Johanna's footsteps followed behind. 'My car's here,' she said. 'You'll be all right?'

'Of course.' Lena had to occupy herself this evening as Johanna was headed straight to her shoot. Lena bid her goodbye and settled on the balcony to watch the sun go down. Swathes of red and orange swept across the sky, leaving behind a soft and inky darkness, ripe with possibility. A thought occurred to Lena and once it took root she couldn't ignore it.

She sprang up from her chair and hurried inside. She showered and redid her makeup, then pulled on a pair of jeans and a sheer black shirt with a hint of cleavage. She considered adding Johanna's yellow blazer for a dash of colour but couldn't risk ruining it. *It's Balmain darling*, Johanna would say, easing it out of Lena's hands any time she wanted to borrow it.

This was Miami, she reasoned. She wasn't going to be cold. She headed downstairs and explored the hotel. First, she scanned the bar as if searching for a friend, then ventured out to the garden. She wandered idly and pretended – as much to herself as to others – that she wasn't scouting for Nico. There was a good chance that the Formula One drivers were stationed at the Ritz and it wouldn't be so unusual if she happened to bump into him. She did a lap of the pool area and headed back inside to casually case the foyer. She perched on one of the plush sofas and stared intently at her phone, as if halted by an important email. When the pretence grew stale, she stared at the lift, as if the doors might open to reveal what she was looking for. Finally, she admitted defeat and retired to the bar. It was the night before the race and even if Nico *was* at the Ritz, he almost certainly wouldn't be drinking. Sighing, she folded onto a stool and ordered a glass of wine.

'Long day?' asked a voice beside her.

She looked up and smiled politely. 'Not really.'

'It's just that you're drinking alone on a Saturday night – in Miami no less.'

Lena held back a cynical laugh. It's not that the man wasn't handsome. In fact, he was almost *too* handsome with his pearly white teeth, squeaky clean shave and meticulous hair. Lena preferred her men more rugged – but in the spirit of Miami, she tipped her glass towards him. 'But I'm *not* drinking alone,' she said.

He grinned and introduced himself as Mark. 'I love your accent,' he said.

She tried to think of something witty to say but settled on a simple 'Thank you.'

'Are you in the US on vacation?'

'Actually, I live in LA.'

'I'm sorry,' he said in mock condolence.

Lena's laugh led them into easy banter. Mark was in the restaurant business and was scouting locations in Miami to open up a Cuban café. Lena listened with interest as he spoke of nearly losing everything when the pandemic hit. The hour drew on, hastened by a nascent chemistry. When there was a natural lull in the conversation, Mark held her gaze, his eyes twinkling with optimism.

'You are dauntingly pretty,' he said.

Lena swallowed, faced with a decision. Was she really a new carefree version of herself? Could she spend the night with Mark and potentially do the same with Nico tomorrow? The thought was wicked and delicious, but the heat of the moment quickly cooled. Mark was attractive and they would probably have fun together, but it was Nico that she wanted.

'Thank you,' she said, angling her head in a show of regret. She slid her feet off the rung of her stool to signal her departure. 'And thank you for keeping me company on a Saturday night in Miami.'

Mark understood. 'It was my pleasure,' he said, lips twisting wryly.

She stood. 'Good luck with the café.' She could feel the pull she had on him as she walked away. It reminded her of the confidence, the sensuality, that she had felt after that evening with Nico. The thought of seeing him tomorrow was intoxicating. She had no idea what would happen but every nerve in her body fired at the prospect of fucking him again. Tomorrow could be the day, she thought. Tomorrow, it would happen.

*

Lena and Johanna were shown to the box, a small enclosure of twelve rows which seated celebrity F1 fans along with corporate sponsors. Johanna had wrangled two tickets through a friend at Cartier. She hadn't been able to get access to the paddock, an enclosed area behind the pit lane reserved for drivers and their teams and the occasional A-list celebrity.

Lena didn't mind, however. Turning up in the paddock was far too strong a move.

She followed Johanna and slid into the back row. She angled her legs demurely and tried hard not to fidget. She had spent an age choosing an outfit, eventually opting for black jeans and a simple white tee. She had aimed for effortless chic, but felt distinctly plain next to the other women in the box: a statuesque blonde with prettily dishevelled hair, and an elegant brunette in a stylish jumpsuit and a hundred thousand pounds on her wrist. It wasn't their clothes but their accessories that set them apart: the gems and stones and shoes and watches. Lena knew that these things spoke volumes and self-consciously hid her chunky boots, which felt more scruffy than effortless.

'Oh my god. That's Tom Ford in the front row.' Johanna dug an elbow into Lena. 'I've wanted to work with him *forever.*' Johanna looked calm but Lena could hear the tenor of glee that others couldn't register. In LA, you were either a star or a fan. Acting like a fan meant you weren't a star and so they had learnt to keep their cool.

Lena squeezed Johanna's hand. 'We'll definitely talk to him,' she said, as if she would have any clue how to approach the hotshot designer.

A roar went up in the crowd and Lena looked to the track. The mechanics surrounding the cars were rushing off the grid. The race was about to start. First, there was the formation lap, which preceded the actual race. Each driver zig-zagged on track to warm up their tyres for better grip. Nico's car was second on the grid behind the Red Bull of Michael Vossen, his championship rival. Lena watched as the cars lined up again on the grid. The crowd fell impossibly quiet. The lights above the grid turned red one by one. The atmosphere was electric, wired to spark at any moment. All five lights were red and, then, after a single heartbeat, flashed off – the race signal to *go*.

Lena pressed in her headphones to listen to the live commentary. It was difficult to follow the race when you could see only a section of the track. Almost immediately, two drivers in the midfield collided. The Alpine of Frenchman Patrice Girard went into the barrier, leaving behind a litter of debris. The crowd erupted in jeers as the safety car was immediately deployed, limiting the pace, and precluding any actual racing. Lena watched the assured way that Nico controlled his car, leaving just enough distance between him and Vossen to avoid the wrath of the stewards. The crowd were loud, desperate for the race to restart. After four long laps, the green flag signalled the end of the safety car, and the drivers were free to race. Nico chased Vossen, inciting deafening roars. For a breathtaking moment, it seemed that he would pull ahead, but Vossen closed the door.

Lena pictured Nico in the cockpit: angry and sweaty, spitting expletives. Or maybe he was cool and calm. It struck her just how little she knew about him, this man that she had flown across the country to see. She had googled him, of course, and learnt that he was French on his mother's side and American on his father's side. It seemed that the latter was enough to secure the support of the Miami crowd who cheered wildly as Nico put pressure on Vossen. On the straight – a section of the track with no turns or bends – Nico activated DRS. The drag reduction system enabled a driver to add extra power when within a second of the car in front. It made overtaking easier and the races more eventful. Nico went wheel to wheel with Vossen, mere inches between them. They almost touched and, then, Nico ran out of room. As they entered the main straight, he stayed close to the Red Bull, then pulled out of its slipstream and out-braked Vossen into the turn, snatching the lead away. The crowd roared their approval. Here, at the most theatrical circuit of the most glamorous sport in the world, they got what they came for.

From there, Nico edged out his advantage through the pit stops. He was on course to win when the safety car was imposed again following another collision. Closing up the field gave Vossen a shot at the lead when the race restarted. He was within a second of Nico for five heart-stopping laps but always too far away to make a proper lunge. Nico had superior pace and, over the final laps, eked his lead to over a second, preventing Vossen from using DRS. He sailed to victory, taking the lead of the championship by three precious points.

The crowd poured onto the track and converged around the podium. Lena wished that she was down there, cheering with abandon, instead of up here, feigning indifference. She watched Nico's face on the two screens that flanked the podium. He was classically handsome, a little more French than American. He looked so different when he smiled: bright and magnetic. Lena felt something stir inside her: not lust; something less heat and more warmth. She wanted desperately to see him again – but not like this, not surrounded by thousands of fans and a cold cabal of VIPs.

She turned to Johanna. 'Do you think they'll be celebrating tonight?'

'Of course!' she shouted over the noise.

'Do you think you can get us there?' asked Lena with a sheepish wince.

Johanna laughed. 'What did I tell you about models? We look good in clothes . . .'

'And you look good at parties,' Lena finished. She kissed Johanna's cheek, buoyant with the mood. She and Nico Laurent had an appointment to keep.

*

They parked outside the mansion, a broad cream building studded with Ionic columns that aped European museums. It had a bright, plastic feel and Lena wondered if this explained why Americans loved Europe so much. The architecture there was actually authentic; here, even exclusive venues had an ersatz quality. Lena and Johanna were escorted into a large reception room with black-and-white Ennerdale tiles and a marble staircase sweeping up one side. Despite the grand setting, the guests were decidedly mixed. She noticed drivers, engineers and team principals, a smattering of journalists and, of course, a swathe of beautiful women. Lena did a mental calculation and pegged herself in the middle. If Nico Laurent wanted to go home with the most beautiful woman in the room, it wouldn't be Lena he chose.

She saw him at the bar and felt something dart inside her – nerves, or anticipation. She fought the urge to approach him.

She would hover on the periphery and wait for him to notice her. She and Johanna weren't easy to miss, especially in these dresses: a sea-green whispery thing, and a scarlet dress that dropped off Johanna's slender shoulders. Lena often joked that she was Johanna's ugly sister, but in truth, they worked well in tandem. For men, a cool blonde and wholesome brunette was a double serving of catnip. They worked the room, both on sparkling form. The entire time, Lena charted the distance between her and Nico. She was heartened to see him deep in conversation with his team principal – nowhere near the numerous beauties.

Johanna yelped when she spotted Tom Ford in a corner. 'I've *got* to talk to him,' she said.

Lena hesitated. She didn't want to hide in a corner and miss her chance with Nico. 'You go ahead,' she said. 'I'll only cramp your style.' She milled around on her own and chatted to a couple of journalists. One of them, Casey, said he worked at the *LA Times* and was interested in seeing *Please Understand*. Lena gave him her details and excused herself as soon as it was polite. She didn't want to get stuck in one place.

Finally, she saw Nico break away from his conversation and head down a corridor. She followed him, quietly mortified by what she was doing. She stopped short when she saw that he was headed to the bathroom. She stationed herself a little way off and pretended to be on the phone. She had her back to him and every time she heard footsteps approach, she casually turned around and glanced up. Every time, it was someone else. She coloured, glad that Johanna wasn't here to see this. A witness would be excruciating. Then, she heard his footsteps: confident, purposeful.

'Okay, I'll see you tomorrow,' she said into her phone and turned. They locked eyes at the exact same time, as if it were predetermined. Lena startled, then frowned as if she was trying to place him. He paused mid-stride, clearly trying to place her too. Lena realised that, despite all her machinations, she hadn't planned an opening gambit. She groped for one now, but ran out of time.

'You,' said Nico – a short, sharp sound that rang with accusation.

Lena blinked, her lips parting soundlessly.

Nico didn't wait for her to speak. He grabbed her upper arm and hauled her into an alcove, out of sight of the rest of the guests. 'What are *you* doing here?' he demanded.

She pulled out of his grip. 'I was in town,' she said, trying for glib but sounding defensive.

'You were in Miami?'

'Yes.' She shook her head to signal her bafflement.

'Why?'

Lena told herself to be calm; to play her cards with care. 'I'm here with a friend,' she said, shifting to a casual tone. 'She's a model and booked a job here. She asked me to come along.'

Nico narrowed his gaze on her. 'And you came to be at this party . . . how?'

'Models look good at parties,' she quipped. She looked up at him, a quirk of a smile playing on her mouth. 'The rest of us have to try,' she added, inciting him into a compliment. She watched his gaze stray to her cleavage and felt her confidence grow.

'And?' he said, irritated by her coquetry.

'And I came along to keep her company.' This wasn't how she had envisioned their meeting. 'Congratulations by the way,' she said, steering them to safer ground. 'I saw that you won the race.'

He scowled. 'Are you stalking me?'

Lena balked. 'What? No,' she stuttered with disbelief. 'I was in town and I was *invited*.'

'That's why you were hanging around outside the bathroom?' he asked coldly.

Lena faltered, caught between indignation and shame. That was exactly what she had been doing. 'I'm not trying to *snare* you if that's what you think.'

'Then why are you here?'

She scoffed. 'I don't have to answer to you.' She moved to leave, but he grabbed her by the elbow, pressing to the point of pain.

'I don't like groupies.' His voice was hard.

'Jesus Christ. You're a prick, you know that?' Her cheeks burned with heat. She was humiliated by what she had resorted to; flying across the country just to get in his circle. It was so fucking embarrassing.

'Hey man, you all right?' a voice asked from across the hallway.

Nico released Lena's arm and took a step back. 'Yeah, fine.'

The stranger turned his gaze on Lena. 'Um, you all right?'

She recognised him as Davide Russo, an Australian Formula One driver. She nodded and angled her face away from him so he wouldn't see the tears in her eyes.

'Just gimme a minute, man,' said Nico.

'Okay.' Davide hesitated, then gestured towards the main hall. 'I'll be just over there,' he said.

Lena knew from the way he said it that it was aimed at her. That small intervention reassured her and she blinked away her tears. As soon as Davide was gone, Nico turned to her and spoke in a savage whisper.

'What happened between us was a one-time thing, so don't show up at my workplace spouting some shit about models at parties. I know what girls like you are like. Stay the fuck away from me.'

Lena was winded by the salvo. Anger rose in her gut. 'You're so full of it,' she said. '*You're* the one who came on to me.'

He smirked. 'So what are you saying?' he asked in a challenge.

Lena was at a loss. She didn't know what she wanted from him. Chemistry? Apology? A time machine to claim back her dignity? 'You're such an arsehole.'

He looked her up and down. 'At least I'm not pathetic.'

The insult stung and, as his footsteps receded, it took all her strength not to break down and cry.

Chapter 3

The light in the room cast everything in a buttery hue: the sumptuous cream carpet and enormous crystal chandelier. A four-poster bed stood to one side, heaped with brocade pillows. Lena sat in an overstuffed chaise longue and tried to calm her thoughts. After her run-in with Nico, she had fled upstairs and into an empty guest room, trying not to cry and ruin her makeup. A tiny, errant part of her thought it was still possible that Nico might change his mind; that he might somehow divine that Lena was more than a groupie. That flicker of hope shamed her even more. Nico was right. Lena *was* pathetic.

She exhaled – a choppy, fractured sound that did little to rally her. She wanted to leave the party, to leave Miami and forget that she had ever come on this sorry quest. She groped for her phone and sent a text to Johanna, keeping it deliberately vague so as not to spoil her spirits.

Hey, I'm taking a breather upstairs. I'm ready to go whenever you are, but no rush. I can always make my own way back. x

She waited to see if Johanna would come online, but there was no activity. She decided to give her half an hour, then make her own way to the Ritz.

'Oh, yeah, for sure!' called a voice in the hallway.

Lena heard advancing footsteps, then watched the doorknob turn. The door swung open and Davide Russo froze at the threshold. 'Oh shit, I'm sorry.' He glanced right and left down the hall and then back inside the room. 'Um, I think you're in my room,' he said.

'Your room?' Lena was confused.

'Yeah,' he said hesitantly. 'A few of the teams are staying here.'

She looked around the empty space and that's when she spotted the clues: an orange duffel bag next to the bed, a Kindle on the nightstand. She sprang up. 'Oh my god, I'm so sorry. I thought this room was empty.' She raised a palm in apology. 'I just needed a moment and this was the first door I opened.'

'It's okay.' Davide's face lit up with his famous thousand-watt smile. 'Please take a moment. I'll go.'

'No, no,' Lena cut in. 'Please. I'll go.' She moved towards the door.

'Hey,' Davide said, stopping her. 'Are you okay?'

'I'm fine,' she said, but he heard the quiver in her voice.

'You don't seem okay.'

'I . . .' She swallowed. 'I just did something really pathetic.'

'You wanna talk about it?'

'Not really.'

He winced with understanding. 'Nico can be a bit full-on.'

'I don't give a fuck about Nico.' The venom in her voice made it clear that this wasn't remotely true.

Davide waited, sensing that she wanted to talk.

'I don't know what I was thinking. I flew over here thinking that I'd see him and that we'd *connect* somehow, but . . .' She fell quiet, embarrassed by her naïveté.

'Don't feel bad,' said Davide. 'We see a lot of this sort of thing.'

But that was the *very* thing that embarrassed Lena – not the transgressive nature of her actions but the sheer banality; the utter predictability. She'd thought that she was better than that. Lena was a writer, not a model or an actress, and had thought that this flimsy fact would somehow serve to elevate her; that it would incite Nico to look beyond the veneer. But no. Lena was just like every other girl who stalked these men just because they happened to be the best drivers in the world.

'I'm going to go,' she said.

Davide stepped aside, clearing her path to the door. 'Okay, but you seem pretty upset. If you want, we can have a drink and talk.' He caught the look on her face. 'No dodgy business, I promise.'

Lena considered this. The thought of going back to the party made her feel ill. 'Okay,' she said, 'but no dodgy business.'

He cracked that grin and ushered her back inside. She took a seat and watched him pour two whiskies from a decanter on the desk. He took the opposite end of the chaise longue and raised his glass. She clinked hers against it and watched him take a long sip before she followed suit.

'What's your name?' he asked.

'Lena Aden.'

'Davide Russo,' he said. He motioned at the door with his glass. 'Look, I don't know what happened between you and Nico, but I can take a decent guess. I suppose the thing I'd ask you is: what are the chances that he's "The One", you know? Sure, he's a handsome fucker but what are the chances that you and he are meant to be together? Pretty slim, right? So why bother getting upset over him?'

Lena felt relaxed by the whisky. 'What the fuck am I doing in Miami?' she said. He curled one corner of his lips as if to say *search me*. She groaned and leaned her head on the rim of her glass.

Davide laughed. 'Okay, enough feeling sorry for yourself.' He waited for her to sit up. 'So what *are* you doing in Miami? Did you come here all the way from England?'

'No. I live in LA. I'm originally from London but moved here five years ago to . . .' She lifted a shoulder as if the answer was obvious.

'To what?'

'To make it big and have fun,' she said sardonically.

He ignored the bite in her tone. 'And *are* you?'

She scoffed. 'No. I'm not making it big and' – she gestured vaguely – 'I'm not having fun.'

'I'm sorry.' Davide's large brown eyes were warm with sympathy.

For the first time, Lena noticed his looks. He was tall and lean with curly brown hair and deep dimples. In his own way, he was just as attractive as Nico. She held his gaze, emboldened by the alcohol. 'Are *you* having fun?' she asked. Could there be a way to salvage this night?

'Not today,' he said with a doleful laugh. 'I retired from the race.'

She didn't speak for a beat, locked in a silent challenge. Here was a chance to prove to herself that her night with Nico wasn't a fluke. Could Lena really be one of those women that she so frequently envied?

She traced the rim of her glass. 'Maybe we can find another way to have fun?' Davide watched her, cogs turning in his head. His lips parted but he didn't answer. Lena let the alcohol take control, *needing* to feel better. She leaned forward and kissed him, smelling whisky and aftershave. If Davide was surprised, he didn't show it. He set down his drink without breaking stride and responded to her kiss. She opened her mouth a little, let his tongue touch her, the warmth making her moan. He pulled her onto him and Lena felt his body respond. She marvelled at how easy it was. So *this* was why the women she envied got what they wanted; they were simply bold.

Davide held her waist as she straddled him. She felt him press against her. He was so hard, it made her breathless. She stripped off his shirt. The skin underneath was tanned and taut. She touched it, quite unable to believe that real men looked like this. She arched against him, wanting him to touch her.

'Hey.' His voice was husky. 'Are you sure about this?'

She shushed him and kissed his lips, rocking on top of him. His hands snaked behind her back and expertly unzipped her dress. He pulled it off her shoulders and groaned when he saw her breasts. She had bought a bra just for this party: sheer black, cut so deep it nearly exposed everything. Davide slipped a finger inside one cup and brushed it over her nipple. He pulled down the fabric and took her in his mouth. Lena pressed against him. He let out a deep moan and then, in one quick and fluid motion, manoeuvred her beneath him. He tugged at her dress, the sound from his mouth aggressive. She could sense him beginning to lose control. The thought unnerved her and her body tensed by instinct. Davide felt her resist and stopped immediately.

'Hey, hey,' he said softly, cupping her chin. 'What's wrong?'

She closed her eyes and shook her head. 'Nothing.'

'Do you want to stop?'

'No, no, it's okay,' she told him.

He clenched with indecision, the heat rolling off him. 'Let's stop,' he said, breathless with sexual tension. He pulled back with a deep exhalation. 'Woo, let's stop.' He slapped his own cheek lightly.

'Okay.' Lena's voice was small and subdued.

Davide saw the look on her face and pulled her up gently. He replaced one bra strap onto her shoulder. 'You okay?'

'Yes. I'm sorry, I just . . .' She blinked back tears.

'Hey, it's okay,' he soothed. 'It's okay.' Gently, he wrapped her in his arms and tucked her head beneath his chin. 'It's okay. You're okay.'

Lena was so exhausted: by this evening, by this week, by the last five years. She felt broken by all the wanting. She nestled against Davide and felt her body give in.

*

A sound rose in the air: the clean jangle of breaking china – a plate handled clumsily or coffee cup slipping loose. Lena stirred and, in her haze, assumed it was Johanna. But, then, she bolted upright for she did not recognise the wallpaper. She was in a four-poster bed in a large and lavish room. She startled to see Davide Russo curled up on the chaise longue. His six-foot frame was bent at odd angles in an effort to fit on it. She exhaled slowly, realising that she still had her dress on. She had taken his bed all night. She moved guiltily out of bed and into the adjoining bathroom. She winced at the sight of herself: the dishevelled hair and smeary makeup. There were marks stamped into her skin from where the dress had pinched all night.

She tried to decide whether to take a shower or simply neaten the mess and leave as she was. Finally, she decided to get out sooner rather than later. From her bag, she retrieved a paltry few items – a matte powder, a lipstick and hairbrush – and did the best she could. The circles under her eyes were more pronounced than usual, but other than that, she looked relatively presentable.

Now for the walk of shame.

She chided herself for the thought, but it was so ingrained in her moral fibre, it would take more than two nights to unpick it. She tugged down the hem of her dress and walked back to the bedroom. Davide was fast asleep. She briefly considered waking him to move him to the bed, but decided to let him be. She scribbled a note on a branded pad.

Davide, thank you for taking care of me. I'm sorry I took the bed.

She left it unsigned and tucked it under the decanter. She hooked her fingers into her high heels and padded into the corridor. She shut the door as quietly as she could and turned towards the stairs. She froze mid-step as she locked eyes with the man on the landing.

Nico Laurent stared back at her. He took in her messy hair and the just-got-fucked state of her dress, and smirked: *I thought so.*

Lena felt a snap of disbelief that it would happen like this. Her lips parted, about to insist that nothing happened, but she caught herself in time. She owed Nico Laurent absolutely nothing. She lifted her chin and advanced along the corridor, swinging her heels in a low, loose arc. She saw the dip of his Adam's apple as he prepared to speak. She felt lit up with energy, every nerve in her body pulsing as she passed by close to him. She willed him to say something, anything, to stop her – but he let her go. She fixed her gaze on the banister, determined not to look back at him. *Come on, Nico. Please.*

She walked down slowly and reached the base of the stairs, no longer in his line of sight. She paused, waiting. For a moment, she truly believed he would follow her, but his tread receded. Lena smarted with fresh rejection. A familiar quote came to her: *The opposite of love is not hate, it's indifference.* That's what Nico felt towards her. Not lust or romance, not even the disdain of yesterday, but pure, unadulterated indifference.

Voices rose in the kitchen and Lena flinched. She didn't

want others to see her like this: her hair dishevelled, dress crumpled and skin ruddy with rejection. She dashed across the foyer into the muggy Miami air.

Inside her Uber, she shuffled across the backseat so that the driver couldn't see her in the mirror. They wheeled out of the semi-circular driveway and along a parade of oak trees. The sunlight winked between the leaves, making Lena squint. She closed her eyes and pretended that it was to ward off the light. It was the third time she had met Nico Laurent and the third time he'd left her teary.

*

Miami International Airport was chilled a few degrees below comfortable, as was the way with public buildings in hot and humid cities. Lena wore a light white T-shirt with denim shorts – a uniform of sorts in Miami – and shivered in the aggressive air-con. She considered pulling a cardigan from her cabin suitcase but she was already running late. She skirted around dawdlers and tourists, side-stepping toddlers and their Trunkis. She reached the departure gate and was relieved to find that boarding had only just opened. She spotted Johanna, who looked every inch the off-duty model in a casual T-shirt, sleek yellow blazer and jeans. She glanced up and snatched off her oversized shades.

'Where *were* you? I thought you were going to miss the flight!'

'I'm sorry. Everything was such a rush this morning. I had to go back to the hotel and pack.'

'Yes, I gathered that.' Johanna appraised her. 'Were you . . .?' She raised a brow.

Lena sighed. 'It's a long story.'

'We've got time.' Johanna threaded her arm through Lena's. 'I had you upgraded so you can tell me on the flight.'

'Seriously?' Lena let out a little laugh. 'Thank you, Jo.' This was exactly what she needed: a few hours with her friend to process the mess. They passed through security and took their seats in business class. Lena stretched, enjoying the extra space. Johanna ordered two glasses of champagne as soon as they took off.

'So, tell me,' she urged, pressing a glass into Lena's hands.

Lena recounted the events of the evening: Nico hauling her into the alcove, his suspicion and disdain, her own mortification.

Johanna scowled. 'What a fucking misogynist. He screws you and then as soon as you want to screw him back, he acts like a fucking moral guard. Who does he think he is?'

Lena swirled the liquid in her glass. 'The Formula One world champion, I guess,' she said wryly.

Johanna stalled. 'Well, when you put it like that.' She flashed a gallows smile, the steam leaving her argument. 'Are you okay though?'

Lena swallowed. As a writer, rejection was a constant in her life – a pain that you learnt to live with – but romantic rejection had sharper edges. It always felt personal. 'I just feel so *stupid*, flying all the way here.' Lena had thought that maybe she wouldn't see him, or maybe he would be with some other woman. She had never expected that they would come face to face and he would baldly reject her. It stung deeper than what was logical.

'Hey.' Johanna touched her lightly. 'Listen to me. I work with the most beautiful women in the world and every single one of them has done something stupid for a man. *Every* single one, so don't you dare feel ashamed of yourself.'

Lena flushed. 'But I *do*,' she admitted. 'He had my ticket, Johanna. He knew *exactly* what I was doing.'

'Okay, so what? You're never going to see him again.'

Lena considered this, but it made her feel even worse. Why was she so hung up on him? She didn't even know him and yet she had pored through pictures and clips. He rarely gave interviews off the race track, and was always calm and measured when he did, giving away nothing of himself. Perhaps that's what she found so intriguing. He was enigmatic – so rare a quality in modern society – and she was drawn to that. He felt like a mystery to be solved.

Johanna waved a hand in front of Lena, breaking her reverie. 'Man, you really are into him, aren't you?'

'Yeah, I think I am.' She squirmed. 'Or *was*. There's no chance of anything happening now.'

Johanna drained her glass and set it down with flourish. 'In that case, we'll just have to find you another crazily sexy, ridiculously successful multimillionaire to whisk you off your feet.'

Lena laughed and the absurdity of the situation hit her. As if *she* – a wannabe screenwriter out of thousands in the city – could capture the attention of one of the most desirable men on earth. If that was true, then Nico was right. Lena *was* pathetic.

Chapter 4

As spring bloomed and LA went from warm to scorching, Lena threw herself into work. She freelanced by day, accepting any and every commission that landed on her desk: a double-page spread on wedding lighting for a bridal magazine, a four-page advertorial for an aviation finance title, productivity hacks for a vacuous business site. By evening, she worked on *Please Understand*. Her thirtieth birthday was now four months away and she was keenly aware that if her script didn't catch attention, her time in LA would be up. Over the last month, she had stayed at the Aston late most evenings, reading and re-reading sentences until she felt cross-eyed. Tonight, however, she had gathered up her pages and come home early.

'Johanna?' she called, tossing her keys on the sideboard. 'Do you mind if I jump in the shower? I've got that charity thing.' She kicked off her shoes. 'Johanna?' She walked into the living room and realised that the flat was empty. She showered quickly and hurried to her bedroom.

She startled when she saw what was in there. On one hanger was the outfit she had originally planned to wear: a monochrome dress with blocky shoulders and long sleeves.

Next to it was another dress: a gold sequinned floor-length gown embellished with a flowing cape. It was structured in the waist and shoulders, lending it a glorious shape even on the hanger. Lena approached it, weirdly shy – like a little girl given a princess dress. There was a note pressed into the hook of the hanger.

Babe, in this town, the only thing more glam than the movies is the arts – and the only thing more glam than the arts is charity. You'll need something better than that dreary monstrosity. Behold the Jenny Packham Goldfinger gown. Please take care of it. I'll need to give it back!
Johanna x

Lena touched the material, thoroughly taken aback. It was a thing of such extraordinary beauty, she hardly dared to wear it – but Johanna was right. The charity gala was to be hosted by arts patron William McGregor, an 'old money' American Scot who was worth more than a billion dollars. Brianna had been invited as the artistic director of the Aston Theatre and had urged Lena to come along. Lena was savvy enough to understand that the party would offer ripe hunting ground for potential patrons. She needed to look like a million dollars and her original dress wasn't up to the job.

She pulled on the *Goldfinger* gown, careful not to snag the sequins. She almost squealed when she saw how it fit. It skimmed her figure beautifully, cinching her in all the right places.

'God bless you, Johanna,' she said. This was a dress prime for hunting.

*

William McGregor's mansion resembled the Royal Albert Hall in London: an Italianate-style circular structure with a domed roof and ornate frieze that wrapped around the building. The Fareham red brick walls, however, looked too bright and clean compared with its British model. Even old money was new here, Lena noted wryly. She was hit with a yearning for the real thing: the bright lights of the Royal Albert Hall as you walked up from South Kensington, the pedalo boats on the Serpentine, the supercars parked by Harrods. Even the whine of the Central Line and the flashing billboards at Piccadilly Circus, which she used to hate. She had been back to London only once since leaving – for her father's funeral – but couldn't face her mother again. Not after what she said that day. Lena pushed aside the memory as she walked into the mansion. She felt a pause in the air as others took in her dress. This must be what it's like, she thought, to be truly stunning. Every room you walked into lost a second of time. She scanned the room for Brianna, or any familiar face. How was it that after five years, she still didn't know enough people in LA. She heard a burst of laughter and looked at a cluster of friends gathered in one corner. Maybe they were colleagues, or indeed strangers. That was the problem with this city. Everyone acted like they knew each other and, by extension, were having a better time than you. She decided to be bold and joined them.

'You look friendly,' she said – her usual opening gambit.

The man closest to her turned around from the group. He looked puzzled and said, 'We are.' The group quietened and, one by one, they looked at her.

'Are you enjoying the party?' she asked.

The man nodded politely. 'We are, madam.'

The smile froze on her face. It struck her that each of them was wearing the same outfit: black trousers, white shirt, a waistcoat, blazer and bow tie. They weren't guests but staff, and she had interrupted their team briefing. Lena immediately coloured and took a step back.

'Well, uhm, have a nice night,' she mumbled. She turned, hoping that no one else had witnessed her faux pas. She lifted a glass of champagne off a waiting tray and gulped half of it down before remembering to pace herself. She was there to help save the Aston and needed to network. She found a group of fellow writers, but quickly grew tired of their jostling; a rearranging of hierarchy with each new name they dropped. She moved off to work the room. Thankfully, her dress was an easy segue to conversation. She lost count of the number of people who approached her to compliment it. Slowly, she lost her self-consciousness and eased into the evening.

As she reached for her third glass of champagne, she felt a hand on her elbow.

'Lena, hi!'

She turned. 'Brianna!' They air-kissed, more for show than anything.

'There's someone I want you to meet.' Brianna pulled her towards her companion, an older, bearded man who wore a white silk scarf and top hat over his black tie. He looked like a founding father – no doubt what he was going for.

'William McGregor. How do you do,' said the man.

'How do you do,' she replied, taking his hand.

'Oh, an Englishwoman!' he cried, delighted. 'A friend and foe all in one.'

Lena laughed. William's accent was entirely East Coast US, but he was clearly keen to show off his Scottish roots. 'Guilty,' she said.

'Well, what a delight. Tell me, is this all terribly ghastly or can you just about stomach our gauche little ways?'

'It's perfectly charming,' she said, hamming up her accent.

'Ah, the consummate English rose!'

Lena smiled, rather enjoying the role of sophisticated lily-white rose. 'Tell me: is Edinburgh as beautiful as they say?' she asked. She knew that he had a home there.

His eyes rounded in shock. 'You've never been to Edinburgh!'

Lena frowned in coquettish sorrow. 'I've never had occasion to.'

'Well, you must join me the next time I'm there!'

'Oh, I couldn't possibly intrude,' she said.

'As my guest!' he boomed. 'I insist.'

'That's so kind,' said Lena, nodding once graciously. Brianna murmured along politely, knowing full well when to let a younger, prettier woman hold court if it meant it could win them funding.

Lena found that she actually rather enjoyed William's company. He was self-aware, sharp, and had an acerbic wit. Brianna subtly drifted away, letting the two of them talk.

William didn't make Lena feel small for knowing less about art than film. In fact, he stressed, his charity was heavily involved in cinema too. Lena suspected he was one of the polished classes that could talk about anything. They were deep in conversation about highbrow horror when William stopped mid-flow.

'Lena, I have someone you should meet.' He called over her shoulder. 'Rosberg!'

'Wallace!' came the voice behind her.

She turned around, her smile on full beam, ready to greet the newcomer. It froze on her lips; turned into a rictus grin. The man looked at her and surprise flashed across his own face.

William urged him forward. 'Nico, have you met Lena Aden?'

'I haven't had the pleasure,' he said without missing a second beat.

'Lena is a preternaturally talented screenwriter. And, Lena, this is Nico Laurent, the reigning Formula One world champion.'

Nico offered his hand and Lena shook it. He squeezed just a little too hard. She felt her pulse quicken and urged herself to calm. She wouldn't let him fluster her, not here, not when she was having a good time.

She turned to William and angled her head prettily. '"Rosberg"?' she asked.

Nico cut in with the answer: 'William likes to pretend that he mixes me up with a former champion. He says it keeps me grounded.'

'And Nico likes to pretend to mix me up with William Wallace, which is stupid because he's dead.'

'And yet somehow better looking,' said Nico, clapping him on the back.

Lena didn't give him a courtesy chuckle. 'Well, I should leave you both to catch up,' she said, handing her glass to a waiter.

'Nonsense!' cried William. 'We see too much of each other as it is. We would much rather talk to you, isn't that right, Nico?'

Nico met her gaze and held it so long that her cheeks began to burn. 'Undoubtedly,' he said smoothly and offered her a new glass from a passing tray.

Lena took a beat too long to respond. 'In that case, I couldn't possibly decline,' she said. Their fingers brushed when she took the glass and she averted her eyes to William.

'Do you watch Formula One?' asked Nico, drawing her attention back.

She grimaced politely. 'I'm afraid not. Sorry.'

'Hm,' he said doubtfully. 'I would have had you down as a fan.'

'Why's that?'

He shrugged. 'You just seem the type.'

Lena bristled. 'It does seem fun, but it's all a bit *quick* for me.'

The corner of his lips fought a smile. 'Touché,' he said.

That small concession made her ripple with pleasure. She turned away quickly lest her own smile betray her. 'And you, William? Are you a fan of boys playing *vroom vroom?*'

He flicked a hand in the air. 'Occasionally, but it's all a bit loud for me.'

Lena could sense Nico smile beside her.

'No, we know each other through the charity,' said William. 'Nico here is one of our biggest patrons.'

'Ah,' said Lena. 'Are you one of those people with a Basquiat casually hanging on your wall?'

'Actually,' said William, 'he's more interested in cinema.'

'Really?' Lena failed to hide her surprise.

'Yes,' said Nico, 'but all very pedestrian compared to your taste I'm sure.'

'Like what?'

Nico shrugged. 'Like *The Meyerowitz Stories*. And also *Marriage Story* by the same director. He's like an uncomplicated Woody Allen.'

Lena did a double take. 'I *love* Noah Baumbach,' she said. Then, to prove that she wasn't just playing along, she added, '*While We're Young* is also very good.'

'I'll watch it,' he said.

Lena studied him, longing to ask him more, but she couldn't be seen to be clingy. Not after last time. She turned to William, detaching herself from Nico's gaze. 'I really must find Brianna, but it was lovely to meet you both.'

William kissed her goodbye and Nico leaned in to do the same. When his lips brushed her cheek, she caught the scent of his cologne and it took her right back to that balcony, his hand slipping inside her dress. She pulled away, her skin hot, and didn't make eye contact again. She hastened to the ladies' room to take a moment to calm herself. She noticed how shiny her skin was and powdered it meticulously. Brianna came up behind her.

'Excellent work, kid.' She raised a brow. 'I think William was rather taken by you.'

Lena gave her a thin smile. 'Let's see.'

Brianna glanced at her watch. 'I think our work is done here, so I'm going to head off. See you tomorrow?'

'Yes.'

'We're starting to cast Hana so it might be a late one,' Brianna warned.

Lena nodded. 'I'll bring snacks.' She loved Friday nights at the theatre when the world outside fell away and the hours ran by like water. She hugged Brianna goodbye as two other women filtered in. Lena wanted to get away from the heat of the party. She wondered about leaving with Brianna but really she wanted a moment alone, to catch her breath and think. She knew from the drive here that the house was surrounded by gardens; an inky expanse in which she could hide. She slipped out of the bathroom and walked through a set of glass doors into the balmy night. The gardens were walled for security and large enough to get lost in but small enough to be found. She wandered towards a bank of trees, breathing in the scent of lavender. In a distant corner, she was delighted to come upon a maze. There was a fine chain across the entrance and a sign that said 'Maze closed'.

Perfect, she thought. She lifted her gown and stepped over the chain. She rounded the first corner and sat on a stone bench, not daring to venture further – not when it said so patently that the maze was shut. She exhaled, wishing she could unzip her dress, which was beginning to verge on painful. She raised her arms and stretched, releasing the tension in her shoulders.

That's when she heard the footsteps: a soft shifting of gravel that steadily drew closer. Lena held her breath, hoping that the sign would ward off fellow guests. But no. The imposter ignored it and entered the maze.

When she saw him, she sprang to her feet, defensive by instinct.

'I was hoping I'd find you,' he said. 'I saw you walking this way.'

Lena stared at him. He had accused her of stalking him and now *he* was following *her*? 'What do you want?' she asked.

Nico assessed her coolly. His gaze flitted from her lips to her collarbone to her cleavage.

Lena scoffed in disbelief. 'You're kidding me, right?'

Nico stepped towards her but Lena stood her ground. In three strides, he closed the distance between them. They were so close to touching, she could feel the heat of him. It came off him in waves and made her flush with yearning. Nico leaned in and the night around them stilled: the cicadas falling quiet, the trees no longer rustling, the distant voices muted. Everything she wanted to say fell away – *stop toying with me, you humiliated me, I don't want this.*

He lifted his thumb to her lips and brushed them softly. The act, so simple and yet so intimate, lit up her nerves. He parted her lips and pushed his thumb inside her mouth. Instinctively, she closed her tongue around it. Slowly, he moved in and out, watching her intensely. Her breathing deepened as he kept that steady rhythm, not speeding up or slowing down. She licked him, soft and teasing, her whole body pulsing from that simple motion.

He eased it out of her mouth, then lifted the folds of her gown and slid his hand beneath. He traced a line up her inner thigh, then stroked the flimsy wisp of her underwear, pressing just where her pussy met the silk. She arched with pleasure, pushing herself against him. A low groan escaped his lips but he remained in acute control. He pulled aside her underwear and rubbed his thumb against her in lazy controlled circles. The sensation was exquisite and she grew warm and wet against him. He was gentle at first, barely stroking her, making her press against him. Then, he added just the tiniest pressure, making her gasp with pleasure. He pulled away and held his thumb to her lips, watched her lick her own juices off it, before he moved back to her pussy. Again, he added pressure, just the tiniest amount to add to the intensity. She could hear herself against him and pressed harder, quaking, desperate for more. He added yet more pressure and she cried out, right on the edge of coming. She felt herself dripping over him. Then, he pushed the tip inside her, barely moving before she exploded against it, coming so hard and forcefully that the ground swayed around her. A guttural cry escaped her, her every nerve pulsing. Nico clasped an arm around her to hold up her quaking body. She folded into his shoulder. As the adrenaline left her, she began to shiver. Nico noticed and wrapped his arms around her. She let herself be held and pretended for a moment that they were lovers.

Her breathing slowed, but she wanted more. She pressed

against him and felt his hard-on. She wanted more from him, wanted to give him everything. She reached down and stroked him, listened to his breath grow shallow and rapid. He groaned, a low, deep sound of keenly controlled desire. She looked up at him – at the firm set of his jaw and the deep frown on his brows – and pressed her lips to his. In doing so, she felt his whole body tense. He kissed her back but the act was rigged with conflict, as if barely keeping grip. His body was a livewire, ready to ignite. His lips moved to her neck, teeth on skin, but it turned into a growl – a harsh, frustrated sound – and he wrenched himself away from her.

Lena blinked, confused. 'Nico?' He shook his head, but she couldn't read the expression there: anger, regret, hostility? 'What's wrong?' He spun and strode away from her. Lena was astounded. 'Nico!' she called after him. 'What the fuck?' When he didn't answer, she righted her dress and stumbled after him. By the time she reached the entrance of the maze, Nico was gone – just a black smudge on the far side of the garden. Lena was dumbfounded. Why had he fled as if stalked by the devil himself? She stared at his receding figure, but her body was still in heat, allowing no room for real reflection. These sessions with Nico, as perfunctory as they were, were the best sex of her life. He had undone something inside her: the leash on her sexuality, and the beast it had set free threatened to consume her. She *needed* release; needed to feel him on top of her, inside her, losing control above her. She knew that if she never saw Nico again, she would never again know a moment of peace.

Chapter 5

Lena wiped the stringy hair from her face, panting hard in the heat. It was late afternoon and the boulevard was filled with runners and walkers. There was an electric feel in the air: LA at the close of a working week. Lena tried to siphon off it, to bolster her own mood. She had been in the flat all day, pent up from the party last night. Eventually, she'd decided to thrash it out on a run.

She checked her watch and ran for another kilometre. Five in the LA heat was akin to ten back home. When she hit her target, she allowed her pulse to slow. Sweat rolled off her skin, now the colour of puce. Breathing heavily, she wandered onto the beach, hoping for a wayward ocean breeze. She paused at the shoreline, careful not to wet her trainers. She watched the waves roll in and was hit with a stark certainty. If she had to leave LA, she would never return to it. It would be too painful to confront its boundless beauty and know that she had failed. The prospect filled her with sorrow and she turned and headed back to the flat, keen to be alone.

There, she found Johanna leaning on the kitchen counter, eating a piece of toast. She was dressed in dark leggings and a white v-neck T-shirt: her outfit of choice en route to a job. Next to her on the counter was an enormous bunch of red roses.

Lena raised a brow. 'Well, you clearly made an impression on *someone*.' She kicked off her trainers and padded over to admire them. They were velvet smooth and smelled exquisite. 'These are gorgeous.'

Johanna smiled smugly, then snatched up the envelope and handed it to Lena, who read her own name on the front. Her heart snared in her chest. *Nico*. She ripped open the envelope and read the message inside.

Lena, you were enchanting last night. I hope we can work together soon.

Confused, she reread the message. She flipped the card over and read the name W. M. McGregor. Instantly, she deflated.

'Seems like *you* made an impression on someone.' Johanna plucked the card from her hand. 'W. M. McGregor?'

'William McGregor,' said Lena. 'He's a philanthropist.'

'I know who he is,' said Johanna, eyes rounding with interest.

'We met last night.' Lena relayed the events of the gala. She was hesitant to share what had happened with Nico but knew that Johanna would never judge her. She explained that he had followed her to the maze and what had happened between them. When she finished, Johanna began to sing 'I Put a Spell on You' by Nina Simone. That was the great thing about Johanna. She always reflected your mood. If you were spitting anger, she would spit hellfire. If you were hooked on a guy, she would book you both a hotel room.

Lena winced. 'I'm not being stupid, am I?'

Johanna lifted a shoulder. 'I mean, that depends. Are you going to fall in love with this guy? If so, then yeah, you're being fucking stupid. If you're going to allow yourself to have the best sex of your life with one of the hottest men on the entire fucking planet, then no. Go and fucking get it.'

Lena shook her head in wonder. 'God, I love you.'

Johanna seemed taken aback. 'I love you too,' she said with a hint of uncertainty as if surprised to find that it was true. The words seemed to elicit fresh concern. 'You're not going to, are you? Fall in love with him?'

'Of course not. I'm not an idiot.'

'Okay, good.' The lines in her forehead smoothed. 'In the meantime, you'd do well to enjoy Mr McGregor's attentions.'

'It's not like that.'

'It's always that like,' Johanna replied wryly. She checked her watch. 'Right, I've got to take off. I've got a night shoot so I won't be home 'til tomorrow.' She kissed Lena's cheek. 'Go get it, bitch.' With that, she was off.

Lena smelled the roses and smiled. Maybe one day, she too would be rich enough to send a $500 bunch of flowers to someone she met in passing. She allowed herself to daydream: flying all over the world first class, being wined and dined, hanging out with the rich and famous – and, most of all, financial security. How improbable but wonderful. She was still in the throes of the fantasy when her phone began to ring.

'Ms Aden?' said a voice, American but formal – a bit like Frasier Crane's.

'Yes?'

'Mr Laurent would like to request the pleasure of your company this evening.'

Lena blinked. 'I'm sorry – *what*?'

'I work for Nico Laurent and he would like you to be his guest this evening. We'll send a car to your apartment at 6pm. Please wear something comfortable and pack an overnight bag.'

Lena was stunned. Nico Laurent was asking her out on a *date*? An *overnight* date? She felt a ping of joy, bringing her out of her stupor. But then, with dismay, she remembered that they were casting the role of Hana at the Aston and there was no way she could miss it. She cleared her throat. 'Um, I'm not available at six. Can I meet the car at eight?'

'I'm afraid that won't be possible. Shall I decline Mr Laurent's invitation?'

'No,' she said too quickly. She winced, agonised by conflict. She couldn't miss auditions, but if she said no now, she knew that Nico wouldn't try again. She had no idea how she would square this with Brianna. It was far too late to reschedule the casting. There were too many moving parts at play – but the actress chosen for the lead *had* to be a team decision. She exhaled. 'Six is fine,' she said, closing her eyes in a grimace.

'Very well.'

'I'm sorry, what was your name?'

'Castor Eliot.'

'Okay. Thank you, Castor.'

The man hesitated. 'You may call me Eliot.'

'Oh, sorry. Thank you, Eliot.'

'You're most welcome, Ms Aden.' He hung up before Lena remembered to ask how he had got her number, or if the driver had her address, or what exactly 'wear something comfortable' meant. 'Comfortable' as in loose and sporty or *comfortable* as in scant and sexy?

She checked the time and saw that she had less than an hour to get ready. She hurried to the shower, cursing herself for going on a run. Her hair always took an age to dry. She was jittery with nerves as she dried off and then rifled through her wardrobe, discarding joggers and leggings and jeans. *Comfortable*. A loose sundress? T-shirt and shorts? She wished that Johanna was here to help. What might a man like Nico want do on a first date? He certainly wasn't a dinner-and-a-movie sort of guy.

Could it be? It struck her that he might take her racing. A skittish thrill moved through her. How incredible it would be to get a racing lesson from a Formula One world champion. Her nerves twanged louder. What *exactly* was she meant to wear? She was running out of time and sifted her clothes with mounting panic. She spotted a cream-coloured pair of shorts and snatched it from the heap. It was tailored and elegant but also casual. She put it on with a pale-blue Oxford shirt and a pair of white Converse. This could be sporty, or it could be tea in Nantucket. Next, she faced the hardest thing: bailing on Brianna. She knew that a text message wouldn't cut it, so she picked up her cell and dialled. She prayed that it would go to voicemail but had no such luck.

'Hi, Lena. The actresses are already lining up. What time do you think you'll get here?'

She swallowed. 'Brianna, I'm so sorry, but I can't come in.'

'What?' There was a beat of silence. 'Why?'

Lena had practised the lie. 'I started to cough this morning.'

'Oh no.' Brianna's voice was freighted with dread. 'Have you done a test?'

Lena scrunched her eyes shut as she told the lie. 'Yes. I'm afraid it's Covid.'

'Oh god.' Brianna sighed. 'Okay, well, I'm sorry to hear that, Lena, but we can't send all these people home.'

She winced. Surely, they couldn't cast Hana without her. 'Can you film the auditions?'

'We don't have the equipment or setup.'

'It doesn't have to be anything fancy. Just ask Ahmed to set up his iPhone on the ring light. He can set it to record.'

'But there'll be hours of footage.'

'I'm sure his phone can handle it.' Lena hated to push, knowing she was at fault here.

When she spoke, Brianna was clearly annoyed. 'Fine, but you know how it is, Lena. You really need to see them face to face.'

'And I will. This is just the shortlist, right? I promise I'll be there to whittle it down.'

'Okay, fine.'

'Thank you, Brianna. I'm so sorry.'

'It's okay. Just get better soon, will you?'

'I will.' Lena set the phone down. Her guilt was muscled aside by a stronger emotion. She was going on a date with Nico

74

Laurent. *She* was going on a date with Nico. As if on cue, a car horn sounded outside. She peeked through the window to find a sleek black sedan parked below her building. She grabbed her bag and bounded downstairs.

The driver waited on the pavement. He wore a dark suit and had the bland, forgettable look of an FBI agent: clean shaven, close-cropped sandy hair, brown eyes, average height and build. He held the car door open for her.

'Hi,' she said, gliding into the back.

'Good evening, Ms Aden.' He got into the driver's seat and smoothly moved off.

She exhaled in an effort to calm her nerves. 'Do you know where we're going?' she asked.

The driver met her eyes in the mirror. 'To the marina.'

'Oh.' Her eyes rounded. They were going out on a boat. So *this* is what it was like to be whisked off your feet. The car glided along Pacific Avenue, the evening traffic already congealing. The marina was just ten minutes away; not much time to gather herself. They came to a stop by a basin. The driver – Chris – opened her door and led her along a pier to a waiting yacht: a sleek tri-deck vessel that bore the name *Ariadne*. On deck, an older gentleman in a butler's uniform stood to attention.

'Ms Aden, I presume?'

'Yes.' She noticed his gaze flicker to her outfit and immediately felt self-conscious.

'May I?' He offered an arm.

Lena took it and stepped onto the yacht. 'Eliot?' she asked, recognising his voice from the phone call.

'Yes.'

She offered her hand. 'It's nice to meet you.'

He shook it obligingly. 'Likewise. Mr Laurent is awaiting you.'

Lena fought to keep her expression neutral as she followed him to the bow. A table was laid for dinner and a bottle of champagne waited in an ice bucket. Nico turned and looked at her and the sun hit his ice-blue eyes in a way that made her falter. He wore navy shorts and a loose white shirt and his hair was tousled in the wind. *Like a literal million dollars.*

Lena took a moment to steady herself. She didn't know how to be with him. In London, she had had a couple of serious relationships – a strait-laced accountant, a journalist-turned-teacher – but dating in LA had been hard and she'd all but forgotten how to be seductive.

Be yourself, she heard in Johanna's voice. It was easy for *her* to say. Johanna was fun and spontaneous and carefree. Lena was thoughtful, academic and other unsexy adjectives. But she hadn't put on an act last night. It was by being herself, by talking of film and sparring with him, that Lena had won this date. Maybe Johanna's advice wasn't so terrible.

'Hi, Nico,' she said. 'You look great.' He smiled and Lena fought to remain casual. She took in his chiselled jaw, the light stubble, his clear eyes, dark hair and brows. Separate to that, he had an energy that was almost palpable: raw, pulsing, magnetic. It made her want to touch him.

'I'm glad you came.' He gestured at the bottle in offering.

'Yes please.'

Nico waved Eliot away and uncorked it himself, holding it

over the bow in case the foam spilt over. She felt the boat move beneath her just as she took her glass from him.

'We're sailing?' she asked.

'Of course,' he said.

Lena loved the hint of Europe in his broad American. 'Where do you get your accent from?' she asked – as if she didn't already know.

'Lots of summers in France,' he said.

'You have family there?'

He nodded with a faraway look in his face. 'Yes. My mother is French.'

'Oh.' She feigned surprise. 'Do you speak it?'

'Yes.' A playful glint came to his eye. 'You're trying to work out if I'm civilised?'

'I wasn't.'

He took a drink of champagne and held her gaze over the rim of the glass. 'You intrigue me.'

Lena flushed. There wasn't a woman in the world who wouldn't enjoy hearing Nico Laurent say those words. She didn't know how to respond and turned her gaze to the sea instead as they left the marina. The sun had started its slow arc towards the horizon but it was still hours from sunset. She watched it glitter like glass on water. She held on to the moment, wanting to remember its beauty and promise, unmarred by what might follow. She faced Nico. There was so much she wanted to ask him – *why do you behave like a jerk? Why did you run away yesterday?* – but told herself to be cool. Too much of herself would put him off. She had to spar a little, keep it light and loose.

'So which film did you get this idea from?' she asked, gesturing outward.

A slow smile curled on his lips. '*The Parent Trap.*'

Lena threw her head back and laughed. 'I was just joking but you actually *did* steal it.'

'I did.' The ice in his eyes thawed. 'Do you mind?'

'No. It's working.'

Another slow grin. He topped up her glass and led her to the dinner table. Eliot appeared soundlessly and Lena grimaced when she saw lobster on one of the plates. She had been vegetarian for nine years.

'For the lady, seared cauliflower, kohlrabi and miso purée, pickled ribbons and seaweed pearls.' Eliot set down her plate. 'For sir, grilled langoustine, shellfish jelly, black radish and sea herbs.'

Lena looked between the two plates.

'I understand you're vegetarian,' said Nico.

Lena closed her open mouth. 'Yes.' She wanted to ask how he knew, but decided to play the sophisticate; to act as if other men did this for her as standard.

He indicated the lobster on his plate. 'You don't mind?'

'No. Not at all,' she said with a little too much enthusiasm.

'So you're a screenwriter. What are you working on at the moment?'

Lena told him about *Please Understand* but was conscious of the fact that it sounded twee. Quickly, she changed tack. 'It's really just a stepping stone,' she said. 'I want to work on bigger things.'

'Like what?'

'Big vehicles like *Inception*, *Gravity*, *Gladiator*.'

'What do you think of Stephen Bay?'

Lena considered this. Bay was a famous director known for big-budget action movies: robots, explosions, bombshells in hot pants. She wouldn't put him in the same bracket as Nolan, Cuarón or Scott, but his films were always rollicking fun. 'He's good at what he does,' she said.

'I know Stephen well. I could introduce you.'

Lena arched her brows. Is this how easy it was for the other half? 'That's kind, but not necessary.' She didn't want Nico to think that she had ulterior motives.

'It's not a problem. I'll put you in touch.'

'Thank you,' she said, humouring him, knowing that in LA a hundred people promised you a thousand things that never would materialise. Friendships here were shallow: everyone was cheery and approachable, but if you needed something beyond dinner and drinks – help moving home, for example – you would quickly realise that you could count your friends on one hand.

'What are you thinking?' asked Nico, bringing back her focus.

Lena gestured absently. 'How much LA has screwed with my mind.'

He was surprised by this admission. 'In what way?'

'Oh, so many ways.'

Nico took a drink of champagne. *God, his lips.* 'Tell me,' he said.

She took a beat to gather her thoughts. 'There's so much good stuff here. LA makes you more outgoing, looser, braver, but it makes you shallower too, and overly focused on status. And what I feel, I don't know if it's the poison of this city or . . .' She fell silent and shook away the thought.

'Or what?' pressed Nico. He studied her expression. 'Tell me.'

'Or if it's that I have something to prove.' Her voice took on a wistful note. 'When I moved to LA five years ago, my parents were completely crushed. I'm their only child and they felt abandoned by me. They couldn't understand why I'd give up a chance to study law to become just another hack in Hollywood.' Lena flashed back to that final day: her father red-faced with stoic emotion, her mother rigid with blame. 'I promised to visit them, but kept putting it off. I was busy and I couldn't deal with the guilt.' Lena exhaled. 'A year after I moved, Dad had a massive heart attack. I flew back for the funeral and Mum told me – not without blame – that his dying wish had been to see me.' Lena looked out at sea, blinking rapidly. 'That's what I sacrificed to be here and if I never make it as a writer, it would all have been for nothing.'

Nico reached out and fit his hand on top of hers. Gingerly, she laced her fingers with his, but Nico pulled back as Eliot approached the table.

'For the lady, grilled red meat radish, cucumber and celery jelly, black radish and sea herbs.' He placed a plate in front of her. 'And for sir, roast venison, parsley condiment, beetroot and red onion with medlar jus.'

Lena was immediately conscious that she had got far too heavy, too fast. This was just the sort of thing that would put off a man like Nico. 'Anyway, it's not that I don't love

LA,' she said, pitching her voice back to breezy. 'I just think it makes you too focused on status, and what you're missing out on and how far behind you are.' She looked across at him, remembering that he was literally leading the biggest race in the world. 'God, I'm talking to the wrong person,' she said with a cynical flick of the wrist.

'No, you're not. I know what it's like to lose.' Nico caught her look of doubt. 'Listen, Lena, everyone's playing the status game. We're just playing at different levels. Do you think Jeff Bezos is satisfied because he's richer than you? No, because he's playing in the same league as Zuckerberg and Musk. I understand what it's like to lag behind. When I lose – which I do – *everyone* sees it, so I know what it's like to be dissatisfied. It's pretty much my default setting.'

Lena studied him. 'Is that true?'

Nico shrugged and focused on the piece of venison that he was cutting up neatly.

'Nico, is that true?'

His fork stilled. 'Yeah,' he said without looking up. 'It's true.'

'Why?'

He continued to cut. 'The usual.'

'Like?' Lena could see that he was uncomfortable and told herself to tread lightly.

Nico's jaw hardened. 'Let's just say there's a reason I use my mother's name,' he said glibly.

'Your dad wasn't around?'

'Oh, he was around.' His voice took on a bitter note. Lena aimed her gaze to the left of him to let this new intimacy breathe. Given space to talk, Nico carried on. 'Dad was a drunk, which greatly disappointed my mother. The French actually know how to hold their drink.'

Lena didn't dare speak, afraid to spook the candour out of him.

'I always thought that when I got to a certain height, a certain weight, that I would stand up to him, but I never did.'

'He was violent?' ventured Lena.

A dark grin. 'That's one way to put it.' Nico's gaze darted to his hand for just a split-second, but long enough for Lena to see it. She blanched, hit with a vinegar sorrow, sharp and acrid in her throat.

'Nico,' she said in a whisper. He made no move to hide it; couldn't in fact, for the small, round burn mark was right in the middle of the back of his hand – a particularly special cruelty for a man as notoriously private as he. Lena took his hand instinctively. He pulled away but she tightened her grip until she felt some give.

'I was the lucky one.'

'Your mother?'

'Gabriel. My brother.' The name softened something in Nico. 'We grew up in the Palisades and, from the outside, everything seemed perfect. We had a big house, a nice car, holidays in Europe. Dad was highly functional and no one thought to intervene. I threw myself into karting; ignored what was happening. It worked well because it gave me an excuse for the bruises.' Nico eased his hand out of hers and fixed his gaze on the blackening sea. 'One time, my mother said that she couldn't take me to practice, but I had a fit.

I was eleven years old and selfish, and said it would be all her fault if I never made it in racing – so she took me and Gabe. There was traffic on the way back – complete gridlock after an accident – and it was late by the time we got home. As soon as we walked inside, we could sense his mood. My mother told me to look after Gabe, to not let him out of my room, but I got distracted. And he got out.'

Lena held her breath, saw the clasp of his throat as he swallowed.

'Dad was really drunk that night – every night, but that night especially because we were so late. Gabe got under his feet and by the time I realised, it was too late. He hit him so hard that Gabe ended up in hospital.' Nico took a short, sharp breath. 'He was never the same again. They did scans, said there was nothing wrong with him, but *I* knew and my mother knew that Gabe came out different. He was a silly kid, you know? Always smiling when everyone else was in a mood. Seven years old and had never thrown a tantrum, but he changed that day. He became quiet and morose; wouldn't say a word for hours. Dad drank himself to death and my mother never recovered. She never blamed me for Gabe, not verbally, but . . .' Nico looped into silence.

Lena felt the urge to hold him, but their relationship didn't yet have that ease. 'Nico, I'm so sorry.' She reached for his hand, but accidentally brushed her wineglass. It skittered off the table and careened to the floor. The sound of breaking glass had Nico on his feet, lightning quick. They locked eyes and Lena saw the high alert there, his whole body rigid in readiness of violence. This, she realised, was a sound from his childhood. Before she could speak, Eliot joined them briskly.

'Please allow me,' he said to Lena. He swept up the glass with a practised hand and mopped up the champagne.

'I'm so sorry.' Lena stood back to give him space.

'Absolutely no harm done,' Eliot reassured her. 'I'll be right back to clear your plates.'

Lena stared at the blot on the decking. 'I'm so sorry, Nico.'

'It's fine.' His voice had lost its softness. He tossed his napkin on the table, then turned and strode to the bow. He gripped the rail and hung his head in what looked like supplication.

Lena approached him hesitantly. She touched his arm, making him flinch. 'Are you okay?' He looked at her strangely, then. Almost accusingly. He seemed on the cusp of saying something, maybe an apology, but then his expression hardened again. 'Excuse me a moment.' He stalked across the deck and disappeared from view. She heard him talk to Eliot in a muted tone. She strained to hear and realised that he was speaking French.

Appelez Sabine s'il vous plaît. A pause. *Oui, maintenant.* Followed by words too soft to hear. Lena waited for him to rejoin her. She leaned on the rail and watched the pleated surface of the sea. She couldn't stop thinking about the scar on Nico's hand: a perfect, glazed circle. What agony he had faced as a child. And guilt about his brother. Is that why he was so aggressive on track? He was still paying penance for a crime that wasn't his. Lena felt a deep sadness for him but also a kernel of pride that he had revealed himself to her. There was something about this evening – the slant of light on the water, the twitch of salt in the air – that set the right tone for intimacy. Lena cursed herself for breaking the spell and hoped that she could salvage it. She let her breath out slowly, daring to imagine that she and Nico could be more than a short-lived tryst. She revelled in the thought, buoyed by possibility.

'Ms Aden?' Eliot's voice cut through her thoughts. 'We'll be mooring soon.'

Lena turned. 'We're not staying on the boat?'

'No,' he said, bemused. 'We're going to Crushes, Mr Laurent's home.'

'His home? Out here?' They were far from shore, closer to the California Channel Islands.

'Mr Laurent is waiting for you.'

'Oh.' She was disoriented. She had thought they would finish dinner and spend the night on the boat, but maybe that was a stupid notion. She hadn't had much experience on yachts. She followed Eliot to the stern where Nico stood with his back to her. Beyond was a large rambling house on what appeared to be a private island. It had a picturesque gabled roof, dormer windows and a wide wraparound porch. Cherry trees lined its edges and scented the air with light perfume. 'You live here?' she asked.

'Some of the time,' said Nico.

'Wow.' Her callowness escaped her. 'It's stunning.' The boat gently pitched as it bumped against the jetty. Nico stepped off and held out an arm. Lena gripped it and followed him out with an ungraceful hop. She could feel the tension in his body, a coiled agitation, but decided not to question it. Better to work it out of him.

They approached the house and she marvelled at its character, light years away from the broad, bland mansions in which they had met so far. She was about to say as much, but then they stepped inside and saw the shiny steel, chrome and leather – all the charm gutted out. She had hoped for a dusty old library with dog-eared books, maybe even a first edition or two given how much he earned, but the house was clean and sleek, like the interior of a very expensive car. Nico led her to a cavernous living room. Mercifully, it was carpeted, taking the edge off all the white marble. A semi-circular cream leather sofa sat in the centre and, in front, a wall-mounted fireplace. It was so much like a showroom that Lena audibly gasped when she spotted the only sign of life: a large silver elongated urn.

'Is that . . .?'

Nico nodded.

Lena approached the trophy carefully. A line of gold trim spiralled down its length and, between, were the signatures of every Formula One world champion. Lena traced a line from Farina in 1950 all the way up to Laurent, each revolution marking a decade of winners. 'This is incredible,' she said, voice soft with awe.

Nico watched, unmoved. 'Come upstairs,' he said.

Lena felt a pang of anticipation that almost felt like fear. She wasn't a natural seductress so, in lieu of technique, followed him up submissively. He led her into and through a bedroom, out onto a terrace, and handed her a fresh glass of champagne. She leaned over the terrace wall and looked onto an infinity

pool. Beyond, sunset torched the horizon. 'This is stunning.'
She turned and let him come to her. She could feel the heat of
his skin and tilted her face to his. For the first time, she was the
one to make a move. It was a tender kiss, soft and slow, and
when he opened his mouth, she almost dropped her drink. He
took it from her and set it aside in one fluid move. He circled
his arms around her waist and lifted her onto the wall, just
like the first time they met.

If you want me to stop, say red.

Lena ached with the need to do it again. He kissed her
neck, then wrapped one hand around it, not quite squeezing.
Her body arched into his, seething with pleasure. She needed
him to undress her, to touch her, to fuck her. She remembered
the feel of his fingers, making her drip with want. She pressed
against him, desperate for bare skin.

An angry sound rose from his chest and he broke away with
startling violence. He looked at her with something indiscern-
ible. Resentment? Regret? Contempt? 'Stay here,' he instructed.
He turned and marched back through the double doors.

'Where are you—'

He slammed the doors shut, leaving Lena alone. Her body
was so keyed up, it ached to the point of pain. She was tempted
to touch herself to relieve the throbbing there. Somewhere close
by, a door whined open. Lena glanced down to try to locate
it. Below, Nico strode to the edge of the pool. Lena was about
to call out playfully when his voice cut in.

'Sabine.'

She followed his gaze and startled when she saw movement in the pool. It was a woman and when she turned Lena

saw that she was naked. She had creamy pale skin and long flame-red hair; not bottle-red but natural. As far as Lena could see, everything about her was natural and yet so gallingly faultless. She emerged from the pool slowly and Lena watched, transfixed. She was curvy but toned: full breasts and a tight, taut stomach. Lena's breath grew shallow as she realised what Nico intended: a threesome with her and Sabine.

Sabine. The name he had said on the boat. Had he summoned this woman here? Her skin was wet but she embraced Nico, dampening his shirt. He kissed her lips and pulled her towards him. The sight raised a complex storm of emotion: confusion, envy and anger – but also curiosity.

Nico traced his fingertips up the curve of her inner thigh. He stroked her pert pussy and Sabine purred with pleasure. Lena was mesmerised. She watched as Nico touched the woman, making her moans deepen. Sabine pressed against his fingers and Lena could tell that he was teasing her, not letting her have enough. He leaned down and took a pink nipple in his mouth. Lena could see his tongue dip in and out, flicking the tip of it. Lena's own breath grew rapid.

Sabine rippled with pleasure and curled her fists to keep control. Lena waited for them to look up, to invite her to join them, but they were lost in each other. Nico closed his mouth around her nipple, sucking it wholly, but taking his time. Each time Sabine moaned, Lena felt a pulse of heat. She imagined leaning down and licking one nipple herself. The thought almost made her moan out loud.

It occurred to her then that perhaps this *was* her invitation; her own private show. She backed away from the edge, towards the French doors. She pulled one open but it didn't move, then tried again to no avail. Confused, she tried the other, then both at once, but they didn't budge. She walked back to the terrace wall. Sabine was stretched out by the lip of the pool with both legs in the water. Nico stripped off and walked in. His muscled chest was gold in the sunset and his hair was flecked with light. He approached Sabine and lifted her legs onto his shoulders.

'Nico.' The word was feeble in her throat and Lena tried again. 'I can't get out.' She waited, but he didn't react to her. 'The doors are locked.' Again, no reaction. 'Nico!'

He pulled Sabine closer to the edge of the pool. He lowered his head and began to lick her. Lena couldn't understand what was happening. From where she stood, she had a full view as Nico licked Sabine – slowly, pleasurably. Lena's gaze flicked between Nico's tongue working in and out of her pussy and Sabine's pale breasts that moved in time with her quickened breath. Nico took his time, taking genuine pleasure from making Sabine gasp.

'Nico!' Lena tried again. There was no way he couldn't hear her. It dawned on her that *this* is what he intended: to have her watch him fuck Sabine. The realisation curled like a fist inside her chest, squeezing hard, contracting her airway, but she couldn't rip herself away.

Sabine moaned louder as Nico's tongue moved faster. She bucked against him, reaching for something to grab in her fists, needing something to ground her. He licked her, long, hard and insistent, making her pant in rapture. Then, she came with a loud and primal cry. He ground her into his mouth, licking until she grabbed at him, sinking her fingers into his hair.

'I need you,' she told him. 'I need *you*, Nico. Please.'

In one fluid move, he lifted himself out of the pool, his biceps flexing with pressure. Lena got her first full look at his cock: thick, hard and smooth. She wanted him – wanted *it* – but he pressed into Sabine's pussy. She bucked against it, rabid with need. He pushed inside her, inch by inch, making her beg for it. He pushed all the way inside and she cried out with pleasure. She rolled on top of him, arching her back so that her glorious breasts were in full form. Nico groaned and reached out to touch them. He brushed his thumb across her nipples, making her contract with pleasure. She rocked on top of him and, then, she came again, her moans stretching into the night air. It was the most exquisite sound that Lena had ever heard.

Nico flipped Sabine on her back again, still deep inside her. He leaned down and kissed her, shockingly tender. Jealousy fired inside Lena. Then, it was Nico's turn. He moved against her and Lena could hear his flesh on hers. She watched him fuck her, thrusting inside again and again, and then, just at the point of coming, he looked up and met Lena's eyes, crying out in pleasure as he grasped Sabine's hair. The look in his eye was wild and electric and Lena felt punched by it. He made a loud, guttural sound and then he collapsed on top of her. She wrapped her arms and legs around him as they lay there in sweat and sex, both of them finally sated.

Lena's mind was like a trapeze, swinging from one extreme to another. She couldn't settle on a single emotion; it all clashed together. The sight of their tangled limbs made her sick with envy and fury. She turned and fled, and this time when she tried the doors, they slid smoothly open. She stood there, baffled, then darted inside and snatched up her overnight bag. Downstairs, she picked her way through the maze of rooms back to the front hallway. She yanked open the door and marched out onto the lawn. But, there, she froze. The yacht was gone. She spun in a circle, quite unable to believe it. Was she *stuck* there?

'Ms Aden,' said a voice behind her. Eliot was on the lawn. 'May I interest you in a drink?' He motioned at the house.

'No, thank you. Actually, I was hoping to get out of here.'

'"Get out of here?"' he repeated, as if he had never heard this colloquialism.

'I want to leave.'

'I understand and, of course, you may. *Ariadne* returns to Crushes at 6am tomorrow.'

'Tomorrow? No. I need to go now.'

'I'm afraid that's not possible, Ms Aden.'

'Can you *just* call me Lena please?' she snapped. Then, catching herself: 'I'm sorry, Eliot. I'm just stressed. Please can you call the boat back?'

'I'm afraid I can't do that. The waterways are dark and unless there is an emergency, *Ariadne* isn't cleared for passage.'

Lena grew agitated. 'Well, what if it *is* an emergency?'

His expression changed. 'Are you hurt?' He hurried over to her.

'No.' She warded him off. 'I'm— I just . . .'

Sympathy moved across his features. 'Ms—' He caught himself. 'Lena, why don't you come inside for a drink and we can see what we can do?'

Frustration sparked inside her, but she knew it was bratty to blame Eliot. 'Fine,' she agreed helplessly. She followed him back inside and down a short flight of draughty steps into a brick kitchen, different from the one above.

'The servant's quarters,' he said with a wry lift of a brow.

Lena offered a weak smile. Eliot gestured at a rocking chair and Lena dropped into it. 'I don't understand why I'm here.'

Eliot busied himself with drinks. When he brought hers over, Lena was surprised to find that it wasn't alcohol but hot chocolate. She accepted it with thanks and used the chance to study Eliot. He had white hair and kind blue eyes, and was a little on the portly side.

'How long have you known Nico?' she asked.

Eliot gently blew on the surface of his tea. 'All his life. I used to work for his father.' A shadow moved across his face.

'Is he . . . kind?' Lena was embarrassed by the needy note in her voice. In LA, kindness wasn't valued. Ambition, hard work and single-mindedness, yes, but seldom kindness.

Eliot had a curious look on his face. For a moment, it seemed like he wouldn't answer, but then he said, 'Not to himself.' He sensed that Lena would probe and quickly intercepted. 'In any case, you should get some rest.' He motioned at her cup. 'Please take that upstairs and get a good night's sleep. Tomorrow, we'll get you home.'

'There's really no way I can leave?'

'Not right now I'm afraid.'

Lena wrapped her fingers around the hot mug. 'Okay.' She stood. 'Thank you.'

'Goodnight, Lena.'

She walked back to the bedroom upstairs. Quietly, she opened the French doors and propped one open with a chair, then snuck to the edge of the terrace. The pool was empty. There was no sign of Nico or Sabine. Were they spending the night together? The thought made her feel so profoundly rejected, just like at that party when he'd accused her of stalking him. She fizzed with resentment and knew that she wouldn't sleep unless she found some way to release it. She eyed the pool, heat rising off it. She rifled through her bag for her bikini, then grabbed a robe from the bathroom and made her way downstairs. At the pool, she stripped slowly. She glanced up, half-expecting to see him watching, but there was no sign of him. She dove into the pool and gasped at the heat. Once her skin adjusted, she swam ten, then twenty, laps but her mind wouldn't clear. It conjured images of Nico and Sabine, the sounds they made still ringing in her ears. She swam on, hoping to quieten her thoughts. Finally, at fifty laps, she began to tire. She swam to the edge of the infinity pool and looked out at the distant lights. She folded her arms over the lip and laid her head on top. One day, she too would own a pool like this. She breathed in the warm fumes and let the tension go. Her muscles relaxed and, finally, her mind did too.

'Hi.'

Lena jerked into wakefulness. The voice had come from above. She turned to find Sabine standing next to the pool. Her red hair was freshly washed and she wore a flimsy silk slip that strained against her breasts.

'I was worried you would fall asleep,' she said.

Lena climbed out of the pool, clumsy in her haste, and wrapped the robe around herself.

Sabine brandished a bottle of champagne. 'Want a glass?'

Lena eyed it sceptically. 'Are you . . .' She hesitated. 'A sex worker?'

Sabine was amused. 'No. I'm a friend of Nico's.'

'A friend?'

'With benefits.'

'So was that show for *my* benefit?'

Sabine arched a brow. 'Why? Did you like it?'

Lena scoffed. 'Doesn't it bother you?'

'Doesn't what bother me?'

'Being used.'

'Au contraire, cherie,' she said in a convincing French accent. 'He is very good at what he does.' A suggestive smile curled on her lips. 'And so am I.'

Goosebumps rose on Lena's skin. 'Is he watching us?'

'No,' Sabine assured her. 'He doesn't do anything without consent.'

'Is that so?'

'Yes.'

'So why did he lock me out on the terrace and force me to watch you both?'

Sabine frowned. 'He didn't.'

'He *did*. I couldn't get in the house.'

Sabine looked up at the terrace. 'Those doors don't auto-lock. Did you lift the handle to open them?'

Lena faltered. When she first arrived, the doors were already open. Nico closed them when he left. Lena had pressed the handles downwards when she first tried to open them. Later, she must have pulled upwards by chance as she fiddled with them. He hadn't locked her out after all. *God, what an idiot.*

Sabine saw her face. 'I told you: he doesn't do anything without consent.'

'Did he send you here?' asked Lena.

'He's gone.'

'Gone?' Lena felt it like a punch in the gut.

'Yes, he has practice tomorrow.'

'But the boat left before him.'

Sabine pointed with the bottle. 'He took the chopper.'

Lena gave a sardonic laugh. 'Of course he did.' Whatever circles Nico moved in, they were way above her own. She shook her head, defeated. This game didn't make sense to her. 'So that's it?'

'Look, why don't we go to the spa? We can get this bottle on ice.'

'No, it's late.'

'We can talk. I'll explain a few things about Nico.' This caught Lena's interest. Sabine sensed it and pushed a little harder. 'Come on. If you get tired, you can go straight to bed.'

Lena knew that she would struggle to sleep. 'Okay,' she said finally and followed Sabine. She seemed to know her way around the labyrinth.

'I love the spa but Nico hates it.' Sabine turned right and walked along another bright white corridor. 'In fact, he hates this house.'

'He does?'

'Yes. He bought it based on the exterior. The listing didn't have internal pictures and he was too busy to visit. He assumed he was buying a creaky old dustbowl. When he got here and saw that it was completely modern inside, he was crushed. He hasn't had the heart to sell it though. I think he wants to restore it, but he'll never have the time.'

Lena was consoled to learn that this taste wasn't his. She followed Sabine through yet more corridors and out onto a square that resembled a Zen garden. She led her to a room with muted lighting and a massage table in the middle. She pulled a bucket of ice from a fridge and stuck the bottle inside it.

'Lie down,' she instructed.

Lena surveyed the table. 'No, I'm okay.'

'I'm a qualified masseuse – and, no, that's not code for *prostitute*.'

Lena studied her. 'Are you really?'

'Yes. Don't make me pull out my certificate.'

At this, Lena smiled. 'Okay, fine.'

Sabine pressed a towel into her hands. 'I'll be back in a moment.'

Lena stared at the closed door, only half certain what was happening. Was this leading to something? Or was it really just a massage? It was all so disorienting. She heard Johanna's voice in her head. *You came to LA to have fun.* 'Okay,' she said decisively. She stripped off her bikini and lay face down on the table, spreading the towel across her bottom.

Sabine knocked lightly and came in. Lena sensed rather than saw her move along the length of the table. She gathered Lena's hair to one side, her fingertips brushing the back of her neck. 'Relax,' she instructed, leaning down, her breath hot in Lena's ear.

Lena let her muscles slacken and murmured in assent.

'The oil is warm,' said Sabine. She spilt a few drops onto Lena's back, making her gasp. 'Tell me if it's too much.' She began to rub it into her skin, drawing long, firm circles from her shoulder blades down to the small of her back. Lena felt the tension leave her. Sabine dripped more oil onto her skin and rubbed until it was slippery. Lena could hear the sound of it: a slick, slapping sound between her skin and Sabine's. Her breathing sped up and she worked to keep it slow.

Sabine moved further down Lena's back, then folded back the towel. She worked on each of her cheeks in turn, kneading and rubbing. She sighed deeply as if pleased by the sight of her. Lena parted her legs ever so slightly to give her better access. Sabine rubbed her thumbs along the crease where Lena's arse met her thighs. With each repetition, she slid her thumbs further into the curve. Then, almost imperceptibly, her fingers brushed Lena's pussy. Lena closed her eyes, taken by the momentum. Her body sang with anticipation, but there was nothing for another few minutes. Had she imagined it?

Sabine massaged her inner thighs and, then, another touch, light and exquisite. Lena let out a moan. She wanted Sabine to understand that, whatever this was, she was okay with it. There was nothing for another few minutes. Then, she felt drops of hot oil on her pussy, making her gasp again. For a moment, they trickled along her skin and, then, exquisite pressure. Sabine rubbed in the oil with two fingers. Lena moaned more loudly, encouraging her. For a few moments, they stayed like that, Sabine rubbing the oil into Lena's pussy as she tried not to squirm with pleasure. She sensed Sabine adjust her position and, then, something warm and wet was on her: Sabine's tongue on her pussy. Lena had never been with a woman before and knowing that this ethereal redhead with her perfect breasts was bent between her legs turned her on like never before. She tried to keep still, to not lose control.

Sabine was slow at first, licking in long, firm strokes. Then, she lightened the pressure, flicking quickly instead. Lena panted with pleasure, unable to grasp which was making her more delirious. Sabine licked and sucked, knowing just where and how to touch her. Lena bucked against her tongue, wanting more of it, wanting to turn around and put Sabine's flesh in her mouth.

Sabine slipped her tongue inside Lena and she cried out in rapture. She lost the reins on her body and writhed wildly as Sabine's tongue moved with her, licking and lapping at her soaking wet pussy. Sabine began to moan and the added vibration sent Lena over the edge. She screamed with abandon, coming into Sabine's mouth. The air itself seemed to pulse, her entire body alight. She collapsed against the table, shivering as her senses returned to her.

She felt weight press down on the table and saw that Sabine had got on above her. She placed a leg on either side of Lena's body, straddling her so that she sat at the base of Lena's spine as she resumed the massage. Lena sucked in a breath. She could feel Sabine's pussy on her skin. It was wet, and made a slick sound as she rocked back and forth with the motion of the massage. Lena felt herself grow even wetter. Sabine rocked gently, oiling her own pussy from Lena's skin. She leaned forward and pressed her breasts against Lena's back. She slid back and forth and the oil made a soft squelching sound between their bare skin. Sabine's breath quickened as she rubbed herself against Lena's arse. Lena reached back, grabbed Sabine's hands and pulled them to her breasts. Sabine moaned and moved faster on top of her, her cries loud and wanton. She squeezed Lena's breast, desperate to stroke them but unable to for the weight of both their bodies. Instead, she bit Lena's shoulder, her movements growing frenzied as she ground her pussy into Lena's skin. She moved faster and faster until the pressure built and then, with a resounding cry, she came against Lena's arse. She collapsed onto her, both of them slick with oil and sweat. They lay there, one on top of the other, shivering with adrenaline. When her heartbeat slowed, Sabine lifted herself onto her elbows so that Lena could turn around beneath her. She lowered herself again so that their breasts pressed together. Sabine took one of Lena's nipples in her mouth.

'Oh, you're not finished?' Lena murmured.

'God, no,' said Sabine. She closed her lips again.

Lena let herself be touched, be controlled, be played like a fucking marionette. Sabine was from another world; a sylph sent to lead her astray and Lena knew that if she was asked at this moment, with her body keyed up like this, she would follow this woman to the very depths of hell.

Chapter 6

Lena's brain thumped in her skull – punishment for all the champagne she had drunk last night. She let the cold shower pelt her skin, shocking her to her senses. She dressed slowly and steeled herself for downstairs. There were two other people in the house – Sabine and Eliot – and she didn't know how to behave around either of them. Her old acquaintance *shame* had come to find her this morning, armed with a dozen questions. *Does Eliot know? What will he think? How many others have there been before you?*

Lena squared her shoulders, trying for defiance. She had had fun last night. She'd had *fun* – and that had been missing from so much of her life. She was tired of being cowed by shame and forced herself to hold her head high as she marched out of her room. On the landing, however, she paused to listen for voices. Hearing none, she padded down the stairs discreetly. In the main kitchen, she found a coffeepot brewing.

'Hello?' she called tentatively.

'Good morning, Lena.'

She spun. 'Hi, Eliot.'

'Sleep well?'

She coloured. 'Yes, thank you.' She tried to read meaning into his question; any hint that he knew what happened. 'And you?'

He tipped his head obligingly.

Lena hesitated. 'Have you seen Sabine?'

'Ms Cadieux left early this morning.'

'I see.' Lena hovered unsurely. 'I guess I should go as well.'

'I've just put some coffee on. Won't you have a cup? We have fresh pastries too.'

Lena smiled, disarmed by his warmth. It seemed that Eliot wasn't as frosty as he had first appeared. She accepted a coffee with thanks and plucked a pain au chocolat from a wicker basket. 'Who is Sabine?' she asked casually.

Eliot sat at the table and took a sip of coffee. 'She is a friend of Mr Laurent's.'

Lena rolled her eyes. 'Eliot, surely you call him "Nico" when he's not around?'

'If that's what you would prefer.'

'I would.'

Eliot smiled a little. 'She's a friend of Nico's.'

Lena thought this over, then decided to be direct. 'And they occasionally sleep together?'

Eliot's mouth pinched in one corner, displeased by this call for indiscretion, but he answered nonetheless. 'Yes, I believe they do.'

'Is she a sex worker?'

'Heavens no. Mr— Nico would be far too worried about the optics. He would lose all his sponsorships.'

'So she's just a random friend that he can call to this island at any time of day?'

'No, she's a nurse.'

'A nurse?'

Eliot sighed, realising that he wasn't getting rid of her any time soon. 'Sabine lives across the bay. She looks after Nico's brother.'

'Gabriel has a nurse?'

Eliot jolted. 'You know about Gabriel?'

'Yes. Nico told me about him on the boat.'

Surprise flashed across his features. Clearly, he was taken aback.

'Why?' asked Lena.

Eliot set down his cup. 'Well, he never tells his friends about Gabriel.'

Lena considered this. 'Eliot, if he has an arrangement with Sabine, why bring me here? Is he just toying with me?'

Eliot was quiet for a beat. 'He told you about Gabriel on the boat?'

'Yes, right before I spilt the drink.' Lena remembered how he'd clammed right up. That's when he'd summoned Sabine. Was he punishing Lena for . . . what? Seeing more than he'd planned to reveal? She looked at Eliot. 'Was he punishing me?' She waited and when he didn't answer, she reached out and touched his hand, making him start a little. 'Eliot, he was punishing me for getting too much out of him. Is that it?'

Eliot gently drew back his hand. '*Punishment* is the wrong word. A defence mechanism perhaps. A reminder to himself that he must keep you at arm's length.'

'Why?'

'That's what balances him: racing, time alone, time with . . . friends. He feels stifled in long-term relationships.'

'I'm not asking for a long-term relationship. I'm asking for . . .' She trailed off, not knowing the end of the sentence. 'I'm asking for some time with him.'

Eliot studied her. 'You have things you care about in your life?'

'Yes. My writing, my career, my friends.'

'And you're proud of who you are – fundamentally?'

She blinked. 'I mean, I'm not happy with where I am in my career but, fundamentally, yes, I'm proud of who I am.' As she said it, she realised that it was true. She was smart and loyal and resilient; generous with her time and money; and compassionate towards those weaker than her – and she *was* proud of that.

'If that's the case, Ms Aden, I would suggest that you get on that boat and never come back.'

Lena blanched. 'Why?'

'Mr Laurent burns the things he cares about.'

The words clanged like a bell, telling Lena to run. 'But, Eliot—'

Briskly, he snapped to his feet. 'The boat will be leaving soon, Ms Aden. The captain is already on board.' He whisked away her empty mug and the half-eaten pastry on her plate. 'Is your luggage ready to be collected?'

'Yes, but—'

'In that case, I shall attend to it. You may go straight to the boat.' He gave her a tight nod. 'Good luck to you, Ms Aden.'

Lena stared at the space he left behind, thwarted once again. She threw up her hands in defeat and headed to the yacht, hoping that things would be clearer once they returned to shore. The captain, who she now realised was the same man that drove her to the marina, greeted her with a nod. Wordlessly, they set sail with just the two of them on board. Lena walked to the stern and watched the island recede to a dot. She felt a sense of melancholy settle over her.

Mr Laurent burns the things he cares about.

Would she be burnt by him? She turned into the wind and let it buffet her skin. Nico made her behave in ways that she had never imagined. Watching him with Sabine had unleashed something inside her. And Lena's own time with her had revealed something she had never known. The realisation was hot like coal, firing deep inside. The promise of more was tantalising, but what was the cost of Nico's orbit? Getting burnt irrevocably? With so much depending on the next few months, Lena couldn't get lost in him.

As they sailed on, she realised that it wasn't her choice to make. She had no way of contacting him: no phone number or email – just this house in the middle of the sea and she wouldn't even know how to find it. As ever, Nico was in control.

*

The bar was dark and bland: faux mahogany tables lined with cushioned booths and wine literally on tap. Lena had never been there before. She had only stepped in after spotting the large screen playing Formula One. There was a clutch of fans on the sofa in front, but nothing like the raucous groups that crowded in here during football. Lena watched from the edge.

It was the penultimate lap of the Azerbaijan Grand Prix and Nico had just been told to pit. Changing his tyres this late in the race gave him the greatest chance of setting the fastest lap and earning an extra point in the driver's championship – sorely needed with Vossen leading the race. Nico had a healthy lead ahead of the driver in third place, but it was a gamble nonetheless. In the pit lane, the Mercedes team descended on Nico's car. Their lightning-quick pit stops were legendary in the sport. But, to their horror, the wheel gun got stuck in the front right tyre. Lena held her breath and watched the seconds tick by as the mechanics tried to wrench it free. By the time they managed it, they had lost seven seconds – an eternity in this sport – and when Nico rejoined the track, he had lost second place to Samuel Peraza, teammate to Vossen.

'And it's a nightmare for Mercedes!' cried the commentator.

Nico's race engineer was heard on the radio: 'Nico, we'll debrief everything afterwards.'

'Just let me race,' he snapped in reply. Lena was surprisingly satisfied to hear the harried note in his voice. It seemed that Nico Laurent wasn't always a hundred per cent in control. She watched as he pulled up behind Peraza with half a lap to go. Rather than wait for the straight, Nico attempted to overtake at the notorious Turn Fifteen. The gathered fans gasped when the two cars came millimetres from touching. Then, Nico pulled forward and the fans in the bar roared with joy. They didn't care that Nico drove under the French flag; to them, he was wholly American.

'And Nico Laurent moves back up into second place,' said the commentator, just as he passed the chequered flag. 'That will be a relief for Mercedes. And he has taken fastest lap, putting him neck and neck with Vossen in the championship. Oh, what a season this is turning out to be.'

Lena watched as Nico parked and lifted himself from the car. Even with his helmet on, it was easy to read his mood – clearly disappointed with P2. He stepped onto the scales to be weighed before he was allowed on the podium. Lena had read that drivers could lose nearly half a stone in a single race.

Up in the cooldown room, Nico mopped his face with a towel and took a swig of water. He raked a hand through his hair, a frown on his brows.

'God, he's so hot,' said a young blonde woman at a nearby table.

'Who is he?' asked her friend, turning around to look at the screen.

'Nico Laurent. I mean, they're *all* hot but he's like a god.'

'Oh my lord,' a third friend chimed in, looking out over her spectacles. 'I would climb all over him.'

The blonde winced. 'Maybe I'd ask him to shower first.'

'Or not,' said spectacles, raising a chorus of laughter.

Lena listened with a sense of unease. It wasn't jealousy but a different emotion entirely: a twisted sense of pride because, unlike this trio of American beauties, Lena had slept with Nico Laurent. She knew what it was like to have him pin her in place, to touch her in ways that made her make sounds that were alien to her. She felt an overwhelming urge to tell them; to lean in chummily and say, *You're never gonna believe me but* . . . The prospect gave her a thrill but it soured quickly to shame. The old Lena would never feel the need to brag about a tryst with a celebrity.

It had been a week since she had seen Nico at Crushes and each passing day confirmed what she suspected: that whatever they had was over – a fierce but brief flash in the pan. This is what she had always feared about casual hookups. That after the high, you'd be left with the sting of rejection. And it *did* sting. To Nico, she was just another body, another forgettable face. He hadn't been beguiled by her charm or intellect. That was the most cringe-inducing thing; that she'd really believed he *would*. She'd really thought that he would see that she was somehow different.

She watched him on the podium, pouring champagne over his two opponents. He took a swig and then poured it over the crowd. She was glad then that she didn't have his number or any other way to contact him, for she knew she would have caved. Standing there transfixed, she was dismayed by her own weakness. With a deep breath, she tore herself away from the screen and walked out into the early summer heat.

*

The writers' room in the Aston Theatre was lit with a hazardous mix of gifted candles and iPhone torches. Normally, the literal nature of not being able to keep the lights on would appeal to the writer in all of them, but Brianna's grave expression chilled their amusement. The Aston's age-old stage lights kept shorting the circuit. They had to be replaced and the three quotes so far were each over $6,000. Brianna was unusually anxious. This was the first time in her tenure that the Aston faced extinction. There had *always* been pressure, but this time – with the spectre of Keller Stone hanging over their heads – it felt like it might actually happen.

Ahmed refreshed the GoFundMe page. They had raised only $800 of their $6,000 target despite a concerted blitz on social media. Lena had felt embarrassed asking for donations on Facebook and Twitter. All her old friends would see and know that she hadn't made it – but they *had* to save the Aston.

'What about William McGregor?' asked Lena. 'He seemed interested in working together.'

'I'm trying to wrangle a date from his assistant,' said Brianna. 'But even if I manage it, there'll be months of hoops to jump through. There always is with charities.'

'Could we get an electrician to do it pro bono?'

Brianna looked at her wryly. 'Only creatives agree to do that. Electricians, you have to pay.' She laughed bitterly.

Lena felt a knot in her gut. If *Please Understand* didn't run, her last shot in LA would vanish in an instant.

Gloria cleared her throat. 'Guys, I know this isn't the best time but I've got something to tell you.' A candle flickered, casting shadows across her face. 'I've got a new job.'

Brianna breathed in through her nose. 'Gloria, you're not serious.'

'I'm sorry. I didn't want to say anything until I knew for sure but I just can't afford this job anymore.'

'Well, where are you going instead? The Geffen hasn't

hired anyone new for a decade and the Orpheum would mean a two-hour commute.'

'I'm going to clean for a while and—'

'Clean?' said Brianna, as if she didn't understand the word.

'Yeah. I mean, it's obviously not what I wanna be doing but this . . .' She shrugged. 'This was all a pipe dream, you know? A Latina with an accent making her way in Hollywood? It was never gonna happen.'

Lena felt the knot harden. Gloria had an exquisite eye for detail and a surgeon's precision in set design. She deserved to be working at the very top level of the industry.

Ahmed hopelessly tapped a key on his laptop. The page on his screen refreshed, the $800 figure taunting him. 'It's *fucked* up,' he said. He looked across at Lena. 'What do you always say? If you can't get past the gatekeepers, build your own house?' He threw up his hands. 'So now what?'

'Could we speed up the process with William?' Lena asked Brianna. 'He seemed to like us. If we can get that meeting, I'm sure we could get the funding.'

'I can try but I don't think we can bypass the charity's protocols. They're there for a reason and—'

'What the fuck,' Ahmed interrupted, shooting up from his chair. He tapped a key once, then twice, blinking rapidly. 'Holy fucking fuck.' He turned the laptop round. There, on screen, was a figure: $6,800. Underneath, it said, '*You have reached 113% of your target.*' He scrolled down. 'An anonymous donor just gave us six thousand dollars!' They gathered around the screen, a glowing square in the dark.

Brianna read out the message from the donor. 'I can't wait to see *Please Understand*. NL.' She straightened. 'NL?'

Lena's stomach flipped over. *Nico. Nico Laurent.* Brianna saw the look on her face and angled her head in query.

Ahmed whooped with joy. 'Now you can stay!' he told Gloria.

She smiled with regret. 'This doesn't change anything, Ahmed.'

'What?' He stared at her. 'Why?'

'This is just to pay an electricity bill. My situation is still the same.'

'I can do some math,' said Brianna. 'Move some budgets around to get you what you need.'

'I'm sorry, guys. I'm so tired of living hand to mouth. I need some stability. Who knows? When you're all Oscar winners, maybe you can look up this old broad but until then, I'm down for the count.'

Lena felt a deep, implacable sorrow. It was profoundly unjust that someone as skilled as Gloria had to bow out. She leaned forward and gave her a hug. Ahmed watched them, his arms crossed in denial. But, then, in seeing Gloria's tears, he leaned over too and threw his arms around her. Brianna looked on placidly.

'Am I interrupting something?'

They sprang apart, startled by the voice in the half-dark. The stranger stepped into the circle of light, met with astonishment.

'What are you doing here?' demanded Lena.

'I came to see you,' said Nico.

Lena pointed at the screen. 'Was this you?'

Nico didn't look at it. 'Does it matter?'

Her colleagues looked from Nico to Lena, back and forth like spectators on a tennis court. They waited for her to respond, but she didn't know how to.

'Thank you,' she said finally, her manners kicking in. Her whole life, she had never caught a break. No one had ever given her a shortcut, a buffer or windfall, or any of those secret ingredients that greased the wheels of success. This was beyond anything she knew – and though six thousand dollars meant almost nothing to Nico, it made Lena well with emotion.

'It's nothing.' Nico shifted and his face was thrown into shadow so that Lena couldn't see his expression when he asked, 'Can I take you out for a bite?'

She looked at him blankly as if he'd spoken a foreign language. 'I . . .' She collected herself and checked her watch – a farcical action, she knew, for who could say no in these circumstances? She looked over at Brianna, who gave her a sharp nod in permission. 'Okay,' said Lena. She lifted her bag from the back of her chair and slung it over her shoulder, trying for nonchalance. She followed Nico out, leaving her colleagues stunned.

Outside, despite the fading light, Nico pulled on a baseball cap and a pair of mirrored shades. 'I hope you don't mind,' he said, pointing at them.

She remembered that Nico was used to being recognised. 'No,' she told him, feeling thoroughly fazed.

They fell in step and for the first few minutes, things were quiet and awkward. 'I owe you an apology,' he said finally.

When Lena didn't respond, Nico stopped beside her. He steered her into Ocean View Park, onto a bench in the shade of a palm tree. He took off his shades and squinted in the waning light that dappled his face through the leaves. 'I'm sorry for what I said at that party in Miami. Davide told me what happened; that nothing happened. And even if it had, I wasn't fair to you.'

Lena flushed with residual shame, remembering the visceral sting of being cast a stalker.

'And I'm sorry for what happened at Crushes. I was . . .' he rubbed a hand across his stubble, 'thrown.'

Lena could see his uncertainty. Like in his reaction to breaking glass, she glimpsed the boy in him.

'The truth is . . .' Nico exhaled, unable to force out the words. 'I want to see you more.'

Lena was rendered wordless.

Nico misread her silence. 'I know I've been impossible but, please Lena, could we maybe have dinner like a normal couple and see where this takes us?'

The word *couple* filled Lena with a luminous, schoolgirl glee. She dug a nail into the bed of her palm and lifted a shoulder casually. 'Okay,' she agreed.

'Okay?' he checked.

'Okay.'

The voltage of his smile threatened to undo her. She stood and hid her face from him. He stood too and laced her fingers in his. And as easy as that, they walked through the park together. They went to Mélisse and were led to a discreet table at the back where he took off his cap and shades. Lena became hyper aware of her own appearance: a plain white tee and jeans, white Converse, her hair pulled up in a messy bun. While Nico asked the server for water, she quickly undid her bun and tousled her hair. She checked her reflection in her wineglass but it warped her beyond recognition.

'What would you like to drink?' asked Nico.

She hurriedly looked at the wine list. 'Um, a glass of the Malbec please.' The server nodded and slipped away. Lena looked at Nico. 'So, is this technically our fourth date?' she asked – lightly, so that he would know she was joking.

'I'm sorry I haven't been in touch. I was in Azerbaijan.'

'Yes, I saw that move you pulled on Peraza.'

Nico was surprised. 'You saw the race?'

'I saw the end. That move was . . .' She couldn't find the word. *Dangerous? Reckless? Suicidal?*

He shrugged. 'The stewards looked into it but didn't find fault.'

Lena was wary of asking about his career; of coming across as a groupie. His wealth and fame felt like a chasm between them. If she focused on it for long, it would reveal the distance between them. 'You still love it?'

'Racing?' His smile lit up his eyes. 'I can't see how I would ever stop.'

'You really were in your element.'

'On the track, you can't think about anything else. Your focus is so raw and sharp, there's no room for any bullshit.'

'So those are the two categories, are they? Racing or bullshit?'

He looked at her intently. 'And there's you.' He winced immediately. 'Jesus, that was cheesy.'

She laughed. 'Just a little.'

He reached out and took her hand. 'I'm glad you came.'

'I am too.'

Lena spent the next hour with this new version of Nico. He was easy and relaxed and although they didn't go into deep talk – kept it all safe and shallow – the chemistry between them sparked. When they finished, Lena reached for her wallet but he closed his hand over hers.

'No. Let me.'

'Are you sure?' she asked, playing out the farce. How do you show a multimillionaire that you appreciate him spending a hundred dollars on a stolen hour with you? He settled the bill and walked her back to the Aston.

'When can I see you again?' he asked, pausing outside the theatre.

'Apparently, whenever you want,' she said wryly.

'Will you text me?'

'I don't have your number,' she reminded him.

He took her phone and keyed it in. 'I'm racing this weekend but could I see you the week after?'

'That sounds good.' Lena looked up at him and held her breath when he leaned in. His lips were soft and tender, barely touching her, letting her come to him. She pressed against him and felt his hands in her hair. *Oh god*, she thought, losing herself in the kiss. *I am all the way gone.*

*

'What. The. Fuck. Was. That?' said Ahmed as soon as Lena rejoined them in the candlelit writers' room.

'What was what?' she asked nonchalantly as she slung her bag on the back of her chair.

Ahmed sprang to his feet. 'Girl, you better tell us what's going on or I'm *actually* going to attack you.'

Gloria looked at him sideways. 'He hasn't been able to focus since you walked out the door.'

'Sorry but how am I supposed to focus when Nico Laurent just casually walked in and picked her up like it's the most normal thing in the world?' He turned to Lena and clasped his hands together. 'Please tell me what the hell's going on.'

'There's not very much to tell,' she said, enjoying his agitation.

'Bitch, you better spill the beans or I'm walking out with Gloria.'

She opened her laptop. 'It's not a big deal. I met him at William McGregor's party,' she lied.

Ahmed slapped the desk. 'I knew I should've come to that. Bri, you should've got me a ticket to that.'

Brianna raised her palms, denying responsibility.

'I *need* details,' Ahmed implored.

Lena rolled her eyes. 'William McGregor introduced me to him and we had a conversation but' – she gestured at the screen – 'I didn't know he was going to do this.'

'Are you *dating* him?'

'No. Of course not.' Lena lifted a shoulder. 'I mean, what does dating even mean when it comes to someone like him?'

Ahmed fell back in his chair with a longing sigh. 'Champagne breakfasts, private jets, exclusive beaches and lazy afternoons aloft a superyacht, caviar, oysters, insane sex, more champagne—'

'Okay, I get it.' Lena grew serious. 'Look, it's all very casual at the moment. He travels a lot. He's busy. I'm busy.'

'Girl, please.'

'It's just a dalliance, okay?'

'"A dalliance,"' he aped in an English accent. 'Oh, how very proper.'

'I'm just going to, you know' – she flicked a wrist in the air – 'have some fun.'

'You deserve to,' said Brianna, her earlier mood now lifted. It wasn't lost on her that this was good for the Aston. 'But do be careful,' she added.

Ahmed cut in. 'Okay, Dour Deirdre. Just let a bitch live, would you?'

Brianna scowled at him but was clearly in good spirits. 'Okay,' she said. She pushed back from the table. 'I'll let a bitch live.'

Lena laughed and revelled in the moment. She didn't know what would happen but vowed not to overthink it. For now, she had her colleagues, she had her script, the lights would come back and the show would go on.

Chapter 7

The next two days were agonising. Lena had texted Nico to say that she had enjoyed their dinner and to thank him again for the donation. Nico had responded with a cursory *me too* – and that was all. Lena had to remind herself to play it cool. She didn't want to pressure him, especially when he had warned her that their time together would be erratic. By the time he got in touch, it was Thursday morning.

I can't make it to LA next week. Will you come to Monaco tonight for this weekend's race? I'll sort out everything.

Lena stared at the message. *Monaco? Tonight?* She scoffed at the impossibility of this. It was a mad idea. She couldn't go to Monaco tonight. For starters, she had to be at the Aston tonight. And tomorrow. She couldn't miss two evenings in a row. Could she? Given Nico's donation, might Brianna let her go? The script was in good shape and they could run the sessions without her. People often went away for long weekends, perhaps not across oceans, but it wasn't entirely mad. She thought about the prospect of a whole weekend with

Nico. Surely, she couldn't decline? She reread the message, then, wincing, she sent him a single exuberant *Yes!* She was simply unable to play it cooler than that.

Great. Eliot will be in touch, came the reply.

Minutes later, her phone rang, Eliot on the line. He spoke to her in a businesslike manner, not alluding once to the last time they spoke. He explained that a car would pick her up at 5pm and take her to LAX. She would fly to Nice Côte d'Azur Airport and travel on to Monaco, spend the race weekend there and fly back on Monday evening. She agreed soberly, but after hanging up, yelled with disbelief. Johanna heard and barged in. When she heard the news, she let out a squeal.

'We need to get serious,' she said, waving at Lena's body. 'I'm booking you a double session at Kazumi's. You need a haircut, manicure and pedicure, and I'm going to assume a bikini wax too.'

Lena cut in: 'But he already knows what he's getting.'

Johanna tutted. 'Lena, you have to operate on a different plane now. You're going to Monaco! With Nico Laurent! You need to look like girlfriend material; not a bit of slap and tickle.'

'Gee, thanks.'

Johanna ignored her tone. 'We also need to sort out your wardrobe.' She counted on her fingers. 'You need something to fly in, something for Friday daytime, Friday evening, Saturday daytime, Saturday evening, the race on Sunday, Sunday evening – though you may not have time to change so let's opt for something versatile just in case – Monday daytime, and the flight back. Nine outfits in total. And, of course, lingerie.'

'I have lingerie.'

'Honey.' Johanna waggled a finger. 'No.'

'I can't afford anything fancy, Johanna.'

'Listen, I'm going to call the PR at Agent Provocateur. I'll tell her that Nico Laurent's new girlfriend is interested in their new line.'

'You can't do that.' Alarm rose in Lena's voice. 'It can't get out that I'm seeing Nico. He'll think I've crowed to the press.'

Johanna gave a knowing laugh. 'Listen, if Keira didn't know how to be discreet, there'd be at least a dozen married movie stars going through divorces.'

Lena made a face, but agreed to a day of shopping and grooming under Johanna's direction. Lena had never been particularly fashionable. While she had a basic sense of style, it was best described as 'classic'. She understood the power of fashion, but had neither the time, money nor skill to put together showstopper outfits. She was glad for Johanna's enthusiasm as they traipsed across LA, preparing Lena piece by piece to step into Nico's world. By the time they were done, Lena looked like a sleeker, richer version of herself.

Back in their flat, they packed together, brimming with expectation. Lena gave Johanna a fierce hug as she readied to leave for her flight.

'Thank you for helping me.'

Johanna smoothed a strand of Lena's hair. 'It was entirely selfish,' she said. 'This way, maybe I'll nab one of Nico's eligible colleagues.'

'I know just the guy,' said Lena, thinking of Davide Russo.

Johanna's eyes lit up. 'Oh really?'

'All in good time.' Lena gave her a playful smile. She turned to the hallway mirror. She wore a ribbed sleeveless top in cream with a knee-length A-line skirt. Classic, yes, but undeniably chic when paired with Johanna's finishing touches: spiked Gucci heels, a Cartier bracelet and an unbranded watch that Johanna had to return in precisely three days.

'I'll take your suitcase downstairs,' said Johanna. 'I don't want you getting sweaty before you get to him,' she added with a wink.

'Thank you but I think I can manage.' Lena gripped the handle and exhaled nervously. She was fully aware that this one weekend could change her entire life. 'I'll see you on the other side.' She hugged Johanna one final time and closed the door between them. She lugged the suitcase downstairs, feeling the sweat bead on her brows. Outside, she was met by Chris, the same driver who had brought her to the marina on the day she had visited Crushes. She thanked him and slid into the backseat. She assumed that he would drop her off at international departures at LAX but instead he drove straight onto the tarmac. There, she was met by a private jet: a sleek Bombardier Challenger 605.

Lena was dumbfounded. She pointed towards it. 'Is that for me?'

'Yes,' said Chris.

'But . . .' She trailed off. There were no customs, no queues, no security. Is this how the one per cent lived? She fumbled out of the car and stood on the tarmac, needing more direction. When none came, she approached the stairs self-consciously. She paused at the bottom, expecting to be told that she was in the wrong place. When no one objected, she gingerly climbed the stairs, up to the body of the jet. A flight attendant greeted her, all white teeth and glossy bun. Inside, there was no one but Lena. It felt obscene, this immense expense on just one person. She looked at the nine empty seats.

'Which one's mine?' she quipped.

'Any you like,' said the woman, whose name badge read Natalya.

Lena took a seat in the middle, brushing her hand over the soft cream leather. Her moral conscience told her that this was outrageous, but a baser, vainer part of her was thoroughly elated.

'Would you like something to drink?' asked Natalya. 'Champagne?' she suggested.

'Um, just some water would be great,' said Lena. Alcohol dehydrated her on flights and she wanted to look her best. Natalya handed her a glass, cool with condensation, and Lena gulped from it gratefully. Once the attendant was out of sight, she self-consciously took some selfies but was too embarrassed to post them. Instead, she watched the sky, unable to believe that this was her life. It was over twelve hours to Nice and though she tried to work, then read, she was far too jittery for any of it. Lulled by the engine, she drifted off to asleep.

When she woke up hours later, she was dismayed to find that her makeup was smeared. After such effort to get her looking perfect, she had gone and ruined it. She unclipped her seatbelt and immediately Natalya was by her side.

'May I help you with something?'

'Yes, um, is there somewhere to freshen up?'

Natalya's eyes skimmed over Lena. 'Of course,' she said with a hint of knowing. 'I'll show you to the bathroom.'

Lena got up and followed her. Inside, she was surprised to find a shower cubicle bigger than in some of the flats she had lived in.

'We land in ninety minutes,' said Natalya, giving her plenty of warning.

'Thank you.' Lena locked the door and laughed out loud. She felt like Alice tumbling through the rabbit hole. She unzipped her toiletry bag and went to work, making sure that she was ready for Nico. She charted the hours until she would see him. She would land in Nice early Friday afternoon and it was a thirty-minute drive from there to Monaco. She had at least a couple of hours to mentally collect herself.

When she stepped off the jet, however, a sporty-looking Mercedes was waiting on the tarmac. Nico was leaned against it, dressed in a navy suit and crisp white shirt, his hair tousled in the wind. He removed his shades and Lena took a moment to look at him. She walked down the stairs – airily, as if this wasn't completely alien to her. Nico pushed off the car as she neared. He kissed her, warm and slow and lingering – not the urgent kiss that she had expected. She felt his tongue and heat rose in her body.

'I'm taking you straight to bed,' he murmured, his lips still on hers as he spoke. He opened the passenger door for her, then slid into the driver's seat. That unremarkable action – the everyday nature of a man and a woman getting into a car – struck her with a force she hadn't expected. She was with Nico, by his side, in his car.

'What?' He noticed her smile.

She fixed her gaze on the windscreen. 'Drive,' she instructed, sensing that he was smiling too.

Nico took off his blazer, rolled his shirtsleeves to the elbow and put the car in gear. Lena noted his ease behind the wheel: relaxed, almost lazy, as he steered through the traffic in Nice. He shifted gears and she watched the tendon in his forearm tense and relax. Lena was transfixed, for there was something intensely sexy in it; something powerful, and masculine. Slowly, she let out her breath. Her body seemed to hum, keenly tuned to the nearness of him. The traffic into Monaco was thick and the silence grew taut between them, charged with everything they wanted to do to each other. She wanted him to reach between her legs, to stroke her, to make her open-mouthed in pleasure. She grew very still, paralysed by sensation: the strobe of her heart going too fast, the strum of something that felt like fear. She closed her hand over the edge of her seat, her fingers pressing divots into the buttery leather. She remembered how he had slipped his hand beneath her *Goldfinger* gown and made her come all over him. She wanted that again; to feel him against her, making her beg for more.

Nico kept his eyes on the road, but his grip on the wheel tightened, his knuckles turning white. Lena's whole body tensed with anticipation, her breathing now quick and shallow. By the time they reached the hotel, she was slick with want. They rode up in the elevator, wordless among company.

Lena had imagined him tearing off her clothes as soon as they were in his suite. Instead, he led her to the bedroom and positioned her in front of the floor-to-ceiling mirror. He slid his hand beneath her skirt and pressed the base of his palm against the nub of her pussy. She rocked against it, the thin material of her underwear already soaking wet. When her movements grew quick, Nico pulled away. She groaned, feeling herself pulse and ache. Nico unhooked her skirt and let it drop to the floor, then reached down to play with her. They both watched his fingers in the mirror as he rubbed the sheer black silk in small, precise circles. Lena moved against him, close to coming, but once again Nico withdrew. Lena panted with disbelief; begged him to continue.

He brushed his hands up her arms, then tugged off her sleeveless top. He traced her nipple through the sheer silk of her bra. They watched in the mirror as it grew hard beneath his touch. He turned her sideways and lowered his mouth to it. His breath warmed the silk, creating a pocket of moisture. Lena arched into his mouth. He breathed in and out, making her twist with lust. When she shook with her need for him, he dropped to his knees and repeated the act, this time against her pussy. He breathed out, creating heat against the fabric, then pressed it with his tongue. Lena cried out, unable to bear the wait. She needed him. She needed release. She tried to push against him, but each time she did, he drew back, only to tease her again, flicking his tongue against the fabric. Again, he closed his mouth over it and warmed it with his breath.

Lena shivered. 'Nico, please,' she begged.

He moved away and kissed her stomach. He dipped his tongue into her navel, licking it ever so slightly.

Lena felt giddy with need. '*Please,*' she urged him.

He met her eyes and pulled aside her underwear. He licked her so lightly that Lena barely felt it. Then, he added pressure, making her moan so deep and long, it sounded like she was crying. He flicked her clit once, then twice, and then, finally, mercifully, he stopped teasing. He licked her in a long, deliberate stroke, making her writhe with pleasure. His mouth was eager, his own control slipping. He licked and sucked, making her buck with need. She was so close to the edge that when he moved away, she cried out in anger. When he finally, gloriously, unzipped himself, all it took was for him to touch her slit before she came all over him.

Nico looked down at his cock as if surprised by how much she had come. It flicked the switch on his self-control. He thrust her onto the bed and stripped. Then, in an act she had craved since that night on the balcony, he finally pushed inside her. She felt such exquisite ecstasy that no sound escaped her throat. And, then, she came with such force, she lost her mind for a second. She screamed with neon abandon as Nico fucked her and fucked her – so hard and so fast, that she felt utterly consumed. Nico came with a hoarse cry and folded on top of her, his bare chest crushing her. He was quivering and Lena pulled her arms around him. She could feel his heart racing and held him until it slowed.

When his breathing calmed, he rolled onto his back. It was the first time Lena had seen his naked body up close and she was entranced by it. Nico was toned and athletic, strong but not beefy like the various Chrises of Hollywood. His skin had a hint of Mediterranean but the hair on his chest was almost blond.

'Are you okay?' he asked, turning sideways towards her.

She nodded, but Nico must have seen a hint of vulnerability, for he slid an arm beneath her and drew her into him. She fit herself against his chest and let her own breathing slow.

She traced a palm over his abs. 'Do you ever eat chocolate?' she asked, lightly kissing his shoulder.

A warm grin broke on his lips. 'Is that what you're thinking about? Chocolate?'

She smiled too. 'I'm wondering how you can keep in shape like this without giving up everything.'

'I eat chocolate when the season is over.'

'And during?'

'During? I'm basically hungry.'

She propped herself up on an elbow. 'Seriously?'

He angled his head in a hedging motion. 'No, but I am one of the taller drivers, so I have to watch my weight or it impacts my pace.'

'How often do you exercise?'

'A couple of hours a day.' He sat up and Lena idly admired the look of his skin against the bright white sheets. He checked his watch and frowned. 'I've got to head to practice soon, but I'll see you for dinner?'

'Practice?' Lena sat up too. 'Isn't that tomorrow?'

He looked at her, bemused. 'Practice is every day.'

'Oh.' She twisted the sheet in a palm. 'Should I come with you?'

'No. I need to focus. Go out. Enjoy Monaco. I'll be back this evening.' He stood and headed to the shower.

Enjoy Monaco? She didn't *know* anyone in Monaco.

Nico looked back into the room. 'Do you need a credit card?'

'For what?'

'For . . .' He waved a hand as if to say *whatever.*

'Oh.' She stiffened. 'Um, no, that's . . . no.'

He nodded and went back in. Seconds later, she heard the low rush of the shower. She felt discomfited by his offer. Is this what life was like for these men's wives and girlfriends? Sickeningly easily? Lena felt a pang of defiance. She didn't want to be like them, latching onto Nico like a stubborn barnacle. She would much rather pay her way. The thought jostled with another; a snippet from an interview with the singer Mariah Carey. In her early twenties, Carey had insisted on paying for half the mansion that she bought with her older, richer husband. *Oh yeah*, she said, looking back at the age of forty. *Quite the silly little girl, I was.*

Lena was wary of succumbing to the same naïveté. Shouldn't she enjoy Nico's money? After all, who knew when he would tire of her? What was special about *her*? She was pretty enough, but LA was filled with beautiful women. She was smart, but men rarely cared very much about that. She and Nico had been brought together purely by chance and their time together could be brief and fleeting. To squander the opportunity was silly and naive.

But then Lena remembered Eliot's expression when she mentioned Gabe. *He never tells his friends.* Nico had taken her into his confidence. Wasn't there a possibility that they really *did* have a connection? Maybe there was a chance, however infinitesimal, that Nico Laurent had chosen her after all.

On race day, the tension in the air was palpable. Nico hadn't slept with Lena the night before – not even in the same room. Instead, they had eaten dinner together before retiring to separate suites. He needed to focus, he said, and couldn't have distractions. Today, she was in the paddock, the long line of makeshift garages that held the cars and teams. They buzzed with mechanics and engineers and more than a few celebrities. On passing the Red Bull garage, she had spotted Tom Cruise. He had caught her looking and flashed her that famous smile. She had hurried along, flustered, to the Mercedes garage. Lena felt in the way there. She had asked Nico if she should sit in the box, but he had dismissed it out of hand. Now she sat awkwardly with Eva Rafaeli, the girlfriend of Nico's teammate Greg Richards. Eva was five inches taller than Lena with long honey-blonde hair and a natural golden tan. Lena was violently thankful that Johanna had curated her wardrobe and look. Without it, she would be thoroughly out of her element here. She tried to make conversation with Eva but the girl frequently broke away to check her phone, laughing at this or that tweet or meme about her famous boyfriend.

The race started well for Nico who had pole position after setting the fastest lap in qualifying. Behind him was Vossen, followed by Samuel Peraza, Vossen's teammate at Red Bull. In fourth place was Greg Richards.

'How long have you and Greg been together?' asked Lena. Eva set down her phone. 'Nine months.'

'Oh, nice. And does this ever get old?'

'What?' Eva looked at her blankly.

Lena sheepishly motioned at the paddock. 'You know, the glamour, the private jets, the champagne and caviar.'

'Oh!' Eva flicked a wrist in the air. 'I mean, my dad was a racing driver, so I'm used to it.'

'Oh, right. I see.' Lena groped for something else to say, but Eva's attention was back on her screen.

On track, the drivers began to pit. Monaco was a difficult track for overtaking, so the teams usually aimed for a one-stop strategy. Nico came in to pit and exited smoothly after a lightning-fast two seconds. He joined the track in fifth place but regained the lead when each of the drivers in front came in to pit.

'And you and Nico?' asked Eva.

'Oh, we're very new.'

Eva made a sound and nodded.

Lena caught the meaning: *of course you are*. Casually, she said, 'I'm sure I'm one of many.'

Eva tossed her hair and shrugged. 'You know how these drivers are.'

'In theory,' she said, hoping to win the girl over with candour. 'Not in practice.'

'Oh, I'd say you've probably got it right.'

'I see.' Lena smiled with forced intimacy. 'So how long can I expect in this tenure?'

'Honestly?' Eva grimaced. 'I haven't seen one of Nico's girls in the paddock more than once.'

Lena flushed. 'Oh,' she said, hating the callow note in her voice. 'Right.' She knew that it might be brief, but *two weeks*?

Eva smiled sympathetically. 'Sorry. I know that's not what you want to hear. If I were you, I'd milk it. He's a great-looking guy. Enjoy it.'

'Yeah,' said Lena softly. 'That's what everyone tells me.' She felt her cheeks burn and turned away from Eva, fixing her gaze on the screen.

The race was reaching its final stages and Mercedes were on course for a one-two, Nico leading and Greg second. The garage pulsed with pre-emptive glee and Lena tried to feed off it; to quieten the knowledge of what Eva had told her. When Nico and Greg passed the chequered flag, the garage erupted in joy. The mechanics and engineers rushed out onto the pit lane.

Lena looked at Eva. 'Do we . . . ?' She pointed after the team.

'Up to you,' she said with a dismissive lift of the shoulder. She walked out to join them.

Lena watched indecisively. She didn't know what to do, so awkwardly followed Eva. She hovered at the back of the group while Eva cut her way through it. Moments later, Lena spotted her kissing Greg's helmet. She checked to see if Nico would look for her, but he was busy hugging his engineers. He looked jubilant, radiant, truly in his element. Lena smiled instinctively. She decided to hang back and let him enjoy the moment.

The drivers were weighed and ushered up to the podium: Nico in the centre, Greg to his right and Vossen to his left in third place. Nico's win put him ahead of Vossen in the championship, though with thirteen races to come, nothing at all was certain.

After the trophies, the drivers popped open the bottles of champagne, dousing one another and the crowd. Eva leaned back and caught some in her mouth. Lena watched from the fringes, separate from the in-crowd. Once the cheer died down, the drivers were commandeered for interviews and briefings. Lena felt like a fifth wheel as she hung around the paddock. She busied herself on the phone but felt conspicuously out of place. Eventually, she peeled away, onto the track itself. It was growing dark now and there was a distinct chill in the air. She listened to the hum of the crowd as they filtered from the circuit. She felt small with uncertainty, cowed by improbability. She walked without purpose and found that an hour had passed by the time she returned to the paddock. Nico spotted her and strode over.

'There you are.' He seemed exhausted but happy and kissed her on the lips. 'Listen, I've still got more meetings. Go back to the hotel and we'll head to dinner in a couple of hours.'

She arched a brow. 'No party tonight?'

'No.' He smiled rakishly. 'I only want you.'

She let him go. 'And I only want you,' she said in his wake.

*

Lena smoothed the electric-blue velvet of her dress. The long sleeves and structured shoulders were deceptively chaste; when she turned around, the backless dress exuded sex. She added Johanna's pearl earrings and watched Nico in the mirror. She tensed with the effort not to ask, but lost the battle with herself.

'Nico?'

He worked one cufflink in. 'Yes?'

'Eva, Greg's girlfriend, said something to me today.'

He looked up, concerned. 'What?'

'She said that your girlfriends never last longer than a single visit to the paddock.'

Surprise flashed across his features. 'She said that?'

'Yes.'

He exhaled sharply. 'Eva is a spoilt little rich girl who likes to mess with people because she's always bored.'

'But was she right?'

Nico sighed and came and stood behind her. He wrapped his arms around her and kissed the space behind her ear. 'Yes, she's right – but why is that important? Do you care that I ate at Mélisse only once with a girl, or went to the opera only once with another? All it means is that they didn't hold my interest.'

'But taking them to the paddock is personal.'

'It's really not. Tom Cruise was there today. Do you think any of us are friends with him? No. It's the glamour that people are drawn to so, yes, I bring along my dates.' He searched her eyes in the mirror. 'But you're more than that.'

Lena remained neutral, not wanting to reveal how glorious those words sounded to her. She turned in his arms and kissed him. His hands found the bare skin of her back and traced the curve of her spine. She felt him grow hard and pushed away. 'We have a reservation,' she chided gently.

'Forget the reservation.'

'Come on,' she said, breaking away from him. 'We'll be late.' He squared his jaw in boyish defiance but followed her out the door.

At Maison Boulud, they were shown to a discreet table in the garden. Nico spoke to the waiter in French and the two of them exchanged a joke, bursting into laughter. Lena looked on, bemused. Nico was far more relaxed in French and for a brief moment, she wished that she could speak it too.

'Does Gabe speak French?' she asked.

Nico tensed at the mention of his brother. 'Yes,' he answered stiffly.

'Do you think of yourself as French or American?'

'Can't I be both?' he asked, relaxing a little.

'Yes, but probably not equally.'

He considered this. 'I'm more my mother than I am my father,' he said finally.

Lena wanted to ask about his mother, but could see that he was uncomfortable and steered them on to safer ground: the race, the championship, his rivalry with Vossen. She loved to watch him talk about work. He was lively and animated, totally unguarded. The whole time she listened, a smile played on her lips.

'How's *your* work?' he asked, catching himself halfway into an explanation of the Halo.

Lena nodded brightly. She told him that they were casting *Please Understand* and that, afterwards, she planned to switch to feature films. She didn't say that she had already tried and failed and was running out of time. 'It's the networking I can't stand,' she said. 'It's all the same people at the same parties having the same conversations and making the same promises. It's all so repetitive.'

Nico arched a brow. 'Even the party where you met me?'

She laughed. 'No. That was definitely new.'

'I never would have guessed,' he said, slipping the tips of his fingers beneath her dress.

Discreetly, she pushed him away. 'So what about you?' she asked.

'What about me?'

'I take it that wasn't a first for you? Having sex with a woman within minutes of meeting her?'

He shrugged in assent.

'Is it . . . normal?'

The corner of his lips twisted in a moue. 'It can be.'

Lena grimaced, knowing that she shouldn't ask her next question. 'So . . . how many are we talking overall?' Nico sighed and Lena could see that the mood was slipping away. 'I mean, you don't have to tell me.' She laughed to show that it was light-hearted. 'I just figured it's somewhere in the hundreds,' she added to test the waters.

Nico shrugged.

'So thereabouts?'

'I couldn't say.'

'Would you say it's closer to one hundred or two?'

'Closer to one.'

'Okay.' She couldn't gauge if the flutter in her gut was shock or relief. 'And you get tested regularly?'

'Jesus,' he said under his breath.

'I just want to make sure.'

'Yes, I get tested.'

'Okay.' She was glad that he hadn't asked for her figure, for it was shockingly low. She topped up his wine, hoping to draw a line beneath the tricky discussion. The waiter brought over another bottle and Lena gratefully proffered her glass. She soon grew tipsy and noticed that Nico was a little drunk too.

'I'd like to dance,' she declared.

'Then the lady shall dance!' he said, waving a hand as if summoning a servant. He called Davide to find out where the drivers were and they set off to join the party. The club was dark, silver and futuristic – like a very large escalator, noted Lena – but the music was good and the drinks were flowing. She spotted Eva dancing with Greg. When they made eye contact, Lena looked away. She had no interest in striking alliances with a woman like her. Instead, she clung to Nico. She was surprised when he led her to the dance floor. Often, men like him – the stoic, brooding type – didn't dance, but he pulled off his blazer and slung it aside. Lena delightedly joined him. They spent the night laughing, drinking, dancing, kissing, and she genuinely couldn't remember a time that she had felt more free.

Chapter 8

Johanna knocked lightly and brought in a tray with coffee and a small plate of pistachio biscuits, her only weakness.

'I couldn't wait any longer,' she said and set the wooden tray on the bedside table.

Lena roused and grinned slowly. She turned and pressed her face into her pillow.

'Oh my god,' said Johanna. 'You've fallen for him.'

Lena moaned into the pillow.

'Jesus fucking Christ.' Johanna dropped onto the bed next to her. 'You've fallen for him.'

'No,' said Lena.

'Yes, you have!'

Lena turned over but covered her eyes. She exhaled, long and slow, to quieten the jittery hum in her limbs.

'Yes, you have,' Johanna repeated.

Lena moved her hands. 'Completely. Gloriously. Irredeemably.'

'Jesus Christ, Lena.'

'I don't care.' Lena sat up and threw a pillow across the room. 'I don't care!' She fell backwards onto the bed, but Johanna pulled her up again.

'Tell me everything.'

'Oh, Johanna.' Lena shook her head with disbelief. 'This is so fucking cheesy, but he's a *man*, you know? He's strong and fearless and assertive. And it's easy to think he's an arsehole but he has this other side, like with his younger brother, and he's just . . .' Lena sighed. 'I'm gone, Johanna. I tried not to be but I'm all the way gone.'

'Fuck. I've never seen you like this.'

'I've never *felt* like this. I know I'm crazy and this is stupid, but I can't stop it. I don't *want* to stop it. I've spent so long doing the proper thing and I'm tired of it. I don't want to do it anymore. I won't.' Lena felt a heady, destructive flare in her gut.

Johanna handed her a mug. 'Okay, drink this and start at the start.'

Lena took a long drink and began a blow-by-blow account. When she came to her exchange with Eva, Johanna interjected.

'Screw that bitch,' she said, hand curled in a fist. 'Eva Rafaeli has been trying to make it as a model for years but, *honey*, getting your Insta-husband to take a thousand photos of you on the steps of Santorini doesn't make you a model, even if he *is* Greg Richards.'

Lena was grateful for Johanna's loyalty. At her urging, she ran through the rest of evening: the extravagant dinner at Maison Boulud, their conversation about his conquests, the swanky club. They were halfway through their analysis when Lena's mobile rang. She snatched it up, hoping to see Nico's name but finding an unknown number instead.

'Answer it!' Johanna urged.

Lena answered breathily just in case it was him. 'Hello, Lena speaking.'

'Hi, Lena,' said a thick American accent. 'Do you have a minute to talk?'

'Yes. Who is this?'

'It's Stephen Bay.' When Lena didn't say anything, he added, 'The director.'

'Yes, of course. Hi, Stephen!' She winced, not knowing if he preferred to be called Mr Bay.

'Nico Laurent asked me to give you a call. I need a new writer for my next project and it sounds like you could fit the bill. Could you come and meet the team today? Around ten at Paramount on Melrose? Ask for Paula Gillard.'

Lena almost spluttered. 'Yes,' she said quickly. 'I'll be there!'

'Fantastic. We'll see you then.'

'Thank you,' she said but he'd already hung up.

Johanna was open-jawed. 'Was that who I think it was?'

Lena stared at her phone, stunned. 'Yes.'

'Oh my *fucking* god.' Johanna jumped upright on the bed. 'This is it, Lena. This is it!' She leapt into the air and landed on her knees on the mattress. 'Things are finally going to happen!'

Lena exhaled. 'I can't believe it.'

'Believe it, bitch. It's happening!' She crowded Lena in a hug, tipping them both backwards. Lena closed her eyes and let herself fall.

*

It took her an age to get ready. First, she tried a burnt-orange shift dress with fusty gold buttons (too formal), then her writer's uniform of white T-shirt and black jeans (too casual), then a monochrome dress with a black blazer (too stiff), then an A-line skirt with a rose-gold blouse (too *realtor*). Finally, she circled back to her writer's uniform but smartened it with heels and a blazer. She gathered her hair in a neat bun and grabbed her laptop bag. She felt sick with nerves as she locked the door and made the half-hour journey to the Paramount studios.

She walked through the yellow arch that marked the public entrance. When she had first moved to LA, she had taken a tour of the studios, but had found it oddly unsatisfying. She wasn't interested in the ersatz glamour of movie sets. She wanted to be where the magic actually happened: in the writers' room. This was her big chance, maybe her only chance, and the knowledge of that was overwhelming. At reception, she was directed past security barriers and told to take lift D to the ninth floor. There, she was directed to an oblong room. Inside, she was met with eight people: six men and two women. She scanned the room for Stephen Bay but he wasn't there.

'Are you looking for Stephen?' asked a trim blonde woman who could be anywhere between forty and sixty. 'He doesn't join these meetings.' She introduced herself as Paula and pointed Lena to a chair, then ran through the rest of the team. Lena subtly scribbled down their names: *Mark, Nick, Tom, James, Ryan, Penn* and *Aurora*. Paula didn't address her again and Lena realised that this wasn't an interview or even an informal chat but an actual real live writing session. She had been thrown in at deep end. She pulled off her blazer, glad that she hadn't opted for something more formal.

She spent the first two hours listening and making notes. The team was working on a film called *The Liminal*, a big-budget action movie pitched as the American James Bond. Sure, they had Ethan Hunt and Jason Bourne, but it was time for something new. The titular Liminal, slated for Chris Evans, could become the first of a lucrative franchise. If Lena could get her foot through the door, she could have everything she ever dreamed of: wealth, accolades, awards.

Lena skim-read parts of the script, trying to keep up. The character of the Liminal was serving a life sentence but had received an offer he couldn't refuse: freedom, as long as he agreed to work as a mercenary for a covert government unit. He was neither a civilian nor official, but existed in a liminal space. She read a few pages of a fight scene between the Liminal and Mr Gray, a tough killer for hire. She did a double take when she saw that Mr Gray was to be played by an Indian actor. These parts were *never* given to Indian guys, who were usually consigned to scientists, nerds and doctors. Lena felt a pang of optimism. Action films were often seen as lowbrow, but maybe they could make a real change here.

Hours passed and Lena became more conscious that she had no official agreement. Was this a test run? Would she be paid for the day? The afternoon crept into evening and none of the writers moved to leave. Lena checked her watch. She was due at the Aston in an hour but couldn't be the first to go. She excused herself and went to the bathroom to text

Brianna: *I'm so sorry but something's come up. I won't be able to make it today.* She didn't have time to think up an excuse, so quickly added, *I'll explain tomorrow.* She exited WhatsApp before Brianna could see that she was online and hurried back to the writers' room. It was clear that she had just missed a punchline because all the writers were laughing. She looked at them expectantly but none let her in on the joke. Silently, she returned to her seat.

They worked line by line through several more pages and Lena snagged on something. In the scene, Mr Gray turns against the villains that hired him when he learns that they plan to kill a young girl. Instead of handing over the MacGuffin – in this case, an encrypted drive hidden in a bracelet – he decides to give it to the girl instead. Lena read the lines and murmured in doubt.

'Something the matter, Lena?'

Her head snapped up and she was met with Paula's expectant glare. She squirmed as the other writers watched and waited. 'Well . . .' She hesitated and Paula arched her brows. 'In this scene, Mr Gray who has just killed about two dozen innocent people at the hospital hands over the bracelet and he says, "These people are not honourable. I do not want their money." I feel like that's an out-of-character thing to say.'

Penn looked at her curiously. 'It's not out of character because he's a killer with heart. He has boundaries.'

'But he's just killed lots of innocent people at the hospital.'

'Yes, but he draws the line at children.'

'I just wonder if . . .' she grimaced, 'we'd have him saying this if he was white.' She felt the air change in the room and quickly barrelled on. 'Like, Indians are often cast as spiritual or wise and sage, or somehow honourable, so him saying that sounds like a bit of a stereotype when it's not in keeping with his character at all.'

Penn squinted at her. 'I really think you're barking up the wrong tree here.'

'Okay, well, imagine if he was white, would you think that line was congruent with his character?'

Penn frowned, half amused. 'Yeah,' he said in the same tone that one might say *duh*.

Lena looked to Paula to see if she understood.

'I think you're reading too much into it, Lena. Let's keep going.'

Lena flushed. 'Okay, sure.' She focused on the script but her vision was swimming. She wished she hadn't said anything. She wished she had just *shut* up. For the rest of the session, she tried to be extra perky and encouraging but it was clear to her that she had alienated the others. She had blown her big chance – and on something so pointless and trivial. She quietly berated herself to the point where she felt on the edge of tears. As the writers began to wrap up, Lena was left deflated. She packed away her laptop, unable to make eye contact as the others filtered out. She was ready to leave when Paula addressed her from the head of the table.

'So we'll see you tomorrow at nine o'clock. If you report to HR, they'll put you on the payroll.'

Lena was slack-jawed. 'I've got the job?'

'Welcome to the team,' said Paula.

Lena blinked. For five long years, this is what she'd been

waiting for. To think it was finally happening made her emotional. 'Thank you,' she said, swallowing the choke in her voice.

'Don't be late.'

'I won't.' Lena pushed open the glass door and calmly made her way downstairs. When she was safely outside, she folded onto a nearby wall and clamped a hand to her mouth. Then, she began to cry – with joy and relief, and the sense of her bitterness lifting. Few of her friends spoke about it: how living in LA, surrounded by success, ground away at you; how it kept you awake at night with the maddening repetition of *why not me? Why not me? Why not me? Why you?* But here she was, at the threshold of success with a future that made her giddy. She grabbed her phone to send Johanna a triumphant text and saw that she had missed a few calls: one from Nico and two from Brianna.

Guilt muscled in on her joy. She knew she should call Brianna but she didn't want to spoil this moment. Besides, wasn't she owed some goodwill? Without Lena, they wouldn't even have the lights on. She scrolled past Brianna's number and called Nico instead. She listened to the line connect, impatient in her joy.

'Nico!' she cried when he answered.

'Lena?'

'You gave my number to Stephen Bay!?'

'He called you?'

'Yes! He called me!' She squealed with joy, unable to keep it in check. 'He called me this morning.' She took him through her day, repeating certain sections for she couldn't quite believe that it had really happened. She left out her gripe about Mr Gray, not wanting to reveal that she had caused any trouble.

'I'm proud of you,' he said when she finished.

She glowed beneath the compliment. 'Well, it was mostly you.'

'I only arranged a trial session. They hired you because of you.'

Lena smiled and was about to speak when she heard a voice near Nico: low, and full of servitude. 'Where are you?' she asked.

'On a plane, heading to Theo's. He's thinking about some changes.' Theo Witte was the team principal at Mercedes, a fearsome figure in racing. 'Listen, Lena, I'm going to be in Prague this weekend for a corporate thing I have to do. I have two tickets for the opera. Would you like to join me?'

Lena felt heat in her cheeks. 'In Prague?'

'Yes. I'll have you picked up.'

Her throat was dry and she had to clear it to say, 'Yes.'

'I'll have Eliot call you.'

Lena hung up in a state of awe. Was this her life now? Phone calls with Stephen Bay and weekends in Prague, offered to her as casually as a mint? She pressed her fist to her mouth, unable to hold in her glee. This *was* her life now. She stood, tossed her phone in her bag and headed home in triumph.

*

Prague was unseasonably cool for June and yet the air-con was turned on full. Lena shivered in the hotel foyer and wished that she had brought a coat. She wore a one-shoulder floor-length gown in pale-yellow silk chiffon – the same dress, Johanna had told her, that Amal Clooney had worn to Cannes one year.

She shifted uncomfortably and looked across at Nico. It had happened several times on this trip: Nico would be nabbed by a fan, then another and another, and Lena would have to wait until he managed to extricate himself. She felt awkward and conspicuous standing there alone in a dress that drew attention. She glanced around the foyer, feigning nonchalance. To her relief, she spotted a face she knew standing by the great glass doors.

'Eliot,' she called, genuinely pleased to see him. She strode over and greeted him with a hug. He seemed taken aback.

'Ms—' He stopped himself. 'Lena, you look well.'

'Thank you! I'm so pleased to see you.'

'And I, you.' Eliot's brown eyes twinkled kindly. 'I trust you are enjoying Prague?'

'I am, yes.' She smoothed her gown. 'These last two weeks have been a little disorienting.' She hesitated. 'Eliot, I know you warned me to—' She broke off mid-sentence, noticing the man next to Eliot. He was about six feet tall with dark hair and stubble, and moody ice-blue eyes. She saw the resemblance immediately.

'You must be Gabe,' she said.

The man nodded and extended his hand. 'Yes, I am.'

'I'm Lena. It's so nice to meet you.' She saw that he was wearing a suit. 'Are you joining us tonight?'

'Oh no,' Eliot replied for him. 'Mr Laurent was out to dinner. He's retiring to his room now.'

'Oh, that's unfortunate.' She gestured in Nico's direction. 'Maybe if Nico agrees, we can have dinner together tomorrow?'

Gabe looked at her nervously. 'Um, I'm sorry, but I don't know who you are.'

Lena coloured. 'Oh! I'm' – she groped for the right wording – 'a friend of your brother's.'

'I see. In that case, dinner would be nice.'

Eliot cut in briskly. 'Mr Laurent, your schedule is full tomorrow.' To Lena, he said, 'Please accept our apologies.' He touched Gabe's shoulder to steer him onwards.

'Oh, okay. Well, I hope I get to meet you properly, Gabe.'

'Likewise,' he said with a small nod that reminded her of Nico.

Eliot bid her goodnight and ushered Gabe to the lift. Lena pictured the two brothers together and felt a rush of affection. She wanted to see who Nico was when he was with Gabe. Maybe she would get a glimpse of tenderness.

'Lena.' She heard his voice behind her. 'I'm sorry. I couldn't get away.'

She received him with a smile. 'It's okay. We're in Prague. We're together. I have no complaints.'

He gazed down at her. 'No complaints?'

'None.'

He took her hand and led her outside where Chris was waiting in the car. Ten minutes later, they arrived at the State Opera, a grand Neo-Renaissance building in the mediaeval heart of Prague. Lena looked up at the ornate pediment where the central figure removed a lyre from the hands of a dead Orpheus. Before she could take it in, Nico whisked her inside.

They headed to the bar, which was mercifully uncrowded given their late arrival. They ordered a glass of wine and a single malt whisky and waited next to a group of four. The two couples were clearly a few drinks in and one of the men in particular fancied himself a raconteur. He was ruddy-faced with alcohol and spoke in a loud bellow.

'And then he comes out of the office and spends ten minutes turning it on. And I'm like, I can't believe they hired such a fucking spaz.'

Lena felt Nico tense beside her.

'So then this spaz comes over at lunch and says to me—'

Nico spun towards the man. 'Don't say that word.'

The man blinked. 'Excuse me?'

'Don't say that word,' Nico repeated crisply.

The man sniggered. 'Why don't you mind your own business, *friend*?'

'That's hard to do when you're the loudest thing in the room.'

'Well, what word do you mean?' The man squinted, feigning ignorance. 'Oh.' He clicked his fingers. 'Do you mean *spaz*? Sorry, *friend*, but you're not in America anymore.' He jabbed two fingers into Nico's chest.

Nico's lightning instincts grabbed the man's hand and squeezed. The man yelped in surprise, but didn't otherwise react, clinging on to bravado. As Nico squeezed harder, however, the man winced in pain. The woman by his side cried out and others in the room turned towards them. The man's skin turned puce and he bent forward in pain.

'You're going to break it!' he gasped.

'Say that word again,' challenged Nico.

'You'll break it!' cried the man.

'Say it.'

The man's eyes watered. 'I'm sorry, okay?' he shouted. 'I'm sorry!'

'Nico.' Lena touched his elbow, but felt it tense even more. The man cried out in pain. 'Nico!' she said with growing panic. After a long second, Nico finally let him go.

The man staggered back and gripped his wounded hand. 'I think it's broken,' he wailed. 'I'm going to sue you.' He pointed at Nico, bold again in the distance between them. 'I'm going to sue you!'

'Maybe we should leave,' said Lena.

'No,' said Nico flatly.

Lena steered him away from the bar. 'What if he knows who you are?' she asked in an urgent whisper. 'He'll almost certainly sue you.'

'I don't care.'

'Nico, come *on*.' She felt frustrated by this self-destructive streak.

'Lena, he's not going to sue me. He doesn't have the balls.'

'Go inside,' she instructed. 'I'll get our drinks.'

'It's okay.' He took her hand. 'They'll bring them to our seats.' He led her along a corridor into their own box. In the dark comfort of their private space, Lena let herself relax. Drinks in hand, they waited for the curtains to part. Lena hadn't told him that this was her very first time at the opera. The chasm between them was already so wide and she didn't want to point it out.

The lights changed and the audience hushed as one. The orchestra stood to receive their conductor who walked onstage to applause. Upon the first note, the lights dimmed on them and moved to the main stage instead. Two men appeared there, backlit by a screen of cherry blossom. Lena had read that the best way to experience opera was to not try to understand it; to just go with the flow. She struggled with the first twenty minutes, but once she stopped looking for the story, she found that she enjoyed it. In the third act, it all came together for her. She watched the woman on her knees, a child in her arms, and the tone of her voice – so high and clear and painful – brought tears to Lena's eyes. She blinked quickly to stem them but one fell to her lap, staining the yellow silk. She touched it lightly and Nico looked across at her. He saw that she was crying, and his own features flushed with emotion. He laced his fingers with hers and squeezed gently. There was warmth trapped between their palms and that's when she knew, with undeniable clarity, that she had fallen in love with Nico.

The audience broke into rapturous applause as the orchestra struck its final note. Lena joined the standing ovation and Nico stood up beside her. He wrapped an arm around her and she leaned into him, swallowing fresh tears.

'You okay?' he whispered in her ear.

She nodded, not trusting herself to speak. Outside, she was quiet, and Nico – perhaps sensing that she needed it – suggested that they take a walk. They headed to the Vltava River and watched the iconic view of Prague lighting up at night. Nico instinctively ducked when a camera flashed nearby, but it was just a couple of teenagers taking selfies together.

'Does it bother you?' she said. 'Being recognised?'

'I hate it.'

Lena frowned. 'Do you really?'

'I just want to race. The fame is pointless.'

'But is it though?' she challenged. 'You get given free stuff and flown all over the world. You go to amazing parties and spend obscene amounts on a private jet. Surely, that's part of the draw?'

Nico gazed at the water. 'I'd still race without it.'

Lena could see that it was true. Nico would risk his life for the sheer thrill of risking it. She sighed softly and leaned against the railing. They fell into a comfortable silence and watched the lights in the distance. Nico noticed that she was shivering and gave her his jacket. She slipped her arms through the too-long sleeves, hit by the scent of him. When she still didn't stop shivering, he motioned in the direction of their hotel.

'Let's go back,' he said.

She leaned up and kissed him, wanting to never forget this heady, perfect feeling. Hand in hand, they walked back to the car.

Chris put on the heating but Lena kept Nico's jacket. She liked the way it sat heavily on her shoulders.

'Do you know what you're doing tomorrow?' asked Nico. He was busy with Mercedes during the day and Lena had to occupy herself.

'There's a mini film festival on the Vltava, which I might check out. They're showing classic stuff like *Space Odyssey* in a double billing with absurd stuff like *Dumb and Dumber* but with curated pairings. It sounds like fun.'

'I'll be done by six, so meet me at the hotel when you're ready and we'll have dinner somewhere nice.'

'Sounds good.' Lena huddled into his jacket. 'If Gabe is free after all, we should ask him to join us.'

'Gabe?' Nico squinted in confusion. 'My brother?'

'Yes, I met him earlier – in the foyer. We didn't get to talk for very long. He was heading up to his room, but I got to say hi. He looks so much like you. At one point, he nodded and it was eerie how much it looked like you.' Lena yammered on, but then noticed that Nico wasn't responding. She paused and looked over at him. 'Nico?'

'I didn't say you could talk to Gabe.' His voice was brittle, ready to snap.

Lena faltered. 'I wasn't aware I needed permission.'

'*You* approached *him*, I presume?'

'Yes,' she said unsurely. 'Well, I approached *Eliot* and realised that Gabe was there.'

'You "realised" he was there?'

'What are you . . .' She trailed off, confused. 'What's the problem?'

Nico assessed her coolly. 'I don't want you sidling up to him.'

'Sidling?' Lena was bewildered. 'Nico, where is this coming from? I wasn't "sidling" up to him. He was just there – with Eliot – and I said hello.'

'Whatever you want from me, that's fair game but my brother is out of bounds.'

'Nico, I don't even know what you're talking about. I only said hello.' Heat rushed to her cheeks. 'You're being ridiculous.

I didn't have an *agenda* for saying hi to your brother.' Nico scoffed and turned to the window. 'Stop ignoring me,' she told him. She reached for him but he batted her away. Lena grit her teeth and reminded herself why Nico was so protective of Gabe. How could she convince him that she had no ulterior motive? This night, this trip – it was already beyond her wildest dreams. What more could she possibly be scheming for?

'Nico,' she said firmly. 'Look at me.' When he didn't, she cupped his chin and turned his face towards her. Then, with courage that was alien to her, she told him the truth. 'Nico, I love you.' She didn't wait for his response. 'I love you and I say that with no agenda or expectation. I say it not because it's opportune or to manipulate you. I say it because it's here' – she held a fist to her chest – 'and it hurts – it fucking *hurts* – to hold it there. It hurts to pretend that this is casual and light and fun for me when I've fallen for you – madly, stupidly and against all my best instincts. Don't you think I know?' She made a bitter sound. 'Don't you think I know how ridiculous this is? How insanely senseless it is falling for a man like you, but here I am. Rendered completely helpless, but if you think that I'm some master strategist, then stop this car and tell me to get out and I'll do it. I'll do it because I don't expect anything from you, but I want you to know that I love you. I just do.'

Nico breathed in and was just about to speak when the car swerved beneath them to avoid a speeding motorcyclist.

'Apologies,' said Chris. He met Nico's eye in the mirror and a look passed between them. Lena caught it and, in that moment, she understood that this scenario had played out here before. These codes and cues were pre-programmed between them. Hurt curdled in her chest. She felt stupid and naive, and brutally exposed. She moved away from Nico and huddled next to her window. Silently, she willed him to speak – not to reciprocate but merely to acknowledge her presence. She waited and watched the woolly lights of Prague flash by in the window. *Come on, Nico. Say something.*

They drove in silence and drew up to the hotel. Lena felt so far from everything: her hometown of London where the ebb and flow worked in time with her very heartbeat, or her adopted home of LA with its yin-yang of light and shadow. Here, in this strange city to which she had never been, with a man who was irrationally angry for a reason she couldn't fathom, she felt cut adrift.

Nico slammed the car door and walked into the hotel without waiting. Lena scurried after him and barely made it to the lift before the doors slid together. There were people inside and Lena felt illogically self-conscious, as if they somehow knew what had happened between them. She held her breath until the lift stopped at their level. Nico stalked out and Lena followed in silence. She was determined not to be the first to speak. If Nico was going to be unreasonable, then he needed to say sorry. If he wanted her to leave, then he needed to tell her directly. Inside the suite, he poured himself a whisky and walked out to the balcony. She willed him to turn, to look at her, to explain what he was feeling.

'I'm going to change,' she said, giving him a chance to engage. She waited a beat and then, with his back still turned to her, went into the bedroom. She eased out of her dress and carefully wrapped it in paper. She heard Nico on the phone to reception and felt a bead of relief. Perhaps room service was his way of calling a truce. She had a quick shower but left her makeup in place. She would scrub that off right before they headed to bed. She heard voices in the living room and slipped into her robe. She pulled a comb through her wet hair and headed out to see what he had ordered. At the edge of the room, she froze.

Nico was by the door, leaning over her. She was whispering in his ear and laughed at his response – a high, taunting sound. His lips were on her neck, his hand on the small of her back.

Sabine.

Ice frosted Lena's spine. 'Nico,' she said but it was only a whisper. 'Don't.' He responded by pushing Sabine against the door, making her gasp winsomely. He lifted her sheer babydoll nightie. She wore no underwear and Lena could see her full pink lips from where she stood. Nico reached down and stroked her slit. Sabine moaned, long and loud. Lena felt the sting of tears and a familiar storm of emotion: disbelief, anger and jealousy – and yet she couldn't look away.

Nico lifted one strap of Sabine's nightie and let it fall off her shoulder. He kissed her collarbone and pulled down the fabric to reveal her breast. Her skin was creamy and her pink nipple was hard and erect. Nico leaned down and licked it, and Sabine took a short, sharp breath.

'I can't get enough of you,' he told her and the words burned through Lena. 'I can't get enough of this skin, this pussy.' He knelt down in front of her and began to lick her. She moaned deeply and pushed herself into his tongue.

Lena told herself to leave; to grab her passport and go but

she couldn't tear her gaze away. Sabine moved against Nico's mouth. He grabbed her arse and pulled it towards him, feeding himself her pussy.

She grabbed a fistful of his hair. 'Show me your tongue,' she said. She waited for him to comply. Then, with Nico not moving, she began to rock back and forth on it, fucking his tongue, using it how she wanted to make herself come. She rocked harder until Nico couldn't take any more. He lifted her onto his shoulders and buried his mouth in her cunt, licking and sucking until she came with a wild, animal sound. In that moment, with her mouth wide open and her flame-red hair thrown across her breasts, Lena wanted her desperately.

Nico lifted Sabine and carried her to the bed, directly past Lena. Sabine caught Lena's wrist and pulled. Powerless, she followed her. Sabine tugged the cord on Lena's gown and let it fall open. She reached for Lena's skin but Nico pulled her back and splayed her on the bed face down.

'Come,' Sabine instructed Lena. She pulled her onto the bed and arranged her in front of her face. She leaned between her legs and licked. Lena was gone in an instant, her self-control slipping off as easily as silk.

Nico pushed into Sabine and she cried out with pleasure. Lena watched the woman between them, satisfying them both. Each time Nico thrust, he pushed Sabine into Lena's pussy, driving her tongue deeper. It was so sexy, it drove Lena rabid with lust. She ground against Sabine and tried to lock eyes with Nico but he wouldn't look at her. He was caught up in fucking Sabine. He reached round and touched her breasts, letting her nipples brush up and down his palms. He bit her shoulder, took mouthfuls of her skin, and fucked her and fucked her until, finally, he came deep inside her. He looked at Lena at the exact moment he came and she saw ecstasy there but also scorn – and then the thought was lost and she too crashed and came.

She lay in a heap with Sabine, thoroughly spent – physically and emotionally. Her heartbeat slowed but she made no move to untangle herself. Sabine's skin brushed hers as she glided off the bed. Her long red hair fell to the small of her back and both Lena and Nico watched as she walked out to the living room. After a minute, Lena heard the front door open and close and realised that Sabine had left.

She stretched in mellow fatigue. Her body felt warm and languid, exorcised of something. She turned dreamily towards Nico who lay on his back, an arm slung across his eyes. She waited for him to say something. Minutes passed but Nico didn't speak and Lena's neediness pierced her mood. As her mind cleared, she understood that Sabine was intended to punish her, a way for Nico to put her in her place, to remind her that she was replaceable, disposable. And Lena had let him do it. She felt a coil of unease over what she had consented to. The silence between them curdled and what had felt like empowerment mere moments ago soured into shame. She willed Nico to apologise, to comfort her, to promise he would never do this again without at least talking to her – but he did nothing. She waited yet more minutes, then wordlessly slipped under the sheets, needing to cover her body. She closed her eyes, feeling used and discarded. Her tears came, hot and painful, and though she tried to be silent, the soft glug of her throat gave her away. Still, Nico did nothing. Lena curled into herself and hoped for sleep. It was hours later, around 3am, that she felt him against her. He pressed his face into the nape of her neck.

'I'm sorry,' he said, his voice cracking. He held her tight and folded himself around her. 'I'm sorry, Lena. I'm sorry.' In her fugue, she fit her hand into his. He squeezed it and exhaled, shaky with relief. Were those tears in his voice? The answer was lost as sleep reached up to take her again.

Chapter 9

Lena took a long drink of coffee to mask her exhaustion. It had been a long, hard week with her days spent on *The Liminal* and her evenings on *Please Understand*. Each project demanded all her energy, leaving her drained at the end of the day. Still, she was grateful, for it distracted her from Nico. After their night with Sabine, Lena had awoken to find Nico gone, a terse note in his place: *The car will pick you up at 10.00 and take you to the airport.* A week had passed and she hadn't heard from him. She didn't allow herself to dwell on this. If she spent too long thinking about how she had opened her heart to him, only to be punished, she wouldn't be able to get up in the morning. Instead, she threw herself into work. She spent every waking hour at Paramount or the theatre, working with a relish akin to mania. She didn't regulate her pace so that when she got to the Aston each evening, she was creatively spent. Often, like today, she was still at Paramount when she should have been on her way.

The team there had warmed to her somewhat. She was beginning to catch their in-jokes and kept her bugbears to herself, wary of being called 'difficult', the kiss of death in

Hollywood. She tried and failed to disarm Paula. Clearly, the older woman was accustomed to underlings currying favour. Lena had to contribute on her own merit and prove to the team that she deserved her place at the table. Today, they were finessing one of the final scenes of the film. CIA agent Akira Sato had made it out alive and was being berated by her corrupt boss for letting The Liminal run. The scene ended in a bit of an anticlimax.

Lena read over the final few lines. 'Hey, guys,' she said, interrupting the chatter in the room. 'You know how early on, Akira's boss threatens her? He leans right into her and she says, "Take yourself out of my personal space – please", obviously it's a badass moment and it works really well. But what if we switched it around at the end? Right now, she says that if anything goes wrong, she will come for him and he just smirks. What if she leans into him when she says it, and he reacts with the same line: "Take yourself out of my personal space – please"? It's a bit of a comedic payoff but it also switches up the power dynamic.'

Paula considered this, miming with her arms as she thought through the scene. She dropped her arms. 'That's genius.'

'It ends the scene and Akira's time on screen on a high note,' said Lena.

'That's actually perfect,' said Penn. He arched his brows in a show of esteem and the others murmured agreement.

Lena flushed with pride. With the scene finally nailed, Paula let them go. Lena declined the offer of Friday drinks and headed to the Aston. She was already ten minutes late as it stood. It would be forty by the time she got there. Her phone pinged en route and she checked it wearily, expecting a text from Brianna.

Lena, will you come to the British GP tomorrow?

Her stomach lurched. The British Grand Prix? Tomorrow? A second text quickly followed.

I'd really like you there.

Despite herself, Lena felt immense relief. Nico was still interested. Very briefly, she considered the delicious cruelty of replying with a single word. *No.* Or better yet, *no thank you,* but she knew she would never do it. A third text came through, this time from Ahmed.

Hey, where are you?? You're going to miss the audition!

Lena swore. She had completely forgotten that the actress they wanted for Hana was coming in for a second audition. She had missed the girl's first one on the day she had gone to Crushes. *On my way,* she replied quickly. She tossed the phone in her bag and ran towards the Aston.

'Sorry, sorry,' she said, bursting into the writers' room.

Brianna's head snapped up, her lips set in a tight, thin line. 'Where were you?' she asked.

'I was caught up at Paramount.'

'Lena, we delayed seeing this girl a second time so that *you* could be here.'

'I know. I'm so sorry. I totally accept the blame.'

Brianna sighed. 'Well, I don't think we can ask her to come in for a third time.'

Lena cringed with guilt. 'Did you happen to film it?' Last time, Ahmed's phone had run out of storage so Lena had never seen her.

Brianna pushed her laptop across the table. 'Okay, this is the girl we think could play Hana.'

Lena pressed play and watched intently. A young girl with hip-length hair emoted at the screen. She had a heart-shaped faced and a sweet look, and clearly had experience. 'She's a great actress.' Lena nodded with credit.

'She's brilliant,' said Brianna. 'She's done some TV and—'

'But isn't she a bit old?' asked Lena. Instantly, she saw that she'd made a mistake. Her question had been casual, but the mood in the room hardened.

Brianna's expression was steely. 'She's come in for two auditions, Lena, and you've missed them both. Maybe if you had attended, you could have voiced your concerns at the start.'

'I know. I'm sorry. I just . . .' She faltered. 'She looks like she's about fourteen. I don't think the script will work if the actress is so clearly older.'

'Well, do you want to start the casting again?' Brianna asked icily.

Lena squirmed. She knew she had no right to criticise their choice after missing both auditions. 'No, I mean . . .' She pressed play and watched another minute. 'She'll do a great job I'm sure.' She backtracked guiltily. 'She's actually brilliant. I just needed to get my head round it.'

'So what do you want to do?' Brianna waited.

'No. Let's go with her. I'm sorry. You're right. She's great.'

'Okay, well, that's settled then.'

Lena wished she hadn't said anything. Casting Hana should have been a milestone, a collective celebration, but she had ruined the moment. They needed the good news. Brianna was more stressed than usual as Keller Stone had stepped up their efforts to buy the building. The rest of the session was tense and by the time Lena left at 9pm, her mind was completely scrambled. On her walk home, she reread the texts from Nico. She remembered the crack in his voice – *I'm sorry, Lena. I'm sorry* – when he spoke to her in the deep of night. She asked herself what she wanted to do. Not what she *should* do but what she *wanted* to do.

She texted him back with a single word. *Yes*.

*

Johanna lingered at the threshold of Lena's room. She began to speak, then paused, hesitated and started again.

'Are you sure you'll get back in time?'

Lena stuffed toiletries in the gaps of her suitcase. 'Yes.'

'So you'll go straight from LAX to Paramount on Monday? What if there are delays?'

Lena looked amused. 'It's not like you to worry.'

'I just don't want you to screw up your chance on *The Liminal*. I know how long you've waited for it.'

'There won't be delays.' Lena hunched sheepishly. 'I'm taking the jet.'

'Oh!' Johanna considered this and a glint came to her eye. 'So you remember how you said that the jet is always empty?'

Lena murmured as she tried to locate her second headphone.

'Well . . . I'm not working this weekend.'

'Mm.' She spotted it under the bed and knelt down to retrieve it.

'I was thinking . . . maybe I could come with you?'

'Where?' She snapped shut the charging case.

'To the Grand Prix.'

Lena tensed. 'The Grand Prix? As in the *British* Grand Prix?'

'Yes. I could throw a few things in a suitcase and be ready in twenty minutes.'

Lena's heart sank. 'Johanna, I'd love you to come, but Nico is really funny about stuff like that.'

'Funny how?'

'Like, he makes a point about "hangers-on" and I'd hate for him to—'

'"Hangers-on"?' Johanna's voice was hard.

Lena winced. 'I didn't mean it like that. I'm not saying *you're* a hanger-on. I'm saying I don't want him to think you are. It has to happen organically or he'll—'

'But *you* inviting me *would* be organic.'

'He wouldn't see it like that, trust me. It's not you. It's him. He has a weird hang-up about it. Remember how he acted after the Miami Grand Prix?'

Johanna stared at her. 'Yes, but it doesn't mean *you* should be weird about it. I don't even have to hang out with you guys. I just think it would be a nice scene.'

'Johanna, it will happen, I promise, just not this weekend. Not without warning him.'

Johanna's skin flushed pink. 'Right. I see.' She pointed at the suitcase. 'Well, enjoy wearing my clothes and shoes all on your own on your private jet.'

'Jo, come on.'

'No, it's all right. I get it.' She shot her a look of cruel pity, then spun and stalked away.

Lena checked her watch and sighed. She couldn't spare any time to soothe Johanna's ego. She zipped up the suitcase, hauled it up and paused at Johanna's door. 'I'll make it up to you, Jo. I promise.' She was met with silence. 'I'll see you on Monday, okay?' She waited, then tutted softly and headed downstairs to meet Chris.

*

The air crackled with heat and the sound of the crowd buzzed through the circuit. Gas and rubber mingled with the scent of Britain in summer: freshly cut grass and yellow flowers. Lena felt a deep sense of comfort; the warmth of coming home after a long absence. She *understood* Britain and didn't feel like a stranger here. It gave her a natural ease as she settled in the paddock.

'Oh, hi,' said Eva with surprise. 'It's nice to see you back here.'

'Hi. It's nice to see you back here too,' Lena said evenly.

Eva spotted someone over her shoulder. 'Oh, excuse me,' she said and walked away. 'Harry! How's Michael? I hope he's improved his backhand.' She did a circuit of the paddock, showy in her chumminess. 'Jason, que pasa? How's Tania? Louis, the tache is looking great!'

Lena ignored her and focused on the screens. A gradual hush fell across the paddock as the grid was cleared, leaving just the cars and drivers. Vossen was in pole position with Greg Richards second and Nico third. He hadn't had a great qualifying session and was annoyed to have placed behind Greg. Following the formation lap, the lights lit up one by one.

'And it's lights out and away we go!' cried commentator David Croft, more commonly known as Crofty. Nico had a good start and pulled ahead of Greg around the outside of Turn One and into Turn Two. The entire garage cried out as they almost touched. When Nico was clear, Eva looked at Lena with a smile.

'It's one–nil to you,' she said with a wink.

Lena smiled back. Had she misjudged Eva? It occurred to her that perhaps the girl was tired of being friendly to a revolving door of Nico's women – here one week and the next, gone. If she saw that Lena was a little more permanent, perhaps she would thaw somewhat. They watched the race and bantered mildly, Lena thankful for their budding comradeship.

At the midpoint, Nico was instructed to come in for a pit stop.

'I can stay out longer,' he said on the radio.

'Negative, Nico,' came the voice of his race engineer.

'I've still got pace,' Nico protested.

'Box this lap, Nico. Box box.'

Nico tore into the pit lane and Lena watched the mechanics

descend on his car, as seamless as ballet. When he rejoined the track, Nico dropped to third place behind Greg. Five laps later, he regained P2 when Greg was asked to box. As the race progressed, however, Nico's tyres began to degrade.

His voice came on the radio. 'I *told* you to keep me out longer,' he said, clearly frustrated. 'I needed those extra laps.'

'Copy that, Nico,' said his race engineer, as calm as the shipping forecast. 'Just push push push.'

Nico said something unintelligible and the radio crackled off. Vossen extended his lead as Nico lost yet more pace. The frustration in the paddock built. Before long, Nico and Greg started to vie for second place. Their race engineers told them to be careful but racing was in their blood and they refused to hold back.

Eva stopped scrolling Twitter and set down her phone. 'It looks like our boys are gonna get in trouble,' she said in a singsong voice. Lena reached for something clever to say to nurture their newfound banter but the moment was quickly lost. A chorus of shouts went up as Nico and Greg came close. Then, with DRS and fresher tyres, Greg pulled ahead safely.

Eva glanced at Lena. 'I guess it's one–all,' she said with a laugh.

They watched the final laps, rigid with tension. Vossen had a ten-second lead and easily took P1. Greg took P2 with Nico closely behind. The paddock lit up with cheers and Lena applauded half-heartedly. A two-three was a good result for the team but Nico wouldn't be pleased. The race had put Vossen back in the lead of the championship by a single point. Eva bounded over to the engineers. She high-fived each of them as if she were part of the team. Lena watched with a kick of envy and busied herself awkwardly. Eva had left her phone on the table and it lit up with a text. The words were upside down but Lena read them instinctively.

Congrats to Greg!

A string of emojis followed. Lena looked away but a second text came through.

And congrats to you for setting your own record. Fucking two guys on the podium. ;)

Lena reread the message, squinting to glean its meaning. A loud laugh went up and she looked over to see Eva joking with two mechanics. She read the message again before the screen went dark. Vossen, Greg and Nico were the three men on the podium. Was Eva fucking Vossen?

The truth rose like a fever and made her vision swim. Eva strode over and collected her phone. As she read her texts, her lips curled in a smirk. She glanced up and Lena's horror must have been clear, for Eva's own face fell.

'Look,' Eva said impatiently. 'Today is a celebration.'

'Are you fucking Nico?'

Eva flinched at the volume of Lena's voice and checked that no one had heard. 'Can we not do this now?'

'Eva.' Lena's voice was hard and dangerous. 'Are. You. Fucking. Nico?'

The girl exhaled dramatically. 'Yes, okay, I am, but who isn't? Come on, honey, this stuff goes on at every race.'

'When?'

'When what?'

'When was the last time?'

She tutted as if Lena was being unreasonable. But, then, seeing the threat in her face, answered, 'Monaco.'

'The weekend I met you?'

'Yes,' Eva admitted.

'When?'

'After the race. He dropped me off and we fucked in his car, okay?'

Lena nearly choked on this. She felt acutely humiliated. Like a clown that doesn't know it's in the circus, a source of scorn and comedy. She burned with it, felt it sting her cheeks. She remembered that night in Monaco. Laughing, drinking, dancing, kissing, and yet he'd fucked Eva in his car mere hours earlier. Had Chris been there? Did he know? To think he had witnessed Lena professing her love for Nico made her quail with shame. She backed away from Eva, but the girl grabbed her hand.

'Where are you going?'

'Home.'

Eva's voice changed to a softer key. 'You won't tell Greg, will you?'

Lena drew back her hand. 'No, Eva, I won't tell Greg.' Her voice held a hairline crack. She turned and walked out of the paddock, determined not to cry. She caught a taxi to the hotel and fled to her suite. She sat numbly on the sofa. There, far away from witnesses, she broke down. She cried for her naïveté and utter gullibility. She could just about accept that Nico had sex with Sabine. The open, transactional nature of it made it almost tolerable. But this. This was something else. She felt so stupid, so deeply humiliated. The thing that burned the most was that Lena was there that day. She was *right* there – at the hotel, waiting for him. Why fuck Eva en route? Rage welled inside her. She jolted to her feet and marched to the bedroom. She tore her suitcase out of the cupboard and threw it on the bed. She shoved her clothes into it, her anger making it bloat. She struggled to close the zip and leaned her body into it. She was just pulling it closed when the door burst open. Nico was still in his racing suit and his hair was lank with sweat.

'What are you doing?' he demanded.

'I'm leaving.'

'No, you're not.'

She lugged the suitcase off the bed and headed to the front door. As soon as she opened it, Nico slammed it shut. That's when she lost control. 'You fucked her,' she shouted. 'In your car! On your way to me!' She wanted to barrel into him and beat him with her fists. She was so close to slapping him when her conscience stopped her dead. 'Why did you do it, Nico?' Her voice was small and broken. 'You've made a fool of me. You've made a fool of everything I believe in. And I just let you do it.' Her voice compressed into a sob. 'I just let you.'

'Okay, look. Let's just talk about it for a second.'

'Tell me why, Nico. I was right here! Sabine was right here! Why Eva?'

'It was a spur-of-the-moment thing. I was high on the win

169

and I needed release. She was there and she wanted it, and it just happened.'

Lena gripped the handle of her suitcase. 'Well, I'm done.'

'No. You're not.'

'Get out of my way.' She reached for the doorknob but he grabbed her wrist.

'You're not leaving, Lena.' He held fast when she tried to shake him off. Anger flashed in his eyes and he pressed her against the door.

'Let me go,' she said through gritted teeth.

'Say *red* if you want me to stop.'

'Oh, fuck off, Nico!'

He pinned her wrists above her. Lena resisted but her body was already responding to him. He lifted her and she instinctively wrapped her legs around him. He took her through and flung her onto the bed. When he reached for her, Lena shoved him away. He made a sound, deep and hoarse, and easily caught her wrists.

'Nico, don't.' She could smell his sweat, the musk of him, and his animal hunger.

'*I* say when we're done.' He wrapped her hair in his hand and tugged, and Lena cried out in surprise. She felt her body react, arching up to meet him. He tugged aside her underwear and slid a finger along the slit of her pussy. He held it up and she saw that it was slick with moisture. 'Open your mouth,' he instructed. When she didn't listen, he brushed it across her bottom lip. The act was exquisitely slow, but released something frenetic inside her – something that begged her to let him in. She opened her mouth and Nico pushed his finger inside it.

Lena licked it in long, slow strokes and felt herself grow wetter. He pulled out and stroked her pussy again, his fingers growing slick. 'I knew it,' he said in a low groan. 'I knew you wanted it. You're soaking.' He put his face between her legs and began to lick her pussy. She moved against him and was right on the edge of coming when Nico pulled away. He turned her over and brutishly spread her legs. He pressed her head into the mattress and unzipped his racing suit. He stroked her pussy with the tip of his cock. She cried out but he forced her still. He rubbed against her pussy, making her writhe and drip. When she was rabid with want, he finally pushed inside of her – with such force, she cried out in an extraordinary mix of pain and pleasure. She lost control, grinding into the bed as he fucked her from behind. She screamed with abandon as he slapped her arse once, then twice, then again and again. She came explosively and felt herself juice all over his cock, his clothes, the sheets. She came with such intensity, she lost contact with reality, and as she came down back to earth, she knew with absolute certainty that she would never escape his grip.

*

Lena swirled her margarita and watched the salt crystals fall, then melt in the liquid. Her mind was clamouring and she needed something to quieten it. Nico had fallen asleep straight afterwards, his racing suit in a heap on the floor. Lena hadn't even showered. She'd left her packed suitcase by the door and come straight to the hotel bar. Sat there alone, her thoughts went to her father, a man who had taught her to respect herself. It's true that his views had been conservative – Lena could see that now – but he had taught her to value herself and her body. What would he think of her now and the way she had allowed herself to be treated? She felt a well of shame so deep and hot, she nearly burst out crying. She gripped her glass and tensed with the effort to steel herself. A gale of laughter rose from a group nearby. Other than them, the bar was mercifully quiet.

Lena sipped the drink, willing it to hit. She set down the glass, then changed her mind and drained it.

'Can I get you another one?'

She blinked in surprise. 'Davide? Hi.'

He broke into that famous grin. 'Hi, Lena. You look like you could use one.'

'Thanks,' she said, tipping her empty glass.

He ordered two margaritas and took the stool next to her. 'Are you okay?'

She swallowed hard and said, 'Yes.'

He studied her. 'Not being an arsehole but you don't look okay.' His gaze fell to the purpling bruise on her wrist.

'It's not how it looks,' she said quickly.

'Then how is it?'

She twisted the stem of her glass. 'It's . . . not how it looks.'

Davide exhaled upwards. 'Lena, what are you *doing* here?' It was judgemental but also kind and soft.

'The same thing as all the others.'

'But you've got your own thing going for you. You're a *writer*. What are you doing here?' The way he said the word *writer* made Lena feel emotional. It was freighted with such worth, such praise.

'I love him,' she admitted. 'I don't think I ever had a choice really.'

Davide didn't argue.

'I mean, is it so bad really? Eva said everyone's at it. Maybe I just need to switch up my idea of monogamy. Men like Nico, men like you, maybe you're not built for it.'

'That's bullshit.'

'What? You've never cheated on a girlfriend?'

'Not all of them. Not the one I really cared about.' He laced his hands on the bar. 'Though she cheated on me so . . .' He lifted a shoulder wryly.

'I'm sorry.'

Davide groaned. 'God, what a pair of losers we are.' Lena gave a short, sharp laugh, but Davide was serious again. 'Lena, please don't lose yourself in this. Don't forget who you are: first and foremost, a talented writer.'

'You don't know that.'

'Actually, I do.' He smiled sheepishly. 'After we met in Miami, I looked you up and read some of your work. Your piece for the *New York Times* on adopting American vernacular was . . .' He nodded decisively. 'You're talented.'

She flushed. 'Thank you, Davide. That means a lot.' She took a careful sip of her drink. All her emotions spat and stewed just below the surface. One false move would send them bubbling over. 'Tell me about the girl who broke your heart,' she said, shifting the focus to him.

He grinned. 'Man, you'll have me crying into my margarita.

I really didn't think that this would be the vibe.' He ordered another round of drinks and they moved to a table away from the bar. There, they sat and talked like old friends as the hours slipped by. When they came to a natural lull, Davide grew oddly nervous. He fiddled with the heavy-cut glass that held the dregs of his whisky.

'Lena.' His jaw tensed with indecision. 'I think you should know something.'

She set down her drink. 'What?'

'Nico's last girlfriend. Not the girls in the paddock – the models, the actresses, the heiresses – but his last proper girlfriend, the one who moved in with him, and met Gabriel, and did the whole thing with him. She lasted a year with him.'

Lena digested this. 'Okay.' She shrugged. 'That's longer than I've been warned about. A year is actually pretty good before a breakup.'

'No, you don't understand. Phoebe didn't leave him.' Davide grimaced. 'She took her own life.'

Chapter 10

Lena hunkered into her chair, acutely aware of the fact that she looked like a mess. She hadn't slept before her 4am flight back to LA. On the plane, she had tried to cover her dark circles with makeup, but they ended up looking caked. Her hair was static from altitude and she hadn't ironed her shirt. Last night, she had stumbled up to the suite to find Nico asleep. His racing suit was on a chair, which meant that he had awoken but hadn't bothered to look for her. She had grabbed her suitcase and left. Now, back at Paramount, she tried to hide the fact that she was hung over and exhausted. She swigged some water and shrank back when Paula looked up from the head of the table.

'Anyone have other ideas?' she asked. They were thinking of South Asian actors who could play the role of Mr Gray. Riz Ahmed couldn't do it and they had to find an alternative.

Lena cleared her throat. 'There are lots of British actors who could work. Himesh Patel. Nikesh Patel. Rahul Kohli.'

'Can they do accents?'

'Yes. Rahul played an American in *Midnight Mass*. Himesh in *Station Eleven*. I'm not sure about Nikesh but—'

'No, not an American accent. An Indian one.'

Lena frowned. 'Why does he have an Indian accent?'

Penn interjected: 'Because the character is Indian.'

'Ethnically, yes, but he's an American citizen.'

'Yeah, but he could still have an Indian accent.'

Lena swallowed her sigh. 'I worry that this happens too often to South Asian actors,' she explained. 'Everyone else in the film has an American accent. Why does Mr Gray have an Indian one even though he's American?'

'Why's it a big deal?' asked Penn.

'Because he's spouting stuff about honour even though he's a trained killer and now he has an accent. We're typecasting him.'

Penn smirked. 'It's just the character.'

'Well, maybe it shouldn't be,' Lena said sharply.

Paula cut in to calm them. 'This is all very lively but, Lena, there's logic behind our decision. The studio thought we could cast a Bollywood actor to tap into the Indian market, hence the Indian accent. There's no other motive beyond that.' Lena arched her brows in doubt but Paula was having none of it. 'Is that understood?'

Lena exhaled. 'I just—'

'Is that understood?'

She gritted her teeth. 'Yes. Understood.' She waited half an hour, then excused herself and went to the bathroom. She closed the stall door, then kicked it three times in quick succession. She slapped a palm against it, feeling the sting on her skin. She felt coiled with frustration, wiry with anxiety. She bent over and let out a silent scream. In the next instant, she straightened and pretended it had never happened. She heard the main door to the bathroom open and footsteps go into the stall next door. She washed her hands and checked herself in the mirror. She looked awful with her crumpled shirt and flyaway hair. She raked a wet hand through it, then dabbed the makeup beneath her eyes and headed back serenely.

*

Lena didn't have time to go home and shower before her shift at the Aston. She felt sticky and unclean, suffocated by the LA heat. The journey from Paramount had been a nightmare with bumper-to-bumper traffic. She unstuck her shirt from her sweaty skin and pushed through the doors of the theatre.

'You're late,' said Brianna. 'Again.'

'Well, good evening to you too.'

Ahmed looked up in surprise. 'What's with the attitude?'

'Why don't you mind your own business?' Lena snapped at him.

'Sit down, Lena.' Brianna told Ahmed and Gloria to go on a Starbucks run and waited until they left. She fixed her stare on Lena. 'I called you earlier.'

'I know. I'm sorry. I was working.' She had seen the calls but had been loath to explain that she would once again be late.

'Did you forget?'

'Forget what?'

'The date.'

Lena scowled with impatience. 'Why is the date—' Dread lurched in her stomach and she paled with realisation. 'It can't be.' She groped for her phone and fumbled to her calendar. She hadn't set a reminder for she'd assumed that they would leave from the Aston together, not foreseeing that she would arrive an hour late here. 'Oh god. Brianna, I am so sorry.'

Brianna's face was thunder. 'Do you understand how hard it was to get a meeting with William McGregor?'

'I—'

'And then you don't do him the courtesy of *bothering* to turn up. I couldn't even hide the fact that I didn't know where you were.'

Lena's scalp was tight with shame. 'Brianna, I'm sorry. I didn't expect to be late and I—'

'That meeting was going to decide the fate of the Aston and we didn't even get to have it. He turned me away. Do you understand how humiliating that was? I got turned away at the door.' Her voice simmered with anger.

'I can call him. I can ask for another meeting.'

'A man like William McGregor doesn't give second chances.'

'But I can try.'

'You haven't been trying for weeks.'

Lena stopped short.

'The rest of us are here. On time. Ready to work. Gloria's doing day shifts as a cleaner. Ahmed is tutoring. We're piecemeal-ing a living because we want to be here. Because the Aston means something to us. Because *Please Understand* means something to us.'

'I'm here,' said Lena. 'I'm sorry. I'm ready.'

Brianna sagged in her chair. 'It may be too late.' She motioned at an email open on her laptop. 'It's from our land-lord. An "unofficial heads-up" that if we don't agree to a rent hike when our tenancy's up, he'll be "forced" to sell to Keller Stone.'

'Can we afford it?'

'We can barely afford to keep the lights on. An extra four hundred dollars a month is hopeless.' She let out a sigh. 'Why'd you have to miss the meeting, Lena?'

She had no good answer. The fact that Brianna was asking not out of spite but grief only made it worse. Lena had let down her team, possibly irredeemably, and she hated herself for it. William McGregor had been their best chance to save the theatre and she had destroyed it. 'So what do we do?' she asked, her voice small and subdued.

'We keep working. And, when the time comes, we go down with the ship.'

'I'm so sorry, Brianna.'

'What I need from you now is focus. I know that Paramount is a big deal for you but we need you here too. I'm not asking you to give that up, but when you're here, you need to be *here*. If you can't do your job, we'll have to find someone who can.'

'I'll do better,' she promised.

'And you'll mean it this time? Because if you can't, Lena, this is the time to say it. You know how hard it is to find replacement writers.'

'I mean it.'

The door whined opened and Ahmed and Gloria returned with drinks – two flat whites, Earl Grey tea for Lena, and an espresso for Brianna. Lena accepted her cup from Ahmed guiltily.

'I'm sorry for being a bitch,' she told him.

Ahmed took a sip of his coffee. For a moment, it seemed

he would ignore her but then he reached into his pocket and shoved his last Rolo across to her. She caught it gratefully. Ahmed nodded and picked up the script. The four of them worked diligently and when Lena left nearly two hours later, her body was sore with fatigue. Her shoulders were stiff and brittle and her mind felt scrambled. Her misstep could lead to the sale of the Aston and she couldn't have that on her conscience. To make matters worse, she'd made a nuisance of herself at Paramount. All in all, it was one of the worst days of her professional life. She was desperate to go home, have a bath and sink a few glasses of wine. She was on her way when her cell phone rang. *Nico.* She stared at his name for a long time before she pressed accept.

'I've been calling,' he said. 'I'm in LA tonight. Meet me for dinner.'

Lena felt a spike of anger. 'I can't. I've just left work and I'm shattered.'

'You're leaving Paramount *now*?'

'No, the Aston.'

'You're still doing that?'

'Yes, of course I'm still doing that.'

There was silence on the line. 'Meet me, Lena. I want to see you.'

'If I say no, who will you call instead?' She hated herself for her pettiness.

'I deserve that.' He was quiet for a beat and his voice took on a boyish tone. 'Please, Lena. Meet me.'

She closed her eyes. There was so much anger in her but also a sickening need.

'Please,' he urged her.

She exhaled. 'Fine,' she said curtly. 'But I don't want to go anywhere fancy. There's a diner near my place. Meet me there.'

'I'll be there in fifteen minutes.'

*

Lena waited in a booth in one corner of the diner. The checkerboard vinyl floor and red faux-leather seating had charmed her when she had first visited several years ago. Now she could see they were tacky, but the milkshakes were still good and it was just one block from home. She drummed the edge of the Formica table to offload her rancour. She wanted to be calm for this.

She heard a short burst of traffic as the diner door opened and closed. She looked up and, sure enough, it was Nico. He wore casual jeans and a shirt, and the slightest hint of stubble. Men in this town were often described as devastatingly handsome and though it was a cliché, Lena saw that it could be true. Nico had the power to devastate her, and it pained her to know that it was likely inevitable.

She didn't stand up to greet him, but he pulled her up. He closed his arms around her and buried his face in her neck.

'I'm sorry.'

'You always are,' she said, pushing away from him, back into the booth. They waited until they got their drinks – Lena, an Oreo milkshake and Nico, tea with no sugar or milk.

'Eva will never happen again,' said Nico. 'I promise.'

Lena drew wide circles in her shake, her gaze fixed on the straw.

'She was nothing to me. The races are so high pressure; it was just a release. An instant release. That's all it was and I made a mistake and I'm sorry.'

Lena stopped stirring. 'Tell me about Phoebe.'

Nico balked. 'Who told you about her?'

'It doesn't matter. Tell me.' There was challenge in her voice, daring him to refuse.

He ran a hand across his stubble and she saw the give in his shoulders. 'We met two years ago at a charity function,' he began. 'She was from *Uvalde, Texas,*' he said in a Southern accent. 'She was . . . unpretentious, so far from everything I knew. She'd had this picture-perfect childhood and was completely genuine, but not in a hick sort of way. She had a good heart and people were taken by her. *I* was taken by her.'

Lena felt an illogical sting of jealousy.

'We started dating and it was . . . special. She came on the road with me but she missed home and she found the lifestyle difficult. She came to fewer and fewer races and I . . .' Nico turned his teacup and positioned the handle ninety-degrees from the edge of the table. 'I ended up sleeping with someone else. When she found out, she got it in her head that she wasn't good enough, pretty enough, skinny enough, so she started injecting herself with all sorts of shit – Botox, fillers, whatever was available. She started losing weight and suffered disordered eating. I tried to help her. I put her in a clinic, but I couldn't be there all the time. I had the championship and I had Gabe and there was already too much in my head. She would call me and cry for hours and I tried for a while, but eventually I stopped answering. I loved her and I wanted her to get better but I couldn't give up everything for her. When she left the clinic, I sent her to Crushes, but everything got too much for her. She took some sleeping pills on the day of my final race. Eliot found her. No one told me. I won the championship that year but I lost her. So that's what happened to Phoebe.'

A dark melancholy settled over Lena. 'Would it have happened anyway?' she asked. 'If you hadn't cheated on her?'

Nico gestured bleakly. 'I can't say, but she always struggled with my lifestyle. Always.'

Lena slumped. She wanted to hate him for leaving Phoebe in her hour of need, but she also understood that Nico was single-minded. She recognised that to be truly great, you had to focus wholeheartedly to the detriment of everything else. Not for a second did she think that Nico could or would give up racing for her. It shouldn't surprise her, then, that he didn't give it up for Phoebe. A small perverse part of her was grateful for that knowledge. She wasn't alone in Nico's thrall. Others had gone before her.

Nico hung his head. 'I'll be better for you, Lena.'

She was quiet, letting his words steep. He reached out and took her hand. His cigarette burn brushed against her fingertips but he didn't flinch. He let her touch it, his jaw rigid with composure. She felt overwhelmed by her feelings for him, weakened and beaten by them. 'This is your last chance, Nico.'

He folded in relief and rested his forehead on her hands. 'I won't screw up, Lena. I promise.' She let herself believe him. He had never before promised her anything.

The waitress, a brunette in her early forties, paused by their booth. 'Can I get you folks anything else?'

Nico straightened with a contented laugh. 'Two Oreo milkshakes please.' With a grin, he added, 'We're celebrating.'

The waitress reflexively returned his smile. 'Coming right up,' she said, lit up by his gaze. Lena observed this quietly and felt a kinship with the woman, both of them rendered powerless.

Nico was unable to hide his cheer. He tapped a concerto on the side of his glass, brimming with energy. They talked and drank and Lena let herself relax. Soon, she was languid with sugar and fatigue and Nico sensed that she needed sleep.

He drained his shake and said, 'Will you come to the French Grand Prix next weekend? We can have dinner on Friday before it gets too manic.'

'I can't on Friday.'

'Why not?'

'I'll be at the Aston.'

Nico frowned. 'Can't you take the evening off?'

'No.' Lena was determined to keep her promise to Brianna.

'I want you there, Lena.'

'And I need to work, Nico.'

'No, you don't. Not as much as you do.'

Lena stiffened. 'There are things I want to do.'

'And that's why I set you up with *The Liminal*.'

'I can't abandon my play. The Aston might be closing and I need to know that I did what I could.'

Nico was confused. 'But didn't the fundraising sort it out?'

'No, that was just for our electricity bill. The building is in danger of being sold.'

'Well, how much do they need?'

'I don't know. Whatever Keller Stone is willing to pay for it.'

'Well, what if I bought it?'

'Okay, sure,' she said dismissively.

'I'm serious.'

She tutted. 'Nico, you can't *buy* the Aston.'

'But I need to see you. I understand that you can't be with me on the road permanently, but I need to be able to see you on race weekends.'

Lena's voice grew hard. 'What are you saying? I have to choose between you and my job?'

'No. You'll still have a job, just not two jobs. I'll pay for the theatre.' He reached for his phone. 'You quit tomorrow and I'll buy it for a million, five million, whatever it costs.'

'Nico, you're being ridiculous.'

'Lena, please.' He gripped her hands in his and lifted them in supplication. *'Please.'*

'I can't do that, Nico. It's my play.'

'And what about the theatre? This is a way to secure its future. For years. Decades. They can still put on your play.'

She stared at him. 'Are you being serious?'

'Just tell me how much they need.'

She shook her head in disbelief. 'You can't do that.'

'I can and I want to.'

Lena remembered Brianna's words. *We go down with the ship.* But what if there was a way to save it? If the Aston was truly under threat, then the selfless thing was to step away; to let him come to its rescue. As for her play, if it was a choice between shutting it down or handing over the reins, then surely she would choose the latter.

'What are you thinking?' asked Nico.

'I can't let you do this.'

'Why not? I *want* to.'

She tensed with indecision. 'I need time.'

'Okay, take the time you need, but please come next weekend. It's *France*, Lena. The country I race for. I really want you there.'

'If I come, can I bring Johanna with me? That way I'll have some company when you're not around.'

He grimaced. 'I'd rather not entertain.'

'You wouldn't have to. She can keep herself busy.'

'I don't need the complication.'

Lena didn't have the energy to fight. 'Fine, but I don't want to sit in the paddock. I don't want to be anywhere near that witch Eva.'

'Done.' His eyes sparkled, the flecks of ice now diamonds. 'This is it, Lena.' He took a deep breath and let it go. 'It's you.'

She didn't ask him to explain; gleaned her own meaning instead: *It's you. You're the one. I love you.*

I love you too, she thought, not able to remember a time when this wasn't true.

Chapter 11

The waves were more rugged here and battered the shore of the island. The cyclical rush and hiss of them added a sense of drama more suited to Gothic literature. The heat of the day had faded and Crushes itself seemed relieved, its walls and windows sighing in the welcome cool. Lena toed the ground unsurely.

'Just walk normally,' said Nico, laughing.

'I can't walk normally when I can't see!'

'I've got you.' Nico steered her across the field behind Crushes with his hands over her eyes.

'Just give me a clue,' she begged.

'No clues. We're almost there.' After a few more metres, they stopped. 'Okay, you can look.'

She opened her eyes and gasped. 'Nico! Oh my god. They're beautiful!'

He grinned, pleased with her reaction. 'They're rescues,' he said. 'Once their racing careers are over, they're essentially regarded as useless.' He stroked one of the horses. 'I guess I felt an affinity.'

Lena laughed. 'Are they related?' Both horses had rich chocolate-coloured coats and healthy, windswept manes.

'No. They're both thoroughbreds but came from different homes.'

'It's okay to touch them?'

'Yes, they're both gentle.'

Gingerly, she held out her hand and the smaller of the two leaned out and licked it. She saw that Nico was watching with a smile.

'Do you want to ride?' he asked.

Lena tensed. 'Ride?' Short of a novelty ride on holiday, she had never been on a horse before. 'Oh, I don't know. I don't really ride.'

'I'll show you. It'll be fun. I promise.'

She agreed tentatively and he helped her tack up her horse, laughing when she started to fit the bridle upside down. He helped her up onto the horse, then mounted his in a fluid move.

'Hold your reins like this,' he said, 'so it can move through your fingers easily but so you can also arrest it if you need.'

'Okay.'

'Lena, look at me,' he said, sensing her nerves. 'Don't worry. I'll keep you safe. I promise.'

'Okay. I trust you.' She took a few long deep breaths in an effort to relax.

'Squeeze your feet against his belly and he'll get going.'

She did as he instructed and yelped in delight when her horse, Cisco, moved off. Nico's horse, Dash, fell into stride beside hers. They rode gently through a forested path and Lena found her rhythm.

'How often do you ride?' she asked.

'Not as often as I'd like. I had an injury a couple of years ago when Dash got spooked in a gallop. Mercedes asked me to stop riding after that.' Lena raised a brow and Nico laughed. 'This isn't riding. This is walking.'

They came to the edge of a clearing and Nico helped her dismount. He secured the horses and untacked them. Then, he took her hand and led her into the clearing. She laughed in delight when she spotted the table in the middle. It was covered in a red-and-white tablecloth and set for a picnic. 'This is . . . unexpected.' When they drew nearer, she noticed that it was set for three people.

'I hope you don't mind some company.'

She turned and saw Gabe walk into the clearing.

'Lena, this is my brother, Gabe. Gabe, this is my girlfriend, Lena.'

Lena's smile spilt into a laugh. She strode towards Gabe and gave him a hug. 'It's so nice to meet you, Gabe.'

'And you,' he said.

Nico steered them to the table and poured three glasses of champagne. Lena watched them interact: the playful way that Gabe teased Nico for being an overachiever, the tender way that Nico made sure that Gabe had eaten enough. It made her heart soar to see them together.

'Do you ride, Gabe?' she asked.

'Yes, I do. Mostly, I like being around them. They're calming, especially for people who have been through trauma.'

Lena sensed Nico tense beside her. 'Which one do you prefer to ride?' she asked smoothly.

'Cisco because he's gentler. Nico obviously prefers Dash,

but only because he sounds more *manly*,' he said in a deep, gruff voice.

Lena chuckled and felt Nico relax. Late afternoon slipped into evening before Eliot arrived to collect Gabe. Lena bid him goodbye with a fierce hug. 'It was so nice to meet you.'

He squeezed her back. 'I'm glad you're here,' he said.

On the ride back, Nico was quiet.

'Are you okay?' she asked, gently stroking Cisco's mane.

He cleared his throat. 'I've never heard him say that word before. *Trauma*. It . . . startled me.'

'Do you think he was talking about himself?'

'I don't know. We don't talk about that time. Not to each other.'

Lena contemplated this. 'Do you think you ever will?'

'Yes.' After a beat, he said, 'Maybe. I don't know.'

'It could help him,' she said.

Nico nodded, then looked across at her. 'Thank you, Lena, for being kind to him.'

'I like him.' She grinned. 'He may be my favourite Laurent brother.' Nico laughed – a high, bright sound that filled Lena with warmth.

'Mine too,' he said as they rode on in the fading light. 'Mine too.'

*

Brianna stared at the contract, which sat amid the four of them like a poisoned chalice. For all her years in LA, and the practised cynicism of an old hand, she was genuinely taken aback. How does one react to a million dollars? One-point-two to be exact. Gloria and Ahmed looked on nervously and darted a glance at each other.

Brianna made a wry sound. 'So I guess you're literally worth a million dollars.'

Lena flushed. 'You can get another writer – several in fact – and get the script in shape.'

'It's already in shape. Lena, are you sure you want to do this?'

Lena knew that the question was a courtesy. Last week, they had rejected the four-hundred-a-month rent hike. Shortly after, they were told that the landlord had agreed to sell to Keller Stone. The sale wasn't yet official but they didn't have much time. 'This will save the theatre,' she said. 'That's worth more than my writer's ego.'

'So he's *buying* you?' Ahmed cut in.

'No, Ahmed.' She willed him to understand. 'He's saving us.' Nico had offered to buy the building for $1.2 million and the contract on the table stipulated a monthly rent of exactly $1. Lena knew what this could mean for Brianna, for Ahmed and Gloria. An actual decent living wage. The space and time to do the work they wanted without begging for scraps to make the rent; the chance to do good, meaningful work; to invest in the next generation of writers, artists and actors.

Brianna reached for the contract and scanned the pages again. 'Jesus,' she said under her breath. 'How am I meant to *not* say yes?'

'So say yes, Brianna. He's already instructed his lawyers to approach the landlord. All going well, you won't have to find next month's rent.'

'I can't believe this.' Brianna's eyes glazed with tears and it unsettled Lena to see her like this. 'All these years of hustling, grinding, begging and surviving, and this *driver* of yours comes along and' – Brianna clicked her fingers – 'our problems are solved.' She regarded the contract with awe. 'And you're sure about this, Lena?'

'Yes,' she said – and it was almost true. Lena was pleased to be helping the Aston, but letting go of her play had shaken her a little. 'You'll take care of it, won't you?' she said, choking up.

Brianna's features tensed with sympathy. 'We will.'

'Okay, well, I'm going to go before this gets all . . .' She flapped her hands and stood.

'You're going already?' said Ahmed.

'Yes. I've got a flight to catch.'

'Will we see you?'

'Of course you'll see me,' she said in a classic LA promise – broken before it even got going. Ahmed stood and hugged her. Gloria didn't wait her turn; just threw her arms around both of them. Lena squeezed them tight. 'Break a leg, guys,' she said, her voice cracking.

Brianna stood too but hovered at the end of the table. Lena nodded at her and Brianna nodded back. With that, Lena walked out of the Aston into the balmy evening. A breeze rose to greet her and carried off her tears in the wind.

*

Johanna lingered in the doorway. Her long blonde hair was pulled into a messy bun and her face was makeup-free. Lena had assumed that she would be out, as was normal for a Friday evening. She could feel her stare on her back as she finished packing. Chris was waiting with the car outside and Lena didn't have much time. She wheeled around the room in search of her laptop charger.

'But your own play is all you ever wanted,' said Johanna.

Lena was falsely nonchalant. 'Yes, but I've got *The Liminal* and there'll be other opportunities. I've always wanted to work on movies.'

'When I met you, you said you heart belonged to the stage.'

Lena tutted. 'That was me being a pretentious Brit. I was probably just trying to impress you.'

'You weren't being pretentious.'

'Well, things change. This is my ticket to the bigger things. Why would I give it up?'

'I'm not saying you should give it up. I'm saying you should have also kept your play.'

'It's complicated.'

Johanna was clearly unconvinced. 'Okay, well, as long as you get me a role in *The Liminal*, I won't argue.'

Lena gave her a tight smile. The two of them had made up after their tiff last week but Johanna's jesting had grown aggressive. It was as if she felt that Lena owed her something. 'You know I don't control that, Jo,' she said lightly.

'I know but it can't hurt to try.' There was an awkward pause.

'I'll try,' she said in another classic LA promise.

Johanna still lingered. Idly, she brushed her hand up

and down the doorframe. 'Hey, what if I came with you this weekend?'

Lena tensed. Hadn't they been through this already?

'I know you said that Nico gets funny about stuff like this, but given how he's buying the *Aston* for you, I figure he'd be okay with this?'

Lena reached for an excuse, not wanting to tell Johanna that Nico had already said no. She didn't want them to hate each other.

Johanna ventured into the room. 'I could do with a visit to Paris to revive some of my contacts.'

'We'll be nowhere near Paris.'

'Okay, then I'll chill with you at the race.'

'I won't have time to chill. I'll be busy with Nico.'

'Then I'll use the time to network. Last time, I met Tom Ford.'

'I'm taking the jet.'

'So? There's space, right?'

Lena squirmed. 'Johanna, I explained this. I can't just add someone to the manifest.'

'So ask Nico to.'

'He won't do it.'

'You're being so weird about this.'

'And *you're* being pushy.'

Johanna flinched. 'How am I being pushy? It's a fucking private jet.'

'Exactly! People who have private jets don't just allow anyone on there.'

'So now I'm just "anyone"?'

Lena groaned in frustration. 'Of course not. Not to me, but to him, yes.'

'I wouldn't be just "anyone" if you'd bothered to introduce me to him. If it weren't for me, you wouldn't have come in a three-mile radius of him.'

Lena stared at her. 'So *that's* what it is? The ugly sister got the prince and you can't stand it.'

'That's a stupid thing to say.'

'Is it? Every time we walk into a bar, they all flock to you. And you *love* it. You don't even pretend you don't, which is what I love about you. But this' – she waved a hand at Johanna – 'this isn't a good look.'

'Don't be so fucking patronising, Lena.'

'Well, don't be so fucking *needy*, Johanna.'

'Oh, fuck you.'

'I'm done playing your sidekick.' Lena regarded her coolly. 'It's true. Models *do* look good at parties, but maybe Nico's not interested in having *window dressing* at his.'

Johanna flinched, her hurt as bright as a slap to the face. 'Understood,' she said. She held up her hands, giving up, and backed out of the room.

Lena ignored the instant twist of guilt. She found her charger and coiled it into the suitcase. She wasn't going to be the one to apologise. She was so sick of LA, of everyone hustling and jostling for status, trying to bleed you for something – even your closest friends. She wouldn't allow Johanna to make her feel guilty for this. It wasn't Lena's responsibility to indulge her every whim.

Nico watched the screen, a pre-emptive smile on his lips ahead of the comic's punchline. They were in the car en route to the track and Lena couldn't believe how calm he looked. She had heard other sportsmen say that they were sick or scared before big matches, but Nico was in his element. This wasn't just a game or competition for him; it was truly where he was most comfortable. They neared the track and she felt the energy radiate off him.

'You're not nervous at *all*, are you?'

He kissed her. 'I can't wait.'

She wanted to ask more but was scared of getting inside his head, of messing with the wiring that told him this race was his. Nico was in pole position ahead of Vossen. Winning this race was key. If he failed, Vossen would extend his championship lead and, as she was starting to learn, so much of this sport was psychology.

At the circuit, the sound of the crowd was deafening. Lena found it daunting but it only fed Nico's energy. He never courted attention like some of the other drivers but he thrived on the atmosphere; on the pure love of the sport. She followed him to the paddock and felt a charge of satisfaction when she saw that Eva was missing. Greg had broken up with her and it pleased Lena that *she* was still here in the paddock.

Nico was ushered away and the race preamble began: the grid walk, the snatched interviews and unexpected celebrities. The glamour of it was intoxicating. Lena imagined being on Nico's arm tonight as he accepted praise for his win. Her stomach fluttered at the prospect. In this game of time, she didn't know how long she had but she vowed to enjoy every minute.

The cars began their formation lap, zig-zagging all over the track before lining back up on the grid. Lena felt her heart-rate climb. These moments, as the lights came on, were the most breathless of the race. One by one, they lit up – and then flashed off in an instant. Nico pelted ahead and put some distance behind him. Vossen swung to the right to avoid Greg and almost clipped the barrier. How easily the victory would have come. But Lena knew that Nico wanted to win on the track – not through crashes, penalties or retirements. Vossen, on soft tyres like Nico, closed the distance between them. Soon, he was able to use DRS, but each time he tried to overtake, Nico held him off.

When Nico pitted, Vossen took the lead, much to the dismay of the French fans who booed and jeered vociferously. With fresher tyres, however, Nico was able to close the gap and retook the lead when Vossen went to pit. The crowd roared their approval and Lena felt sick at the prospect of Nico losing in front of them.

The pattern began to repeat itself on the second pit stop. Nico was in the pit lane when Vossen took the lead. As Nico rejoined the track, however, two drivers in the back of the field collided, resulting in a safety car – which meant no overtaking. With his position protected, Vossen went in for his second pit stop, essentially gaining it free. Nico had just lost first place. He was stuck in second for five torturous laps and Lena could sense the tension harden.

Nico's voice came on the radio. 'It's been five laps. The track is clear. Why do we still have a safety car?' He sounded unusually stressed.

By this point, there were only seven laps to go and Nico's chance of regaining the lead was diminishing quickly. After another excruciating lap under the safety car, the drivers were finally cleared to race. Nico chased down Vossen but, with fresher tyres, the younger driver fought him off. They went wheel to wheel but Vossen refused to cede. Panic went up in the paddock as the two cars came a whisker from touching. Nico drew level and for a moment the cars seemed suspended, their pace matched exactly. The tension was unbearable, heightened by the roaring crowd. Then, after a breathless beat, Nico pulled ahead. The paddock lit up with noise as panic gave way to euphoria. It echoed out across the entire circuit. Nico Laurent was back in the lead.

But Vossen wasn't ready to yield and they drove nose to tail. Then, as they rounded a corner, Nico made a mistake. He locked up his front wheel and ran wide. Vossen roared past, leaving Nico in his wake. The paddock was mute with shock as Nico recovered and sped after Vossen. They entered the final lap of the race and Nico pushed harder than was sensible. With DRS, he came excruciatingly close to Vossen. The Mercedes mechanics were on their feet, every one of them shouting.

Come on, Nico. Come on.

He came inches from Vossen – and, then, they were over the finishing line, the chequered flag sealing their fate: Nico second and Vossen first. Lena sank in her chair and the entire team deflated. A stunned shock befell them. Nico had overcome multiple setbacks – the safety car, Vossen's free pit stop – only to come up empty for an unforced error, slipping further behind in the championship. That was the thing that unnerved Lena. Nico could tolerate others' mistakes, but this was entirely his and he would punish himself for it.

She watched as the mechanics and engineers consoled one other. Theo, the team principal, threw his headphones against the wall, his features laced with fury. Everyone fell quiet. When Theo raged, you stood by and let him. The energy crackled, close to igniting. Lena shrank back, feeling like a trespasser. In silence, the team filed out towards the podium. It was a Red Bull, Mercedes, Ferrari finish with Christian Lecourt in P3. The Red Bull team was ecstatic and the Ferrari mechanics were in high spirits, enjoying their comeback after years in the doldrums. Mercedes, however, were downbeat. One single retirement would put them at risk. From here on, their performance had to be flawless.

Lena joined the team and watched Nico take second place on the podium. He hung his head and she saw the twitch of his fingers, compulsively rubbing his cigarette scar. She wanted to reach out and stop him, to lace her own fingers with his and hide his scar for him. She wanted to tell him that he was worth so much more than a title, but she knew it would make no difference.

Nico accepted his second-place trophy and shook the presenter's hand. Next to him, Vossen lifted the winner's trophy. Nico looked on respectfully, then, as was custom, picked up his bottle of champagne. He shook it into a healthy fizz, then poured it over Vossen's head – sporting through his crushing disappointment. He leaned over the railing and poured some on the crowd below him. Lena tried to catch his eye but she was insignificant in the sea of fans. The post-race interviews were difficult as Nico was asked again and again about his mistake.

'I don't know what to say,' he told them. 'Michael had an excellent race. We were unlucky but it was my error that cost us the race. I want to say sorry to the team and to all the fans who came out today. I promise we'll come back faster and stronger in two weeks' time.' When he finally finished his duties to the press, he strode to the paddock. Lena sprang up to greet him but he went straight to the post-race briefing. She waited for an hour until he emerged, changed and showered.

'Nico,' she called to him. When he looked up, she could see the storm in his eyes. 'Are you okay?'

'Not now,' he told her. He marched to the car, Lena barely keeping up. He held the door open for her and got in the other side. As Chris manoeuvred out of the car park, Nico leaned forward and put his head in his hands. Lena wanted to reach out and touch him, but he was wound so tight, she felt that he might snap. She had never been in a position like this. In that moment, she wished that she was acquainted with the other F1 wives and girlfriends. Maybe they could tell her what to do, or what to say to soothe him. She was the girlfriend of one of the world's most elite sportsmen and she had no idea what to do with it. In need of guidance, she sent a text to Eliot: *what can I do?*

The reply was almost instant. *Let him be.*

She grimaced but settled back in her seat, giving Nico space. He didn't speak for the entire drive. It was only back in their suite that he even acknowledged her. He poured himself a whisky and turned to her from the balcony.

'Can you ask Eliot to get you another room for a couple of hours? I need to be alone.'

Lena was stung. She fought the urge to go to him, to hold him, to beg him not to push her away, but she heeded Eliot's words. 'Okay,' she agreed softly. She paused in the doorway. 'I think you were brilliant,' she said.

He turned towards the view and Lena retreated to a second suite. Eliot had already given her a key at the start of the race weekend. She paced the living room, tension coiled inside her. She sat at the desk, pulled out her laptop and opened the latest version of *Please Understand* – an instinct whenever she had some down time. Then, with an acid tang, she remembered that the script wasn't hers anymore. She no longer had something she owned. The thought left her adrift. Ever since she could remember, she had always had something that was just hers. Even in the early days, when writing all those mercenary articles about wedding lighting or life insurance, she'd always had something that was hers – and now, there was nothing. She closed the laptop again and prowled around the suite. Like Nico's, it had two bedrooms, two bathrooms and a spacious living room. She peered into the champagne bucket and then inside the fridge. She went out to the balcony where daylight was turning to dusk. She considered going for a wander, but she wanted to be here when Nico was ready to talk. It was hours later that he knocked on her door.

'Get ready,' he said. 'We're going out.'

She looked down at her T-shirt and jeans. 'Where?'

'To the party. I need to show my face.'

'Okay, I'll need some time to get ready.'

'Fine.'

Lena hesitated. 'Do you want to talk?'

'No,' he said plainly. 'I want to go out. I want to forget today.'

'Okay. I'll need about forty-five minutes.' She grabbed a few things from her suitcase, which was still in Nico's suite, then hurried back and sprang into action. She had to minister what he needed tonight: a fun-time party girl who could lift his mood. She pulled on a forest-green sequinned minidress with long sleeves and a deep neckline – her trademark look of classy but sexy. With clear tape, she secured the neckline to her collarbone, twisting this way and that to make sure it didn't spill open. She applied her makeup and finished with a strong red lip. Nico knocked on the door after exactly forty-five minutes. When Lena opened it, he blinked in surprise.

'You look stunning,' he said.

Lena lit up. 'You look pretty good too,' she said. He wore a grey suit with a white shirt but no tie and a light-blue pocket square that set off his eyes. She took his hand and fell in step beside him.

At Mazikeen, they were escorted to a roped-off section of the club separate to the main floor. It was packed with drivers and their partners. Those who were single had cherry-picked some women to join them. Nico downed a whisky, then another, then a third in quick succession. Lena watched with concern, then quietly chided herself. He didn't need a babysitter. Tonight, he needed an equal; someone to keep things fun and light and ease him into humour. She picked up a glass of champagne and started to keep pace. Soon, she was pleasantly giddy and joined some of the group on the dance floor. It was a much-needed release, not just for the losers but the winners too. They were one week away from F1's mid-season summer break and everyone was in a loose and heady mood. She found herself dancing with Greg Richards and felt a pang of satisfaction that Eva wasn't there. As they danced, his hands found the small of her back and she let him hold her there. The music intensified and he pulled her closer and pressed her body to his. She felt the heat of him and was so taken by the mood, it didn't occur to her that Nico would mind, or even notice. Greg was drunk and leaned into her neck, using her for support.

'I'm so happy,' he said. 'Are you happy?'

'I think, so, yes!'

He blinked as if seeing her for the first time. 'You're so beautiful.'

Lena laughed. 'Thank you!' She stared up at his warm green eyes. 'So are you.'

A dancehall song from the Nineties, 'Murder She Wrote', came on and a cheer went up from those who remembered it. The two of them gave in to the music, the heat between their bodies making them both sweat. Lena turned and when he pressed into her back, she could feel that he was hard. Something stirred in her conscience but it was too remote to bring her out of the mood. Greg's hands were on her hips and he moved them slowly up her body. That's when she felt a firm grip on her arm.

'Ms Aden? Mr Richards?' It was a smartly dressed man, in his early fifties, with perfectly coiffed hair. He looked like he might be the owner of the club. 'Come this way please.'

In their drunken state, both of them followed, giggling as they swayed. On the stairs, Lena nearly slipped and Greg grabbed her hand to tug her upright. They followed the man up into a private room, still holding hands and laughing. The light in the room was muted and the music audible but not intrusive. Lena saw Nico on one of the sofas and quickly let go of Greg's hand. Near him sat Christian Lecourt, one of the Ferrari drivers.

'*Quelle œuvre d'art*,' Nico said to Christian in French.

Christian stared at her. '*Absolument.*'

Lena felt her cheeks burn. 'Nico.' She cleared her throat. 'I was wondering where you were.'

'Come here,' he told her. She hesitated, then moved to sit beside him but he pointed to the sofa opposite. He waited until she was seated, then turned to his teammate. 'Come on, Greg.' He beckoned him closer, next to Lena. 'Beautiful, isn't she?'

Greg looked at her. 'She's stunning.'

'Do you want to touch her?'

Through her fug, something pinged in Lena. 'Nico.'

'Answer me, Greg. Do you want to touch her?'

Greg didn't look at Nico; fixed his gaze on Lena instead.

'I fucked your girl, Greg. Don't you want to fuck mine?' The air in the room crackled. Lena felt pressure in her ears, like a sound at too high a frequency. 'Touch her, Greg.'

'Lena,' slurred Greg. 'Do you want to?'

'*Touch* her, Greg.'

Greg blinked, then reached for her, seemingly in slow motion. He slipped his fingers beneath the neckline of her dress, then locked eyes with her. Encouraged by the way her lips parted, he traced his fingers down, across her butter-smooth breast. His nails grazed her nipple, making her gasp. She felt Christian's eyes on her and bit her lip for him. There was something intoxicating about being wanted by every man in the room. Greg pulled her dress off one shoulder, revealing her right breast. He made a low groan of a sound, urgent with lust. He leaned down and, with exquisite gentleness, took her nipple between his teeth. His tongue flicked the tip once, twice, then again. Lena arched to give him better reach, preening beneath his touch. He closed his hot mouth around her, making her quake with pleasure. He licked and sucked her breast, making her wet with want.

'*Qu'est-ce que tu en penses?*' Nico said to Christian.

Lena sensed Christian move closer and felt his weight beside her on the sofa. He pulled at the other half of her dress and she heard the soft sucking sound of tape coming loose from her skin. He freed her arm from the dress and rolled it down. Then, he too, leaned down and took a breast in his mouth. Lena quivered with pleasure. When she locked eyes with Nico, he gave her a look she recognised: lust and contempt.

'Say *red* if you want to stop,' he said.

She closed her eyes and sank into the sofa, and that act of submission was all the permission they needed. Christian lifted her and took her over to a white leather divan akin to a king-size bed. There, with Lena laid out beneath them, the two men grew aggressive. They lit on her in a blur of skin and sweat and sex. Greg knelt between her legs as Christian pushed his way into her mouth, both of them rabid with want. She let them manoeuvre her: Christian now pressing the nape of her neck towards Greg below her, pushing his way inside her as Greg fucked her mouth. She lost control of her mind; let her body descend into a dark and pulsing rapture. She came again and again, screaming with abandon. But beneath the narcotic bliss, something roiled in the depths of her mind, trying to break the surface: *Red. Red. Red.*

Chapter 12

Dawn filtered through the room in muted blue-toned hues. Lena was still in her dress, her arms clumsily threaded back through her sleeves. The fabric was twisted and the sequins felt like scales on her skin. Her mouth was cottony and her head felt heavy and bloated. She blinked, disoriented, and tried to get her bearings. With a sick jolt, she realised that she was still on the white leather bed at Mazikeen. She lifted herself onto her elbows.

'Nico,' she called out. Her voice sounded small – cracked and pathetic. She looked across the room, expecting to see him there, passed out with Christian and Greg. 'Nico,' she called again when she saw that the room was empty. As she listened for his voice, an awful possibility revealed itself. Had they left her there? Her conscience refused to compute this. There was simply no way. She groped for her phone and spotted it on the sofa on the other side of the room. Pathetically, she searched for signs of life – a phone, a wallet or discarded jacket – but the timbre of the silence told her the truth. No one else was here. She had been left there alone. A childlike whimper escaped her as she shuffled off the bed.

She set her feet on the floor and it was when she realised

that she still had her heels on that she burst into tears. They hadn't even done her that kindness when they had finished with her. It was *that* more than anything else that made her feel like garbage. She limped to her phone and saw that she had no calls or messages. Her hands shook as she dialled Nico's number. Numbly, she listened to it ring until it went to voicemail. She waited two minutes and tried again, but Nico didn't answer. Humiliation stung her cheeks. Shame, or the spectre of it, had played such a big part in her upbringing, but she had never felt it so purely. She felt like a piece of trash: used and discarded. It wrung her of her confidence, her self-worth, her sense of who she was – and for what? Because she had danced with Greg? Was the poison so deep inside Nico that it infected *everything*? She covered her face and sobbed. Deep, sad, angry tears to rid herself of this feeling.

The door whistled open and Lena's head snapped up. A thin woman in a cleaning uniform looked in. She made a small *oy* sound and began to retreat.

'Sorry,' said Lena by instinct. 'I'm . . .'

'I'll wait downstairs,' the woman cut in, speaking to the air next to Lena's head. She backed away, letting the door swing shut.

Lena felt disgraced. She looked around for something: a coat, a scarf, or some other armour, but she only had her sequinned dress. Gingerly, she righted it. She tried to stick the tape back to her skin but it sloughed right off. She couldn't bear the thought of walking into her hotel like this. Clumsily, she thumbed through her phone and called the only person who could help.

'Lena?' He answered immediately.

'Eliot.' A sob escaped her.

'Where are you? I'll send Chris.'

She sobbed again. 'I'm at Mazikeen. It's a club but I don't know where.'

'It's okay. Stay there. Chris will be there soon.'

'Okay.' She searched for something else to say, to give voice to what she was feeling. When nothing came, she thanked him and set down her phone. She clutched her dress to her chest and hobbled to the door. The space outside smelled of ice cubes and metal. Goosebumps rose on her skin as she slunk down the same stairs that she and Greg had climbed yesterday, both of them giddy with laughter. *A fun-time party girl*. Lena's heels clacked loudly as she crossed the empty dance floor. She waited by a window and flinched every time she heard the cleaner in some unseen corner.

Chris pulled up in his black sedan and hurried to usher her in. When they locked eyes, she saw not judgement but compassion there, and it made her want to collapse.

'I'm okay,' she said even though he would never ask. Inside the car, she inspected herself in the rearview mirror. Her face was streaked with makeup, her lips a smear of red like a child who'd stolen strawberries. She rifled through her bag for a wet wipe but there was no way to salvage this.

'Chris, do you have a facemask?' she asked.

He nodded and opened the glove box. He pulled one free of its plastic packet and handed it over to her. She gripped it tightly, tethering herself to this gifted armour. In a glaze, she watched the streets slide by. Her mind was blank, working remotely, and she let herself be lulled.

When they reached the hotel, Chris hurried to open her door. Lena put on the mask, literally ashamed to show her face. As she rode up to the penthouse, a flick of anxiety convinced her that her key to his suite wouldn't work. She held her breath as she pressed it against the black panel. The light turned green and she pushed her way inside. Nico was on the balcony with a glass of whisky. He turned and looked at her with an expression she couldn't read.

'You're back,' he said.

Lena didn't reply. Instead, she went to the shower and stayed beneath the scalding water until her lungs felt full of steam. She wrapped a robe around her and gathered up her toiletries. Back in the bedroom, she began to pack. Nico watched her curiously.

'The jet won't be ready for a couple of hours.'

Lena carried on packing. She heard his throat work in the silence.

'You're angry with me.'

'Angry?' She spun towards him, her voice a whisper of disbelief. 'Angry doesn't even begin to describe what I feel. I am disgusted. I am *revolted*. I am fucking *livid*.'

'Why?' he asked blithely.

'Don't gaslight me, Nico. You took me up there and you *fed* me to them.'

He squared his jaw. 'I might have got carried away.'

'Carried away?' she mimicked acidly. '"Carried away" is throwing up in the bathroom after one too many drinks, it's maybe having a drunken fumble. It's not offering someone you supposedly care about for two other men to fuck.'

'So you didn't want to fuck Greg?'

Lena bristled. 'That's why you did it? You wanted to punish me for *dancing* with another man?'

'You're free to do whatever you want, Lena. Just like you did last night.'

'Don't you dare do that. Don't you dare blame me.'

Nico's voice was cool with challenge. 'Are you saying you didn't want it?'

In his expectant gaze, Lena groped for her answer. It was soft like clay and she had to feel it to work out its shape. The truth was that she *had* enjoyed it, hadn't she? That heady, potent feeling of being desired by three men; of submitting to them; letting them do what they wanted to her. There was something liberating in the act of submission, in surrendering so wholly to pleasure. But in the clear light of day she knew that it wasn't what she would have chosen for herself.

Nico saw the conflict in her features and the look on his own changed. 'Are you saying it wasn't consensual?' When she didn't answer, he gripped her arms above the elbow. 'Lena, are you saying it wasn't consensual?'

She swallowed her hurt. 'No, but it's not what I would have chosen for myself.' She felt an immense sadness close over her. 'This life is not what I would have chosen for myself.' Her mind snagged on that thought and when she turned it over again, she found a sense of clarity. 'It's *not* what I choose for myself.'

Nico watched her carefully. 'What are you saying?'

Lena took her time to answer, wanting to be sure. She held his gaze and said, 'I don't want to see you anymore.'

His expression didn't change. 'That's not true.'

'You left me there,' she said, quiet at first. She curled her hands into fists, but had vowed never to hit him.

'Left you where?'

'At Mazikeen!'

'What are you talking about? I didn't leave you there.'

'I woke up there this morning!'

Colour drained from his face. 'Lena, I thought you were sleeping in the suite next door. I got caught up with Theo at the club. I told Chris to find you and bring you home.'

'That's a lie.'

He strode across the room and snatched his phone from the bedside cabinet. He scrolled for a moment and then his features changed, from assuredness into horror. The phone slid from his hands and landed on the bed.

'What?' When he didn't answer, Lena went over and checked the phone.

Chris, I've been caught by some sponsorship bods and don't know how long I'll be. Pick up Lena please and take her to the hotel. She's in the Engine Room upstairs. Thanks.

Next to the message was a red exclamation mark in a circle and, underneath, the words *Not Delivered*.

Nico covered his face. 'Lena, I didn't know.'

'I can't do this anymore.'

'You can't leave.'

'Do you have *any* idea how I felt waking up on that cheap white leather, stinking of other men? They left me there, Nico, passed out with my heels still on. They didn't give a fuck – and neither do you.'

'I thought you were next door!' He gestured at the green sequinned dress that lay in a heap on the bed. 'When you came in, I thought you hadn't yet changed this morning. I didn't know that they—' He scrubbed a hand across his face. 'I didn't know that we left you there.' He clasped his hands together. 'Lena, I am so *so* sorry.'

'I'm done, Nico. I'm done feeling like this.'

'You're angry. I understand that, but please don't do this.'

Lena turned away from him. She tried to carry on packing but Nico snatched the T-shirt in her hands. 'Lena, you're not doing this.'

'You have taken so much from me. My work, my pride, my dignity. I'm not letting you do it anymore.'

'No.'

'Find a way to say goodbye, Nico, because this is it.' She reached for the T-shirt but Nico gripped her wrist.

'Lena, you don't understand.' He fixed his ice-blue gaze on her. 'You don't understand, so I'm telling you now.' He exhaled softly. 'I love you.'

Lena's heart snared in her chest, mutinous with need. 'Don't,' she told him.

'I love you,' Nico repeated.

'Don't you fucking *dare*, Nico.' Her voice was charged with threat.

'I love you, Lena.'

'Fuck off, Nico!' She shoved him away and he hit the wall with force. A wildness lit up his eyes before he could subdue it. In that moment, Lena glimpsed the boy he used to be and felt her heart breaking. 'I love you, Nico.' Her voice cracked. 'But you make me hate myself.'

'I'll be better, Lena.'

'No. You won't.'

'Don't go,' he pleaded. Lena pulled the suitcase off the bed. He strode over, gripped her hand in both of his and raised it to his forehead. 'Please don't do this, Lena. Please.'

She pulled back gently. 'I'm always going to care about you.'

'Then don't leave.'

She backed away from him.

'Lena, I can't do this by myself.'

She walked to the door.

'Lena. Don't!'

She gripped the handle and just as she turned it, something heavy hit the opposite wall, then shattered across the room. It sounded like a mirror breaking but she didn't turn to look. Instead, she shut the door behind her. She leaned against it and closed her eyes, her chest racked with tears. She dug a fist into her thigh to try to hold them back. She put on her shades to hide her distress and set off down the corridor. At reception, her hands shook as she returned her keys.

'Ms Aden,' she heard a voice behind her.

She turned. 'Eliot.'

He ushered her to one side. 'I wanted to check that you were all right.'

'I'm leaving.'

He glanced at her suitcase. 'I gathered.' He paused as if he was weighing something up. 'He won't make it easy.'

She nodded. 'Thank you for taking care of me.'

'I hope you don't think ill of me, Lena – staying with him. I knew his father and I saw what he went through and I feel it's my responsibility to . . .' He trailed off because what could he say? Look after him? Rein him in?

'Take care of him for me.'

'I will,' he promised.

She leaned in and kissed his cheek. 'Goodbye, Eliot.'

'Goodbye, Ms Aden.'

*

Lena tugged her suitcase into her flat over the lip of the doorway. It skittered across the wooden flooring and barrelled into her ankles. She swore in pain and abandoned the case in the corridor. That's when she noticed the stack of boxes balanced against the wall. For a second, she thought she was in the wrong place. Frowning, she manoeuvred around the boxes towards Johanna's room.

'Jo?'

Her housemate looked into the corridor. Her hair was tied in a bun and she wore a tatty old sweater. 'Oh, hi.'

'What's going on?'

Johanna eyed the boxes. 'I'm moving out.'

Lena blanched. 'What? *When?*'

'End of this week. I'll pay my half of the rent until my notice period is up. Then you'll have to find somebody else.'

Lena was aghast. 'Why didn't you say anything?'

'You've been kinda busy.'

Lena bristled. 'Is this because we fought?'

'No, I've been thinking about it for a while.' She gestured vaguely. 'There's a models' house here in Venice Beach and they've been trying to get me to move in for a while. I didn't want to leave you, but you've got your own things going on now, so I felt it was time for me to move on.'

'But so soon?'

'Yeah, sorry about that. One of the models is moving out and they want the room filled asap.' She shrugged a shoulder. 'But like I said, I'll cover my half of the rent until the notice is up.'

Lena didn't want to admit how hurt she was that Johanna would leave like this. They had been housemates for five years. For her to leave so casually felt like abandonment. 'What's the flat like?' she asked.

'It's closer to the beach and larger. I'll get the crap bedroom given that I'm moving in last, but it'll be good for my career to bunk with other models. We look out for each other.'

Lena felt chastened by this. She didn't know whether to try to change Johanna's mind, but the boxes in the hallway were pretty final. 'I'll miss you,' she said meekly.

'I'll be nearby. You'll see me all the time,' said Johanna in her own classic LA promise. 'Anyway, how was the race weekend? Sorry that Nico lost.'

Lena flushed. She had expected to come home and tell Johanna everything. She thought that they would sit on the sofa together and talk out the pain. Instead, she was met with this weird, strained formality. 'It was good,' she lied.

'Great.' Johanna motioned at the boxes. 'Right, do you mind if I get on with it? There's a shit-ton to get through.'

'No, of course not.' Lena made a show of checking her watch. 'I've got to get to Paramount anyway. Is it okay if I jump in the shower?'

'Sure,' said Johanna.

There was an awkward pause before the two of them parted. Lena dreaded the thought of replacing Johanna. Finding a decent housemate in LA was akin to magic. Thankfully, Lena's job at Paramount would cover the rent if she needed time. With the rest of her life in a mess, she would pour her energy into *The Liminal*. She no longer had to juggle the Aston and was ready to work all hours. With this in mind, she ignored her body's plea for sleep and showered and dressed quickly.

She reached Paramount just as the clock struck noon. The writers' room was strewn with paper and two rounds of coffee cups. Their bitter tang hung in the air, mixing with the sunshine. Lena slid into her chair and opened her laptop.

Paula stared at her. 'Lena? What are you doing here?'

'You said I could come in at twelve today,' Lena reminded her.

Paula frowned. 'Didn't you get a call this morning?'

'Um, I might have, but I was in the air.'

Paula impatiently tossed her pen on the desk. 'Follow me please.' Lena set down her bag but Paula waggled her fingers testily. 'Bring that with you.' Lena glanced around at the writers but none met her eye. With a budding sense of dread, she followed Paula outside.

'Lena, you should have received a call this morning. And, frankly,' she pointed at Lena's lanyard, '*that* should no longer be working. Your contract here has been terminated.'

Lena flinched. 'What? When?'

'This morning. Stephen called. He doesn't want you on the picture anymore.'

Lena's cheeks burned with heat. 'Why?' she asked pathetically.

Paula clucked. 'Come on, Lena. Let's be real, shall we? It's not like you were here on merit.'

The words were like a slap in the face. Of course she knew that Nico had made a phone call but Lena had done good work on the script. 'I'm good enough to be here, Paula,' she said with more conviction than she felt.

'Perhaps. But so are thousands of other writers. Why should you get to jump the queue when people like me and them' – she pointed at the writers inside the room – 'fought tooth and nail to get here?' She tutted. 'You think we were cold to you. Well, guess what? We were. You had a few good ideas, yes, but you didn't "deserve" to be here. If you did, we wouldn't be booting you off just because you broke up with your boyfriend.'

'Paula, I need this job.'

The older woman smiled unkindly. 'There's always Starbucks,' she said, knowing full well that, in LA, hundreds vied for those jobs as well.

'This isn't fair,' said Lena, knowing that it came out a childish whine.

'No, you being here in the first place wasn't fair. Now, things are fair again.' She pointed at Lena's lanyard. 'Give me that, go downstairs and talk to security. They'll be expecting you.' She held out her palm expectantly.

Lena felt winded. Paula clicked her fingers impatiently

and that small unkindness threatened to undo her. Passively, she took off her lanyard and handed it over. Paula stalked into the writers' room and snatched up the receiver of the conference phone. Through the glass, Lena looked at the other writers, trying to infer if they felt the same as Paula. None of them looked at her – and not in studied avoidance but total nonchalance. The sting of humiliation made her eyes water, but she was determined not to let them see it. Calmly, she made her way along the corridor and waited for the lift. Downstairs, she was taken off the system by security and walked out through the yellow arch. There, back on the street, she felt entirely disoriented. A bitter, juvenile part of her wanted to call Nico and ask how he could be so fucking petty. The adult in her understood, however, that she had no right to be there. For the last five years, she had been at the loser's end of nepotism in Hollywood. She knew how painful it felt, how gut-wrenching, how completely debilitating, to be passed over in favour of somebody's daughter, sister, girlfriend. Paula was right. Lena didn't deserve to be there. The fact that she had pretended to, even for a few weeks, made her feel ashamed. She took a long look at the arch, committing it to memory. She had a bleak suspicion that the next time she saw it, it would be years from now: she with her husband, a fellow lawyer perhaps, and their two children on a tour of LA film studios. She would look up at the arches wistfully and tell her children how mummy had once worked here, very briefly, and how, for a fleeting, beautiful moment, she had really believed that she would make it in the toughest town in America.

*

The wave rolled onto the shore, extending its lazy reach towards Lena. She let it skim her toes before its graceful retreat. Beneath her, the hot sand was cooling and she was unduly grateful for this. The heat, the sun, the ubiquitous beauty were at odds with her melancholy. Today, she yearned for dreary Britain. She contemplated the prospect of moving back to London. She would have to swap this ocean for something grey and concrete – the colour and matter of failure. She imagined the daily journey to Holborn: the fraying tempers of a hundred commuters packed onto the Central Line, the artificial air and sulphur lights. The thought chilled her soul. She gathered a fistful of sand and watched it slip through her fingers. She couldn't do it. She couldn't adopt that life and act like this one hadn't mattered. She couldn't give up. Not yet. Not when she still had two months left. She stood up and dusted off her hands. There was one thing left to try.

She headed back up the beach and tramped a familiar route to the building. She pushed open the heavy black door and gingerly ventured inside. She heard familiar voices and felt herself fill with warmth. She knocked like a stranger and heard movement inside. After a moment, the door opened.

'Lena?' Brianna's voice was tart with surprise.

'Hi!' Lena said brightly. She walked in without being invited and brandished the donuts like a peace offering.

'What are you doing here?'

She pointed at her old chair, feeling weirdly shy. 'Can I sit down?'

'Yes,' said Brianna as Ahmed and Gloria watched curiously.

Lena splayed her fingers on the table. 'Okay, I'm not going to try to style this out. I want to be honest with you. My contract on *The Liminal* wasn't extended so suddenly I've gone from two jobs to zero. So . . . I wanted to ask how you would feel about me coming back.'

Brianna made a sound as if in pain. 'Actually, you've gate-crashed a meeting.'

Lena cringed showily. 'Sorry! I can just hang back 'til you're done.' She pointed at a tatty chair in the corner.

Brianna shifted. 'Actually, Lena, we need some privacy.'

'Privacy? From me?' She looked to Ahmed and Gloria. 'Why?' No one spoke for a beat. 'Why?' she repeated.

Brianna tapped a pile of paper on the table. 'We received a new contract this morning. From Nico Laurent's lawyers.'

Dread pushed on Lena. 'He hasn't backed out, has he?' If so, the Aston would almost certainly be lost.

Brianna grimaced. 'No. Not exactly.'

'Then what?'

'They have added a stipulation that we halt our production of *Please Understand*.'

Lena gaped at her. 'What? Can they even do that?'

'If it's written into the contract, then yes.'

'But that's . . .' She swallowed hard to compose herself. 'That's not fair.'

'I'm sorry, Lena. I don't know what's happened between you two but clearly it's unfortunate.'

'Well, can you push back? Tell them you refuse?'

'We tried that.'

'And?'

'And they said they would pull out of the sale.'

'Could we get the press involved? Tell them he's basically blackmailing you?'

'Lena—'

'Nico values his privacy. If he thinks he might be exposed for this, he might—'

'Lena,' Brianna interrupted more firmly. A hush fell on the room. 'It's too late.'

Lena's throat was dry and painful. 'What do you mean?'

Brianna sagged. 'We've already signed the contract.'

Lena choked on the news. She couldn't believe that they had shuttered her play. 'You said you would look after it.'

'It was sacrifice your play or sacrifice everything.'

'But you had other options, Brianna.'

'Like what? Our only other option was William McGregor and that didn't work out.'

Lena smarted with guilt. 'So that's it? The play is done?'

'Could you maybe talk to Nico?' said Ahmed.

'No,' Lena replied without even looking at him.

'What happened between you?' Gloria asked tentatively.

If anyone else had asked, Lena would have told them to mind their own business. Instead, she said, 'It's complicated.'

Brianna spoke with clinical sympathy. 'I'm sorry, Lena, but to answer your question: yes, the play is done.'

'So what now?'

'Now we get on with another show.'

Lena straightened. 'Okay, then let's do that.'

There was an awkward pause. 'Lena, I'm afraid you need

to go.' Gently, Brianna added, 'The contract also specifies that you can no longer be here.'

Lena let out an involuntary sound, almost like a hiccup. 'And you signed that?' she asked, impossibly hurt.

'You had already left us.'

'But you *knew* that something had gone wrong. And still you signed it?'

'What choice did we have? It was you or the Aston.'

'So that's it? You just threw me under the bus?'

'You'd already made that decision, Lena.'

'Right. I see.' She was quiet for a moment. 'Well, it was nice working with you all. Good luck with your next show.' She pushed back from the table.

'Lena.' A chorus rose from Ahmed and Gloria.

'It's okay. I get it,' she snapped. When she looked at their faces, however, the sourness turned into sorrow. 'It's okay,' she said more softly. 'I get it.' She coughed her tears away. 'Look, I don't have a speech prepared, so I'm probably going to sound really fucking clichéd, but I want to say that being in this room with you has been the best time of my life. I'm heartbroken that my play won't get to see this stage, but each of you has made me a better writer and I'll never forget that.' She bit her bottom lip to stop it quivering. 'It's been an honour. It really has. So thank you.'

Ahmed began to speak but Lena shook her head. She snatched up her bag and fled. Outside, she paused on the steps of the theatre, needing a moment to steady herself. In just one day, Nico had managed to separate her from everything she valued. She had no housemate, no income, no prospects. How quickly her life had unravelled. Eliot had warned her that he wouldn't make it easy, but she hadn't expected the reprisal to be so swift and strong. She hadn't known it would leave her crippled. She slid down onto the stoop. She felt suffocated by the thought of her next steps. She would have to pack up her life into boxes, find the money for a plane ticket and go home to a hundred *I told you so's*. London. Grey. Concrete. The colour and matter of failure.

Chapter 13

Lena's throat was dry, clogged from all the passing traffic. The fumes were dense and left her feeling itchy. She heard the rumble of the bus before it turned the corner. It came to a stop beside her, belching out exhaust. Inside, it smelled of stale fast food and engine oil, and she pressed her nose into her scarf to try to block it out. She turned up the volume on her headphones to drown out the sound of a man on his phone. This journey was an assault on all the senses: the hard plastic chairs, the thick stream of graffiti, even the metallic taste on her tongue. She hunkered down for the forty-five-minute drive, a deadening passage of time during which she could not write or even read – just blankly listen to music. A large man collapsed on the seat next to her. She grimaced when the damp film on his bare arm brushed against hers. She shimmied closer to the window as his sweat slowly dried on her skin. By the time she reached Palgrave, patches of it dotted her arm. She manoeuvred around him and practically tumbled out of the bus in relief.

She swiped into a large brick building and took the clunky lift up to the fourth floor. Palgrave Content Solutions boasted its location in a 'converted warehouse' but really there was no conversion, just fraying Seventies decor pasted over an industrial past. It smelled of cold cement and looked sickly under strips of fluorescent lighting. Lena settled into her cubicle, which sat next to the window. She looked out at the haze, which revealed a cluster of buildings: downtown LA. Some days, like today, she couldn't bear to look at it. It reminded her daily that she had failed to keep her own promise. She had turned thirty last week and still she was here in LA. Gone was her vow that she would escape the jaws of this city. Her place at law school had been rescinded and it had felt like a lock turning in a key, pronouncing her a lifer.

She waited for her laptop to boot up. She was allowed to bring her own instead of using the second-hand machines that Palgrave gave them as standard. The company, which posed as a cutting-edge AI-generated content solutions agency, was actually a collection of failed writers barely making a living. Lena was a 'staff writer' but her role comprised very little writing. Instead, she had to review content generated by OpenAI. Whether fifty-word descriptions of hotels, or listicles for buzzy new websites, she had a quota each morning and all her output was logged and monitored. At first, it was painful, this collapse of her creativity, but after almost three months in the job, she no longer felt the nerve endings. There was no lancing pain; just a low and remote ache.

She opened her docket for the day. She had to approve a minimum of eighty-four press releases for product launches, mainly in the automotive industry. She clicked open the first one, scanned it and approved it. In the early days, she would spend time restructuring sentences to make them sound more natural, but PaceCheck told her that she was working too slowly. Now, she might take out a stray exclamation mark, but otherwise let things slide as long as they weren't obvious errors. She opened a second press release, scanned it and approved it. The morning passed at that steady, mechanical pace. At lunch, she ate at her desk: a homemade sandwich, bruised apple and cereal bar. Her pace dropped in the afternoon once she knew she would hit the day's target. She was reviewing her ninetieth press release when a shadow fell over her screen. She turned to find Jerry, one of the other staff writers. He was good looking but had a sandy-coloured moustache that gave him a furtive air.

'Hey, Lena. Some of us are heading to Tassili's. Wanna come?'

She feigned regret. 'Oh, thank you, but I can't.'

'Come on. Just one drink? It's Friday.'

'I've got plans,' she lied.

'You always have plans.'

She mimed flicking her hair. 'Players gotta play,' she said.

He looked at her, amused. 'Okay, let's go with *that*,' he said sardonically.

She laughed. 'Maybe next time.'

'Sure,' he said dubiously. 'Well, have a good weekend.'

She waited until Jerry and his group were gone, wary of being caught in the lift with them. It's not that she disliked her colleagues. There was strong camaraderie there – all of them self-aware – but Lena didn't want to socialise. She felt like a duller, sadder version of herself and she didn't want others to witness it. She didn't want them to think that this was who she was. She appreciated the fact that Jerry still asked, but she would much rather hide at home.

On the bus journey back, she braced herself, for it was this stretch of the day that she found the hardest. As they neared Venice Beach, her mind would map Nico everywhere: the restaurant where they had their first date, the diner in which he spoke about Phoebe, the large Tag Heuer billboards for which he was contractually obliged to model. For a while, every passing Mercedes would remind her of him – a sure-fire track to madness. The memory of him pressed constantly, and she had to work to block him out – a subroutine in the back of her mind. Headlines would blurt his name without warning, screens would blaze his face, and he would come to her in dreams. Her body would respond to him, the exact pitch of ecstasy keyed into her memory. In the first week after she'd left, Eliot had called her to tell her that Nico was in a bad way. She had asked him not to call her again and, mercifully, Eliot had listened.

The bus lumbered to a stop to let Lena out. She walked to her flat, feeling mentally drained in the way only mindless work could do. Inside, she kicked together a pair of trainers belonging to her housemate. Kyle, Johanna's replacement, was a waiter and aspiring actor. He had the flat-nosed, rugby appeal of Channing Tatum and, as far as Lena could tell, was a decent actor. They didn't have much in common and Lena was thankful that his irregular shift pattern meant that they hardly saw each other. She missed Johanna dearly. They had made up and saw each other regularly, but it was different not having her around all the time.

Lena dropped her bag on the floor and collapsed onto the sofa. In the first weeks after Paramount, she would doggedly open her laptop and stare at a blank page. She believed that it would save her, would keep her going and persevering – but nothing came. As the weeks drew on, she grew pent up and frustrated. Then, eventually, she stopped trying. Now, she reached for her phone and mindlessly browsed Instagram. She clicked her own profile and scrolled to a specific crop of pictures. A bittersweet feeling wheeled up when she saw a happier version of herself relaxing on a private jet, a telltale elbow in the frame but never Nico's face. At his behest, she hadn't posted any pictures of the two of them. It was like they had never even happened. She pictured him with Sabine, his hands on her milky skin. She felt a sharp pang of jealousy. She missed him intensely. She couldn't imagine meeting a man who measured up to him. She was thoroughly depressed by this thought and curled up on the sofa, not even able to find the energy to turn the TV on. There, in a soup of her sweat and LA grime, she readied for another night on her own.

*

The sharp trill of the doorbell made Lena bolt upright. She had fallen asleep on the sofa and winced at the pain in her neck. The sound came again in two impatient bursts. She stood groggily and teetered to the door. She checked the spy-hole and opened the door with a groan.

'Lena! What the fuck!' Johanna took in the state of her. 'We're meant to be leaving now.'

'Leaving?' Lena said dumbly. 'Where?'

Johanna marched inside. 'I texted you. We're going out.'

'Out? Johanna, no.'

'You need to get back out there, Lena! You've been pining after Nico for *months*.'

Lena flushed. Johanna didn't realise how much these throwaway comments stung. She hadn't told her what had happened at Mazikeen. Instead, she had fashioned it as a romance fizzled out: boy meets girl, boy and girl fall in love, boy gets bored of girl. Accordingly, Johanna was less delicate than she might have been otherwise.

'It's the opening of a new club. It's all female-owned and promises a better club experience for women.'

Lena groaned. 'It sounds awful.'

Johanna bundled her down the corridor. 'It's going to be amazing. For starters, the entire male contingent of Elite Models is coming. There'll be plenty to go round.'

'I do *not* want to get involved in any of that.'

Johanna tutted. 'No one's talking about getting involved. Jesus, you don't have to marry every man you sleep with. That's where you went wrong with Nico. You don't try to tame a stallion; you ride him 'til you're sore.'

Lena shrugged out of her grip. 'Johanna, I'm not in the mood.'

'I'm not taking no for an answer.' She pushed Lena into the bathroom. 'You have five minutes to shower. I am timing you.'

'Listen—'

'Four minutes, fifty-nine seconds!' She promptly closed the door.

Lena caught sight of herself. Her hair was greasy and matted, and there were veiny circles beneath her eyes. This would take some effort.

'I don't hear water!' called Johanna.

'Okay, okay!' she called back, bullied into action. She showered quickly and scrubbed her face with the Drunk Elephant cleanser she saved for special occasions. She dried off, moisturised and hurried to her bedroom. On the bed, Johanna had laid out an outfit: a silk dress in racing green with cut-out panels at the waist. It struck Lena that it was the dress she wore on the night that she met Nico.

Johanna clicked her fingers in Lena's face. 'Come on, chop-chop. You need to bring your A game.'

Lena's focus cleared. 'Okay, let's fucking do this.'

Together, they did her hair and makeup, and poured her into the dress. When they finished, they stood in the mirror shoulder to shoulder. Lena's green was dulled by Johanna's siren red.

She arched her brows dolefully. 'Turns out I *am* your sidekick after all.'

Johanna laughed but it quickly trailed to silence.

Lena shifted. 'Jo, I'm really sorry about what I said that day.'

Johanna waved an elegant hand. 'Look, we both said things we didn't mean.'

Lena nudged Johanna's shoulder. 'You know I love you, right?'

'I do.' Johanna nudged her back. 'Now let's go fuck some shit up.'

They bundled into an Uber, high on anticipation. As they walked into the club, Lena made a decision to have a good time. She threw herself into the crowd. She mixed with strangers, chatted, networked and charmed. She pretended to be someone else – someone with a higher profile, a better career, a better life – and it seemed to work. People gravitated towards her. They keyed her name into their phones, bought her drinks and asked her to dance, and Lena remembered the side of LA that so many people loved: the carefree, happy, hopeful side. Someone offered her a pill but she waved it away. She was happy to just drink and dance. Close to midnight, the owners – two ex-models turned entrepreneurs – readied to officially open the club, christened Midnight's Children. Checking the time, they started an official countdown.

'Ten! Nine! Eight! Seven!'

The crowd joined in and Lena sensed someone at her elbow. She looked up to see a model that she had danced with earlier.

'Hi,' he said sheepishly.

'Hi!' she said, laughing.

'Six! Five! Four!' the crowd chanted.

Lena held his gaze and smiled.

'Three! Two! One!'

He leaned in and kissed her and Lena kissed him back. It was a little uneven, but improved by the mood. They separated and broke into laughter. Moments later, they were forced apart by the shifting crowd. He mimed a broken heart and she threw up her hands. *Sorry!* she mouthed, allowing herself to be swallowed by the crowd. It carried her to the balcony where the winking lights of LA spread like a carpet beneath them. The poisonous beauty of it almost brought tears to her eyes. In that moment, she realised that she wasn't ready to admit defeat. She wasn't ready to retire to a life of checking soulless copy. Maybe what she needed was to shift her thinking. She heard so often about moonshots and Hail Marys, the overnight successes and meteoric rises. Maybe small, incremental improvements were enough. Maybe she would finish *Please Understand* and maybe the earth wouldn't move, but then she would write another show and another and build an audience that way. Even Noah Baumbach had toiled for years in obscurity.

Johanna was suddenly by her side and the two of them fiercely shared a hug.

'We're gonna make it, aren't we?' said Lena.

Johanna squeezed her. 'I really think we will.' The stars twinkled in the distance, as if they too were in agreement. The Pixies' 'Where Is My Mind?' began to play in the background and Johanna was lured away by the promise of drink and laughter. Lena was about to follow when she felt her phone vibrate. She frowned at the 'Unknown number' and answered it reluctantly.

'Lena.' The voice sounded hollow, as if speaking into a glass bottle. 'I'm sorry to call like this but something has happened.'

In her drunken state, it took her a moment to place the voice. 'Eliot?' she said, confused.

'Lena, Nico's hurt.'

A tendril of panic uncurled in her gut. 'What's happened?'

'He's been in a crash.'

The panic spasmed. 'Japan?' she asked, mentally rifling through the grand prix schedule. Since Lena had left him, Nico had won all five races with ever-riskier moves.

'No,' said Eliot. 'Here in LA. He was doing 120 on the freeway.'

'Oh my god.'

Eliot was quiet. 'He's critical, Lena. Will you come?'

She felt her stomach cramp. 'Yes,' she said in a strangled choke. 'Yes, Eliot, of course. Where is he?'

'Cedars-Sinai. Where are you? I'll arrange a car.'

'It's okay. I'm on my way.' She hung up, then pelted inside and pushed her way through the crowd. Bursting onto the street, she took deep lungfuls of air to stop herself being sick. *120mph. On the freeway. Had he lost his fucking mind?* She felt a lance of dread at the prospect of the answer.

*

Lena tore into the hospital, her heels clicking on the shiny vinyl floor. Her alarm animated everything: the swing of the walls around her, the flicker of lights overhead. She collided against the front desk, moving too fast to apply the brakes.

'Hello, I'm looking for Nico Laurent please.'

The receptionist fixed on a smile. 'May I ask your relationship to him?'

Lena faltered. 'I'm a friend,' she said.

'I see. I'm sorry, but we can only speak to his family.'

Lena's alarm grew louder. 'Please. I'm meant to meet his family here. Can you at least tell me what ward he's in?'

'I'm afraid I can't disclose that.'

Lena was protesting when she heard her name behind her. She spun round and flinched. 'Sabine.'

'I'll bring you to him.'

Lena followed her to the lift. A dozen questions clamoured

in her brain. *Is he okay? Is he awake? Did he say anything? Can he still race?* Lena knew that if Nico couldn't race, his life would lose all meaning. The lift doors slid shut and Lena and Sabine faced each other.

'How has he been?'

Sabine grimaced. 'Since you left, he's been . . . erratic.' She shifted uncomfortably. 'Listen, Lena, I'm sorry if anything I did with him hurt you. That was never my intention.'

Lena was surprised to find that she was touched by this. She slumped against the handrail. 'To be honest, I'm glad that you're there. I'm glad that he has someone to call when he needs to. I never wanted him to be alone, or to suffer. I just . . . I couldn't be the one to do it.' Lena saw a shadow move over Sabine's face. It struck her that she had never thought to ask. Gently, she said, 'Do you love him?'

Sabine waved a listless hand. 'No, I don't. When I first came to look after Gabriel, I thought I did. It's kind of impossible not to.' She gave Lena a lopsided smile. 'But I've done enough therapy in my life to know that a man like Nico is . . . unattainable, so it became just about sex for me.'

'As simple as that?'

Sabine scoffed. 'Listen, we're told as women that love and sex are intertwined, that we're not like men, that we're invested, but that's just a way to keep us in our place. I love having sex with Nico, but I don't love Nico.'

Lena's eyes glazed with tears. 'But *I* do,' she said. The dam burst on all her repressed emotion. She loved Nico violently. She wanted him desperately and it made her sick with longing.

'I know,' said Sabine softly as the doors pinged open.

Lena followed her to a private waiting room. When Eliot turned, Lena saw that his eyes were red. With him were Chris and Gabriel, blank-faced with worry. Danger had always been there on track, but it had felt theoretical. Drivers in Formula One were built differently. They had a high tolerance for risk and that somehow filtered through to the people who loved them. They were all bound by the illusion of invincibility. How else could they live with the risk? The fact that it was Nico's life *off-track* that put him in the hospital felt like a cosmic joke.

Lena pictured the doctors working on him. Would they see the cigarette burn on his hand? A clot of emotion rose in her chest, making her physically shake. Eliot noticed and came to her. She curled into him and tried to keep a leash on her tears. He led her outside to a private corner and let her dissolve in grief: a pre-emptive grief for the news that could come, a residual grief for what had happened that night. *Red* on the tip of her tongue.

'Do you think he can get help?' she asked through her tears.

'Yes, but he has to want to.'

The depth of her grief, the fury of her hope, told her everything she needed to know. 'Then I'll wait,' she said.

Eliot nodded bleakly. 'I think that would be best.'

*

It was 2am when the surgeon came to see them. The five of them – Lena, Gabe, Eliot, Sabine and Chris – all stood up to greet him. He was a tall man with elegant hands and spoke in an English accent.

'Nico lost a lot of blood. There was internal bleeding and he has a fracture in his right leg, but he's stable.'

'Is he awake?' asked Eliot.

'No. We had to sedate him for the pain but we hope he'll be conscious soon. There will be a period of recovery, but it's good news.'

Lena folded into her chair, slack with relief. One by one, the others followed suit, stunned that death had passed so closely. In that moment, Lena was envious of the religious. They had a framework to deal with this. They could join hands and pray, or offer up their thanks. All Lena had was chance – and that was entirely arbitrary. She covered her eyes, entirely exhausted.

Over the next two hours, their motley crew rearranged itself: Gabe asleep on Sabine's shoulder, Eliot by the window, Chris procuring food and Lena getting coffee, then a shift in roles with Sabine now by the window. At 5am, a nurse padded into the room.

'Is there a Lena Aden here?'

She leapt to her feet. 'Yes. That's me.'

'Nico is asking for you.'

Lena felt a well of relief. She turned to the others. 'Gabe?' she asked, offering him the chance to see his brother first.

'You go,' he told her.

She followed the nurse gingerly. They walked along an aisle between two rows of chairs and paused by a dark brown door. The nurse knocked and let Lena enter. The square room was over-lit, casting dark shadows under Nico's eyes. She moved to his bedside, not knowing how or where to touch him. She gripped the side rail, a poor proxy for contact.

'Nico.' The word was gummy in her throat, freighted with tears.

'I didn't know if you would come,' he said.

'Of course.' She drew in a shaky breath. 'We could have lost you.'

'I'm okay,' he said. 'I spoke to the doctors. There's a chance I can race again in six weeks' time. That's three, maybe four, races missed. If I can—'

'Nico.' She touched his arm. 'Not yet.' He fell quiet but she could see the cogs turning in his brain, matching dates with steps, plotting his path back to the track. He had fought hard for this championship and wouldn't give it all up. 'There's time,' she told him.

He gathered the blanket in his right fist. 'Are you here to stay?' he asked quietly.

'For tonight, yes.'

'So it worked,' he said.

Lena didn't laugh. Her eyes were glassy with tears and she blinked rapidly to hold them back. 'Gabe's here. I'm sure he would like to see you. And Eliot and Chris.' She paused. 'And Sabine.'

Nico nodded. 'Okay,' he said and closed his eyes. 'Just give me a minute with you.' He held her hand and exhaled – a long, slow sound of contentment. Then, he sank into sleep.

Chapter 14

Lena was faintly aware of movement around her: the distant jangle of a metal trolley, the stop-and-start rush of air conditioning. Her back ached from sleeping in the chair and her mouth was dry and gummy.

She straightened and checked the time – 6.30am. 'Nico?' she asked the room.

'Still asleep,' said Eliot.

Lena ran a hand through her hair and winced at its lankness, her vanity not quashed entirely. She rifled through the contents of her clutch: a single lipstick and a small container of blotting powder – not enough to rescue her face. She dropped the items back into the bag.

A shadow moved over her, blocking the morning sun. Lena squinted up and saw that Sabine was holding out a small plastic bag. Lena took it and found a set of mini toiletries inside: shampoo, conditioner and shower gel along with a zipped fabric bag that was filled with makeup.

'My foundation will be too light for your skin but the rest will work,' said Sabine. 'There are showers in the gym in physio.'

Lena stood and kissed her cheek. 'Thank you, Sabine.'

At the gym, she showered and redid her makeup, careful not to stain Johanna's green dress. The silk had endured beautifully, dropping right back into place. Lena felt an intense gratitude for the women in her life: Johanna but also Sabine, who had come to her aid with a small but meaningful gesture. When Lena returned to the waiting room, Eliot was in the doorway.

'He's awake,' he said. 'Gabe's in there with him now.'

The pressure in her chest eased and she hugged Eliot instinctively. This is what happened when death passed close. It bonded you not only to the one you almost lost but to everyone who loves them too. A collective pardon. Lena stepped back and cleared her throat. Everyone in the room – Eliot, Chris, Sabine – was composed and she didn't want to get emotional.

Footsteps sounded behind her. 'Lena, he's asking for you,' said Gabe. The shadows beneath his eyes were stark and his cheekbones seemed more pronounced. Lena squeezed his arm and made her way along the corridor. She was newly nervous as she walked into Nico's room. Last night, relief had thrust her onward but, now, in the clean light of day, she felt on high alert. She was pleased to see that he was sat up, colour back in his face. His unruly hair and stubble gave him a rakish air and his eyes looked somehow bluer. Lena hovered by the side of his bed, unsure if she should touch him.

'I didn't realise last night that that's the dress.'

Lena looked down instinctively at the folds of silk.

'That's the dress you wore the first time we met.'

'Yes.'

Nico exhaled softly. 'You looked so beautiful, Lena. I couldn't help myself.'

With surprise, she realised that they had never talked about that night. Wasn't that part of the pleasure of being in a relationship? Revisiting how you met and those early heady days. Confessing how you felt, what you thought, whether that remark was a flirtation, if that hand on an arm was an overture or merely an innocent gesture. You would build your history together and maybe one day you would pass it to your children and grandchildren, each permutation differing a little – darkness recast as moonlight, rain blotted out. Remembering an early courtship was meant to be a pleasure, but theirs had been one-sided and so Lena had never asked about it. That first night had moved her world off kilter, but to him she had felt disposable, fleeting, repeatable. His small admission now was the first time Lena understood that she had had a hold on him too.

'Thank you for staying,' he said.

Lena thought of his half-drugged joke last night. *Are you here to stay? So it worked.* She watched Nico closely and said, 'Talk me through what happened on the freeway.'

His features darkened. 'I lost control of the car.'

Lena hesitated. 'On purpose?'

He stared at her. 'Of course not on purpose.'

'Doing 120mph on the freeway wasn't an accident.'

Nico looked away. 'I wasn't trying to kill myself if that's what you're asking.'

'Then what?' Lena's voice grew sharp. 'How did this

happen?' The look on his face chilled her. 'Nico, please tell me you didn't do this on purpose.'

It took him a moment to answer. 'You know that the championship means too much to me.'

'Then why? Explain it to me.'

'I wasn't doing very well after you left. I was still winning races so no one could tell, except maybe Eliot, but I was in a bad way. Losing weight. Not sleeping. Not eating properly. Drinking.' He paused. 'Like my father.'

Sorrow moved in Lena's chest. There was no one Nico loathed more than his father. 'Were you drunk?' she asked.

Nico's lips worked in silence. 'No, but I was on the edge.'

'Why were you going so fast?'

'The racetrack is the only place in the world where I'm not thinking. The only place I forget to hate myself for everything I've done. To Gabe. To you. To Phoebe. To everyone I have ever loved. I was trying to get to that place. I just wanted to stop thinking for a while.'

Lena held herself together, held herself tight, so that she wouldn't fall right into him, back to where she started. 'Nico, I think we should get you some help.'

'You can help,' he said plainly.

It hung in the air between them, his plea for her to come back to him. Lena took a physical step back. 'I can't.'

He tried to lean forward and winced from the pain.

Lena wanted to go to him but she knew that if she touched him, her resolve would slip away. She loved Nico, but she couldn't extract whatever toxin was inside of him without poisoning herself.

'Don't give up on me,' he pleaded.

Her whole body pulsed with weakness – one touch away from caving. She forced herself to recall that morning at Mazikeen. Waking up still in her heels. The childlike whimper so foreign in her ear. The hot sting of shame. 'I can't,' she said, needing to put distance between. 'I'm sorry.' She took another step back.

'Lena, wait.'

'I can't,' she repeated. Then, she turned and fled.

*

Lena felt the sweat seep into her dress. What had possessed her to wear wool on a day like this? Octobers in LA weren't like back in London and she was melting in the twenty-six-degree heat. She glanced at PaceCheck and saw that she was too slow. On Monday, the day after leaving Nico, she had missed her target for the very first time since starting at Palgrave. It happened again mid-week. Now Friday, she was skating close to her first disciplinary hearing.

She scanned a press release about digital technology in car headlights, removed a comma and clicked 'Approve'. She couldn't find a rhythm as her mind wandered to Nico again. She had heard from Eliot that he was recovering well and would soon be discharged from hospital.

'Lena,' Jerry hissed from across the aisle. He gave her a pointed look and she saw that their supervisor was casing the floor. She nodded her thanks and focused on her screen. She worked steadily for the next few hours and hit her target by a narrow margin. She couldn't mess this up. It was the only source of income she had. At 5pm, the room began to empty out, the workers kept there by neither fun, loyalty nor money.

Jerry stopped at Lena's desk. 'Tassili's?' he asked.

Lena looked at him regretfully.

'Plans?' he asked.

She nodded and he gave her a wry smile. Their Friday night exchange, shorn down to shortcut.

'Okay, see you on Monday,' he said.

'Yes. Monday.' The thought of coming back here – of going through the same routine and swapping the same pleasantries – made it hard for Lena to stand up, pack up and leave, to keep going, but what was the alternative? To sit here and watch the glorious sunset over her view of LA? That was a worse torture. She forced herself up and into the creaky lift. Outside, she had to run for the bus and felt her skin grow slick with sweat. The ride home was slow and agonising, and by the time she got there, she was practically humming with stress. She let herself into her building and walked up to the second floor. When she saw who was on the landing, it took her a second to place him – her brain catching up on seeing him out of context.

'Gabe? What are you doing here?' She glanced around, searching for Chris or Sabine. 'Did you come here alone?'

'Chris brought me.' His tone was weary, clearly tired of being babied. 'Can I come in?'

Lena was conscious of her greasy skin, her sweaty dress and lanky hair. She felt sloppy and cheap next to Gabe's air-conditioned tailoring. She let him inside and brought him a drink, then took a few minutes to freshen up quickly. She sensed that she would need to be composed for this. In the living room, Gabe waited awkwardly. He was the same height as Nico but slimmer and looked gangly on the compact sofa. Lena sat in a chair and waited.

'I've been wondering,' said Gabe. 'How is it that I'm the sensible brother when I have literal brain damage.' A corner of his mouth lifted, but he was alone in his gallows humour. Lena found no relief in it.

'What are you doing here, Gabe?'

'Nico has always looked after me. Today, he needs me to look after him.'

Lena lightly touched the base of her glass. 'Is he okay?'

'Physically, he will be. He's being discharged into the care of Mercedes's medical team. They've got him a place in Beverly Hills because Crushes is too remote.' Gabe shifted on the sofa. 'But, Lena, I've never seen him like this, not even after Phoebe died. I don't think he's going to get better without you.'

'Don't do that.' Lena kept a lid on her anger. 'Don't turn up at my door and blackmail me.'

Gabe was impassive. 'I'll do what it takes to help him. He's my brother. He has literally put his body between me and harm, so I'm going to do what it takes.'

Lena shook her head. 'Gabe, you brother is brave and tough and principled, but he's damaged.'

'We both are.'

The plainness of his words slugged Lena in the chest. 'I can't be his punchbag.'

'If you knew what he's been through, you would give him another chance.'

245

'How can I know when neither of you will speak about it?' After that night on the boat, Nico had never again talked about his childhood.

Gabe was quiet for a beat. 'Lena, can you think of a day from any point of your life when your body was in jeopardy? Like, actually frozen in terror?'

Lena thought of all the times that she had felt in danger: late night walks from the Tube to her home, men calling out from vans, that time a man snatched her bag from a passing bike. They were all fraught with risk, but terror? Real freeze-in-your-path terror? 'No,' she answered.

'Okay, so Nico and I. We felt that more often than any child should. I don't mean tiptoeing around the house and being careful not to disturb our dad – but real jeopardy. As in, I heard my brother scream in pain on a monthly basis.' Gabe paused and cleared his throat. 'When a body feels that much terror so often, the brain sort of rewires itself, so that your guard never comes down. You say my brother is damaged. He's not damaged, Lena. He's broken. Our father broke him.' Gabe exhaled sharply. 'Nico thinks I changed but, Lena, so did he. He says that I used to be a funny, silly kid, but I took my cue from him. Nico was always so quick to laugh.'

Lena felt a well of emotion. She could count on a single hand the number of times she had seen Nico laugh with abandon.

'He was a brave, fun kid, but when Dad started drinking, he snuffed all that lightness out of him. He deserves happiness, Lena. Please don't give up on him.'

She blinked and soundless tears spilt onto her cheek. 'Gabe.

He took everything I care about from me. How can I trust him?'

'You start by telling him how you feel.'

She leaned forward and covered her face. 'I'm so fucking angry.'

'Then tell him, Lena. Show him your rage.'

'And then what?' She lowered her hands.

'Pick up the pieces of him and see if you still want them.'

*

The ground floor of Cedars-Sinai was buzzing with activity, LA in full swing on a Saturday evening. Up on Nico's floor, however, all was calm and quiet. The only sound was the nurses' soles softly padding on the plastic floor. Lena gripped the box of chocolates. Her British sensibilities forbade her from coming empty-handed, but now the gesture felt awkward and formal.

She knocked on the open door. Nico hoisted himself up with his arms and Lena watched his muscles contract. She flashed onto a memory: the night of the Monaco Grand Prix, she and Nico in bed after hours of drinking and dancing. She had woken in the night with Nico asleep next to her. Only half conscious, she remembered thinking that he had the most beautiful body she had ever seen. Even now, even after everything, she found herself drawn to it.

'Lena, you're here.' There was relief in his voice and Lena wondered if he had truly expected anything else.

She placed the chocolates on the bedside table and sat in

a high-back chair. She folded her hands in her lap, then, feeling overly prim, unfolded them again. 'Gabe came to see me,' she said, by way of explaining why she was here.

'When?'

'Yesterday.'

Nico frowned.

'Can I ask you something, Nico?' She didn't wait for an answer. 'Do you hate me?'

He blanched in surprise. 'Why would you ask that?'

'Because sometimes I really think you do.'

'I don't hate you, Lena.' Quietly, he added, 'I hate me.'

The words made Lena ache, for she knew the reason behind them. 'Nico, what happened to Gabe wasn't your fault.'

'Don't patronise me.'

'I'm not patronising you.'

Anger flashed in his eyes. 'I'm very clear on what happened, Lena. I was told to keep Gabe in his room. I didn't. And Dad put him in hospital. Cause. Effect. Simple.'

'Your dad put him in hospital. Not you.'

'That's semantics.'

'It's not semantics.' Lena grimaced at the sound of her raised voice. Swiftly, she closed the door. 'Gabe sees you as his guardian. He loves you. He worships you, so why play the martyr?'

The word made Nico flinch. 'Fuck you, Lena,' he snapped.

A bitter sound escaped her. 'That's right. *Fuck* Lena because she's just a fuck-toy that I can pick up when I'm bored and throw out like trash when I'm done. *Fuck* Lena because she's always ready and willing, empty like a vessel. *Fuck* Lena

248

because she's just a cheap fucking whore.' She scoffed. 'How delusional of me to ask if you hate me. That would require a tiny fucking modicum of you giving a shit.' Her lips twisted. 'No. You don't hate me. You're indifferent to me.'

The words startled him and, for a second, he just stared at her, still computing them. Then, his features softened, tender in denial. When he spoke, however, his words were hard and urgent. 'Lena, you don't believe that.' He tried to heave himself closer to her but his leg cast wouldn't budge. 'I *love* you. You know I do.'

'I don't think you do, Nico. How can you? After everything you've done to my life? Intentionally. Methodically.'

'I do love you.'

'Then why? What goes through your head? When you pick up the fucking phone and click your fingers and say that I can never work at the Aston again? Or take my job at Paramount so I can't afford to pay my rent? The malice of it. The pettiness. The cruelty. Why did you do it?'

Nico didn't speak for a minute. 'For control,' he said finally. 'For so much of my life, I've had no control.' Colour rose in his neck and laced up his cheeks. 'When Dad decided to put his cigarette out on my hand, there was nothing I could do. When he broke my ribs, there was nothing I could do.'

Lena blinked. He had never told her about the ribs before.

'When he beat Gabe, there was nothing I could do. Control is how I make sense of the world. On the track, off it, with women, with friends, with Gabe. As soon as I lose control, rage takes its place. I was lashing out, Lena. I was teaching you a lesson.'

'Is that what you were doing at Mazikeen? Teaching me a lesson?'

Nico hung his head. 'When I saw you dancing with Greg, something unhinged in me. I wanted to go over there and punch his fucking lights out and that's when I knew how much you meant. It screwed with my head, so I did it to assert control; over you, over how I felt about you. I couldn't possibly love you so much because look at what I was doing to you.'

Lena's shoulders curled inward, failing at her effort to be stoic. When she spoke, her voice cracked with hurt. 'I have never felt so cheap.'

Nico's features creased with anguish. 'Lena, it kills me that I made you feel that way when you're the most precious thing I've ever had.' He covered his eyes with a palm. His shoulders moved rapidly and she heard the glue in his throat as he swallowed once, then twice, then again. When he finally looked at her, his skin was flushed with unshed tears. 'Forgive me, Lena.'

'I am so angry at you, Nico.'

'We can work through it. Please.'

'And what happens the next time you feel threatened? The next time you need to *assert your control*? What will you do to me then?'

'I'll be better.'

'I don't think you can.' Lena thought of what Gabe had told her. That Nico had been quick to laugh, always thinking of new adventures. That boy had grown into this man and it broke her heart. She looked in his watchful eyes and felt her composure waver. 'I need some air,' she said, rising to her feet.

Nico reached out and caught her wrist. 'Don't go.'

'I just need some air, Nico.' She pulled out of his grip. 'I'll come back.' Outside, she took the lift to the ground floor and made her way to the courtyard. She walked in slow circles around the perimeter, her thoughts getting no clearer. On her fourth circuit, a familiar figure emerged from the dark.

'Ms Aden.'

Lena stopped. 'Eliot. Hi.'

'May I join you?'

'Yes. Please do.' They walked a circuit – both of them silent for a long while. Eventually, Lena spoke first. 'Eliot, when we first met, you told me something about Nico. You said that he burns the things he cares about.'

Eliot remained neutral. 'I'm afraid I may have spoken out of turn.'

'But you were right,' said Lena. 'Do you think he'll get better?'

Eliot took a while to speak. 'It's not impossible.'

'But it's improbable?'

He gave her a quiet, diplomatic smile.

Lena felt so lost. 'I don't know what to do.'

'I fear, Ms Aden, that you're too old to follow a reckless heart and too young to understand that it's the only thing to do.'

Lena stopped and searched his face. 'What are you saying?'

He tipped his head as if it should be obvious.

Her tears were near the surface, making her voice unsteady. 'I love him, Eliot.'

'I know.' He steepled his fingers, then gently suggested, 'Perhaps you should go and tell him.'

Her face creased with emotion. 'Do you really think I should?'

Again, he tipped his head.

Lena took a long, shaky breath. She nodded, her decision finally made. Then, she turned and sprinted. She ran upstairs and skidded to a stop by his room. They locked eyes and the knowledge passed between them, quick and intimate. And, then, they were kissing and Lena couldn't believe that they had ever stopped.

Chapter 15

Lena dashed around the house, snatching up stray glassware. She'd never had a maid before and felt compelled to do a quick tidy-up before the woman arrived. She straightened the shoes in the hallway: one pair of Converse and a heeled pair of sandals donated by Johanna. She neatened the living-room cushions, folded the throw and plucked up a yellow blazer, also Johanna's. She inspected it closely and dusted off the sleeves, then hung it in the hallway. She felt a punch of affection for her friend, who had loaded her with expensive clothes so she would 'look the part' in Beverly Hills. Lena and Nico had moved into the house after he was discharged. The Mercedes team had set him up with a raft of experts – doctors, physios, a personal trainer, nutritionist, masseuse and therapist – and the house was filled with constant activity.

The jangle of the maid's keys made Lena scurry away. She hated herself for the way she acted in front of the woman: the overly jovial tone, the nervous hovering, the need to somehow prove that she hadn't grown up with money, that *I'm more like you than you think!* She preferred to stay out of the way altogether and retreated to the garden. The wide, blocky lawn was manicured beyond any character and lined with plastic-perfect bay trees. Nico sat at a white table in the centre, watching the Saturday qualifying for the US Grand Prix in Austin. He noticed Lena and set down his phone.

'The maid's here,' she said by way of explaining what she was doing out here. Their relationship had a strange new shyness. The power dynamic was off kilter and it made them unsure of each other. 'How's the pain?' she asked, joining him at the table.

'Manageable.'

She motioned at his phone. 'What's happening in Austin?'

Nico grimaced. 'Vossen has pole position. If he wins the race, he'll close my lead to fifteen points. If he wins the next two, I won't be able to catch him.'

Lena didn't speak. She knew it was futile to try to convince him to give up on the championship. The drive to get better for the final race was getting him out of bed each morning. If he could heal in time for Abu Dhabi, and Vossen didn't win both races in between, Nico would still have a chance. 'Who's P2?' she asked. Vossen would have a better chance at victory if his teammate was behind him.

'Lecourt,' answered Nico.

Lena tensed on hearing the name of the Ferrari driver. Something skittish darted in her gut and Nico clearly sensed it.

'Lena. That night at Mazikeen.' His throat worked in silence. 'Did you not want it?'

Lena was quiet for a beat. 'I wanted to please you.'

'That's not an answer.'

She hooked her fingers into the holes of the Regalia tabletop. 'Physically, in the moment, yes, I wanted it. But emotionally, I only ever wanted you.'

Nico leaned forward so abruptly, it made Lena startle. He grabbed her hand and squeezed it to the point of pain. 'Lena, I'm going to make a promise to you. I will never, ever put you in a situation like that again. I'm going to take care of you.' His grip tightened. 'I'm going to undo the fucked-up things I did. I'll get your job back at Paramount. I'll talk to my lawyers about the Aston and I'll—'

'No,' she cut in.

'No?'

'No, Nico. I don't want my job back at Paramount. It was never mine to have. And you can't buy me a career in theatre.'

'Why not?'

'Because it's not up to you. It's not up to you to take care of me. *I* take care of me.' This was why she had kept her job at Palgrave and why she had sublet her room in her flat instead of ending her tenancy. Flimsy though it may be, it was still a safety net; her tiny claim to independence. She relaxed her hand in his. 'But there is one thing you can do to make me happy. I want you to have therapy.'

Nico was confused. 'I am having therapy.'

'I don't mean your team-appointed therapist. Her only job is to sign you off to race. I mean a proper one; one that can help you work through what happened to you.' Gently, she brushed his scar. 'What your dad did to you.'

A muscle twitched in his jaw. She could feel the tension in his arm, ready to snatch his hand away. His whole body was rigid with refusal. But, then, his shoulders softened. He nodded. 'Okay.'

'Okay?' she checked.

'Okay.'

Lena felt lifted. *This*. This meant something. 'There's something else.' She pulled her hand out of his – gently, and without blame. 'I don't want you to sleep with anyone other than me and Sabine.'

He drew back in surprise. 'Sabine? No. I don't have to do that.'

'You do,' said Lena. 'And it's okay.'

'It's not okay.'

'It *is*, Nico. I'm not always going to be around. I want to start working again. I want to do something with *Please Understand*. When you're on the road for weeks without me, I want to know that it's Sabine you'll call and not some other woman.'

'Lena, no. You don't have to do this.'

'I do, Nico. You know I do.'

He shook his head. 'I don't want to hurt you.'

'But you will, which is why I'm asking you. Promise me.'

'I won't sleep with anyone else.'

'Except me and Sabine.'

'Except you,' he hesitated, 'and Sabine.'

Lena was surprised by the effect of this. The worry lifted off her, as light as a bird off a wire. She could live with this. Revel in it, even. She trusted Sabine. And in doing so, trusted Nico too. For the first time since meeting him, she believed that maybe they could last.

'I love you,' she told him.

'And I love you.'

His smile felt like sun on her face. She scooted her chair next to his and curled into him. He kissed her hair and gently stroked the nape of her neck. 'You okay?' he asked.

'Yes.' She felt his stubble graze her scalp. 'Or at least I will be.'

The maid walked into the garden and the two of them instinctively parted. She eyed them with suspicion and bustled back into the house. Lena tutted wryly. 'The one time we're having a tender moment.'

Nico pulled her back to him. 'I promise you more of them.'

She relaxed against him. There, beneath the blazing LA sky, she allowed her heart to let him in. No more defences.

Chapter 16

Lena filled three glasses: a beer for Gabe, a gin and tonic for her and iced water for Nico. She settled into her chair and stretched luxuriously. It was just the three of them this evening. No cooks or cleaners, no doctors or therapists, no corporate bores from Mercedes. She caught Nico's hand beneath the table and gave it a gentle squeeze. He looked over and smiled, and Lena felt a rush of love.

'So then, in French, Mum says, "Just because my children have American accents, it doesn't mean they are stupid. We understood every word you said." The *horror* on the man's face!' Gabe fell about laughing.

Lena fed off his cheer. She had heard this story before, but Gabe and Nico had so few happy memories from childhood and so she let them retell it.

'Gabe, do you remember when we went to that gallery afterwards?' asked Nico, laughing pre-emptively.

Lena listened and felt a sense of lightness. Since that moment in the garden two weeks ago, she had noticed a new kindness in Nico; a solicitude that he had never shown before. In the past, she had sensed that if she needed him, he would send someone else in his stead – Chris or maybe Eliot. This new version of him was tender in ways the other was not. He would touch the small of her back when he sensed that she was uneasy, or kiss her hair when she was exhausted from another long day at Palgrave. Yesterday, she had been washing dishes when Nico had come up behind and wrapped his arms around her. The simplicity of that moment – not sexual or intentional – but just a fact of them being together had made her marvel. She watched him now in the golden light and felt the urge to touch him, to feel his skin on hers, to bury herself in him.

Gabe drained his drink and set down the glass. 'I should get going,' he said.

'Why don't you stay here tonight?' asked Nico.

Gabe stood. 'No, I need to get home.' A smile played on his lips and Lena understood that he had read what was on her mind.

Nico heaved himself up using the armrests but Gabe waved him back down. 'Don't get up. I know my way out.' He gave Nico a hug, kissed Lena and headed into the house.

Lena leaned back and watched Nico. She loved what sunset did to his face. She liked the way he tried to blink off the light, his brows lightly knitted. He saw her watching and reached out his hand. She touched her fingertips to his and then, without a word, she slid out of her chair and down on her knees in front of him. She saw the surprise on his face and smiled. She tugged at his belt and slid it all the way out of the loops, throwing it over her shoulder. She undid the top button and slowly unzipped him. It had been a month since the accident – three months since they had last had sex – and he was clearly ready, already hard in his jeans. She took him out and a sound escaped her lips – soft and content. She lowered her head and ran her tongue slowly, deliberately, over the length of him. He groaned and rose off the chair to meet her but she stopped him with a palm. She teased him with her tongue, then stopped and waited, hovering, letting him feel her breath. When he shuddered, she licked him again in long, measured strokes. He rose again but she pushed him down and held him there. She moved her tongue in maddening circles around the head of his cock, and it was only when he was panting with lust that she took him all the way into her mouth. She felt him pulse as she moved to a rhythm. His breath quickened and he began to buck.

He grabbed at her hair. 'Wait,' he said, his breath shallow and desperate. 'Wait. Lena, wait.'

In that moment, she felt so exquisitely powerful, she almost didn't listen.

'Wait,' he repeated in a growl. He planted his hands on her shoulders and physically forced her back.

Lena rocked back on her heels in a daze. Nico pulled her towards him, making her lose balance so that her knee struck the grass. He yanked her up and onto his lap. Roughly, he tugged up her skirt, then pulled aside her underwear, the white cotton now warm and damp. He pressed two knuckles against her pussy, making her gasp. She ground against them, wanting more. Nico grunted and though Lena wasn't certain if it was in pleasure or pain, she didn't stop to check. She lifted herself off him slightly, just enough so that he could press against her and, then, instinctively, exquisitely, inside her. She cried out as he pushed all the way in. Nico, not yet fighting fit, was forced to let Lena take control. She rocked against him, her moans deep and sensual as she took what she needed. She moved faster, crying with abandon into the glorious LA night. It felt like an exorcism, or something close to religious, and when she came, it felt like a rebirth – the colours too bright and the sounds too loud for her tiny mind to process. She collapsed against him and Nico held her tight, bringing her into his own cocoon.

There, they spent the coming weeks, soothed by a curative intimacy. They talked and laughed and healed – and that's how, a mere six weeks after his crash, Nico Laurent was back on track for the final race of the season. Back in the cruel, corrupting clutches of the world's most glamorous sport.

Chapter 17

The air was hot and acrid like a dying bonfire. Red and green flares lit up the circuit, flaming in the colours of the UAE. The Abu Dhabi crowd was feverish. Theirs was the final race of the season. Champions were made here. The Mercedes paddock was tense. Nico had to win this race or he would lose the championship. Mercifully, he had qualified in pole position, ahead of Greg in second and Michael Vossen in third.

It's lights out and away we go! Crofty's familiar refrain marked the start of the race. Nico's clean getaway immediately gained him a half-second lead. Vossen attacked Greg on the hairpin and easily moved up into second place. The jeers in the paddock were muted. This would be a race of nerve and it was only just beginning. Vossen began to chase Nico, but the Mercedes had superior pace and Nico got a long way clear in the first half of the race.

On lap thirty-five, however, a retirement on track triggered a virtual safety car. It handed Vossen a cheap pit stop, allowing him to reduce the gap between him and Nico. On fresher tyres, he bore down on his rival. It soon became clear, however, that he didn't have the pace to close the gap before the end of the race. Barring disaster, Nico was on course to win.

On lap fifty-three, however, Nico's fortunes changed dramatically. A crash at Turn Fourteen triggered another safety car. Mercedes did not dare call Nico in to pit. If he came in for fresher tyres, Vossen would almost certainly stay out and take the lead.

With nothing to lose, Red Bull called Vossen in and gave him fresh tyres. This put Nico in a precarious position. If the safety car ended, Vossen would have four full laps to overtake, and Nico would be a sitting duck in his older tyres.

Over the next two laps, the safety car stayed out as the last of the debris was cleaned up. Lena watched on breathlessly. On lap fifty-seven, however – the penultimate lap – the green flag signalled that the drivers were free to race again. Vossen moved like a scalded cat as he chased after Nico. Lena watched on breathlessly. Nico had fought so hard to be fit enough for this race. To lose it – and the championship – on an error in strategy would be deeply unjust. She ground her teeth with nerves, unable to quite believe the cruelty of this sport.

Vossen attempted to pass into Turn Five, but Nico held him off. They entered the final lap and for a heart-stopping moment, it seemed that they would collide. If they both crashed out, Vossen would win the championship. The aggressive way in which he drove indicated that this may well be a possibility. Wheel to wheel, they rounded the final corner. Lena's heart thumped in her chest as Nico took the final straight. Vossen fought him all the way to the line. Then, in a glorious homecoming, Nico shot past the chequered flag a whisker ahead of Vossen.

The paddock erupted in a roar. Nico had just won his second Formula One World Championship. Lena threw herself into the arms of a nearby engineer, both of them shrieking with glee. Testosterone overflowed as the men celebrated with bear hugs, back slaps and raucous noise. Lena watched them with a dawning sense of peace. Nico was back where he belonged and had brought her along with him. They had come such a long way since that first night on the balcony. She watched him on the podium and was mesmerised by him. It terrified her to know that he might one day tire of her. She pushed the thought away. They were together now and not like before. This was no longer a tug of war. They were in love – complicated at times, but real. She felt a bright frisson of hope. Maybe it would all work out. Maybe she, Lena Aden, against all odds, was the woman who would settle down with World Champion Nico Laurent. She laughed out loud at the prospect.

She was jostled out of her thoughts and let the crowd carry her. There was delightful chaos as engineers, mechanics, journalists, stewards and fans buzzed around in the afterglow. Lena felt someone grip her arm and turned to find Nico. The look on his face was something she had never seen before and that's when she knew: Nico Laurent was hers.

'I love you,' he said – quietly, as if it was just him and her. He kissed her and closed his arms around her. For the first time in her life, Lena felt utterly content.

'I love you,' she said but the words got lost in his chest, between him and her, where they would be safe.

The club was a cavernous pyramid with textured walls made with long strips of timber, copper and black basalt. Off the double-height dance floor were myriad rooms filled with wood and leather. To Lena, it looked like a very large sauna co-opted by a fetishist. Still, it was the most exclusive club in Abu Dhabi and she was in the mood for fun. Nico was alight with energy. He bought champagne for everyone in the club and drunkenly hugged the other drivers – including Vossen. His energy was infectious and a cabal of drivers followed him and Lena to the dance floor. She felt magnetised by him, drawn to his body. As they moved together, Lena caught Greg's eye from across the dance floor. Both of them looked away at the same time – but not before she caught his expression. Hurt? Or maybe regret? It hadn't occurred to her to ask him if he was okay. Had he made a conscious choice that night or, like her, been carried by the mood and alcohol? She shook the questions away. That night was a wound that hadn't quite healed right and she feared it might reopen if she were to touch it. Instead, she listened to the beat, let it dictate the rhythm to her body.

The next time she saw Greg, he was surrounded by models and dancers, as were the other drivers. They shimmered on the dance floor, in all flavours and colours, getting close, trying their luck. Lena wanted to warn them: *Be careful, girls. Be careful what you wish for.*

Cheers went up one side of the club and Lena looked over to a table freshly laid with coke. Guests flocked over to it – no drivers, she noticed, but plenty of others. Those who remained on the dance floor pressed against each other as the music loosened their inhibitions. The bass was something rhythmic and Latin, designed for sweat and secrets. Nico's touch made her feel impossibly sexy. He grew bolder, touching her in places that made her moan out loud. She was tempted to ask him to take her somewhere private. She wanted his hands on her skin, his tongue somewhere dark and deep. Just as it became unbearable, Lena spotted Theo Witte making a beeline for Nico.

'No!' she called out to him. 'Not now, Theo!'

He broke into that big-bear grin of his. 'Sorry, Lena. There's a sponsor I really need Nico to meet.'

She groaned. 'You're killing me over here.'

'He will be back to bring you to life,' said Theo, deadpan in his strong Austrian accent.

Nico leaned into her. 'I don't have to go.'

She shook her head regretfully. 'No. Go. It's okay.'

'Are you sure?'

'Yes.' She gestured up towards the mezzanine. 'It's probably best I get some air.' She collected a negroni from the bar and headed up to the terrace. Outside, she leaned over the crenellated wall and looked across the city. The heat left her body and her mind regained some clarity. The intensity of the dance floor gave way to a sense of nostalgia. She looked out at the night sky, disoriented by this city. In LA, she knew the direction of home, could see familiar stars and find pieces of herself in the cityscape: where she had her first job interview, the very first diner she went to, the Aston, Paramount, a scape of hope and dreams – some crushed, some still blooming. But, here, in Abu Dhabi with its glitz and dust, she could find no footholds or strongholds to chart her place in life. She laid her head on the balcony and sighed.

'Hey,' said a voice behind her.

She straightened quickly. 'Davide? Hi.'

'Congratulations,' he said. 'You must be stoked for Nico.'

'I am, yes.'

He motioned at the wall. 'Mind if I join you?'

'Please do.'

He fit himself into his own crenel and looked out over the horizon. 'Funny old life, isn't it?'

'Yeah.' She sighed, wistful. 'Sometimes, I have no idea what to do with it.'

'What do you mean?'

'Money. Security. Luxury. I don't know what to do with it. I feel kind of lost with it.'

'Why?'

'Like take this club. Do you know that it's owned by the son of a famous communist? And we're here popping thousand-dollar bottles of champagne? Once, I would have balked at that, or laughed at it, or *something* other than drunk it.' She caught the look on Davide's face and covered her own with her hands. 'Ugh, I'm totally ruining the vibe.'

'No, you're not, but you're allowed to have fun, Lena.'

'With thousand-dollar bottles of champagne?'

'Oh, come on. We're just letting off steam.'

'I know. I just thought this would all feel . . .' She lifted a shoulder. 'Better.'

Davide studied her. 'You're not happy?'

'No, I *am* happy. I've never been happier. I just feel a little adrift.' She looped into pensive silence. They were both quiet and watched the lights wink in the distance. After a while, a soft smile curled on her lips. 'I think I know how to fix it though.' Her smile grew wide. 'I've always known.'

'What's that?'

'I need to show my play, Davide. On stage, even if it's for one night only. The actors were already cast. They already know the script. It's up to me to just get it done. I can't . . .' She gestured towards the party. 'I can't just do *this* all my life.'

'I think that's a good idea.' Davide smiled warmly. 'Have you told Nico?'

'No, but I will – on another night when things aren't so crazy.'

'For what it's worth, Lena, I hope he makes you happy. Because you deserve it.'

'Thank you, Davide.' She hugged him, quick and fierce, then pointed towards the party. 'I better . . .'

'Yeah. Go,' he said.

Lena turned and headed back, brimming with fresh energy.

Chapter 18

Lena sat in the darkened theatre. The stage lights revealed a girl standing in a hospital waiting room. She picked up a deflated football from the motley collection of toys and tried to kick it along the corridor. Her shoulders sagged when it barely moved two feet.

'They're all going to blame me, Dad. But it's not my fault.' She turned to the man behind her. 'It's yours.'

He replied in Sylheti, a language that Lena knew the audience wouldn't understand.

The girl continued. 'You think it's just a game, but it's the *final*, Dad. My team needs me.'

The man smiled sweetly, unable to understand his daughter. She spoke soulfully and tried to express her frustration at being asked to be the adult.

Lena looked around to gauge the reaction of the audience. After that night in Abu Dhabi, she had been gripped by a sort of fever. She had asked the two actors originally cast as father and daughter if they would be interested in putting on *Please Understand* for one night only. The actors had already learnt the script and eagerly agreed. Everything else – the set design, makeup, styling – had to be done on a budget. Nico had offered to fund it but Lena had declined. She wanted to do something for herself and had used up her meagre savings to hire a small community theatre for the evening. The Aston had been an option, but Lena wanted a fresh start.

On stage, the scene changed to the one where bailiffs turn up at Hana's door. Lena saw herself in the girl. Her childhood had been so limited and she wished she could tell her younger self that it would all be okay; that one day, she would be putting on a show in LA; that she would be dating one of the most successful men on earth; that she would have a wonderful group of friends who had come out to support her. Brianna, Ahmed and Gloria were here. Even the writers from Paramount had come. Johanna was on a shoot but promised to come to a future show 'come hell or haute couture'. Jerry and a few of her colleagues from Palgrave had made the trip as well. Lena was touched that so many of them had come, and just a few days from Christmas too.

When the lights went out, the small space lit up with applause. A few people stood up and the actors thanked them with a gracious bow. A few more followed suit, and then a few more. Lena looked around and flushed with pride. Still, people continued to stand and before she could process what was happening, Lena had her very first standing ovation. She choked up, brimming with warmth and gratitude. The show was something she was truly, genuinely proud of. She had pulled this off, if nothing else in the world. If her career went nowhere, she would know that she *did* something here; she changed a part of LA if only for one night. It wasn't as indelible as a star on the Walk of Fame but she had done a tiny piece of work that she could forever be proud of. She wished that Nico was there to share it, but Theo Witte had commandeered him to wine and dine Mercedes executives at the Beverly Wilshire.

'Lena!' Ahmed crowded her with a hug and handed her a glass of cheap Prosecco – all they could afford on her budget.

'You did it!' said Gloria. Lena saw tears in her eyes.

Brianna joined them too and squeezed Lena's hand. 'It was a triumph,' she said.

Lena choked back her surprise. To Brianna, praise was sacred and, unlike others in theatre, she was careful and sincere with it. 'Oh, Brianna. You don't know how much that means.'

'We have to bring it to the Aston like we planned originally.' Brianna cast a quick glance around the audience. 'Presuming your driver would be okay with that?'

Lena hesitated. When Nico had first donated to the Aston, she had rippled with pride, but now she wished that he had never got involved. She wanted something separate from him and the fact that he owned the building made her wary of working there even though she loved it. 'Thank you,' she said, 'but I think it would get complicated.'

Brianna understood. 'Okay, but if you change your mind, we would love to have you.'

Lena thanked her warmly. Over the next hour, she mingled with the crowd, accepting praise with grace. *So this is what it feels like*, she thought. She wanted to hold on to it, this moment of pure, uncomplicated happiness. She hoped there would be many more but she also knew that, in LA, nothing was guaranteed.

When the crowd thinned out, Ahmed caught her eye from across the room. He pointed at his watch and mimed ten minutes. Lena winced and cut a path towards him. She had promised to join him at a mutual friend's Christmas party, but was talked-out for the evening.

'Oh no. You're bailing, aren't you?' he said, reading her expression.

'I'm so sorry. I'm totally beat.'

'But you promised we'd celebrate tonight!' He pulled a face. 'I'm not saying that warm Prosecco in this tiny hall isn't rock 'n' roll, but you deserve a proper night out – and this way we do it on my friend's buck.'

'I'm sorry.' Lena grimaced. 'You'll know other people there, won't you?'

'Yeah, but that's not the point. This should be a night you'll remember.'

'I will remember this one.' She kissed his cheek. 'Forever.'

His pout thawed into a smile. 'Okay, fine.' He gave her another hug. 'You were brilliant and I love you.'

'I love you.' She squeezed him back, then said goodbye to her final few guests.

Out on the street, it was one of those nights when she wished this city was walkable. She felt wired and wanted some time to unwind. Maybe at home she could open a bottle of wine and take it to the garden. Tomorrow, she would chart her next steps. She spotted her Uber and darted across the street to meet it.

'Good night, miss?' said the driver, Dieter.

'Yes, very good.' Her smile was wistful. 'Actually one of the best.'

He grinned at her in the rearview mirror. 'Those are hard to come by.'

'They are, Dieter,' she said. 'They really are.'

They fell into companionable silence as they drove across LA, snaking along the large, wide roads towards Beverly Hills. Dieter put on some music: *Tracy Chapman*, one of Lena's favourite albums. The mournful tones of 'Baby Can I Hold You' filled the car and Lena closed her eyes and listened. By the time they approached the tall row of mansions, she was dozing off.

Dieter parked outside a tall iron gate. 'Do you want me to ring the buzzer, ma'am?'

'Oh, no, it's okay. I'll just walk through.' She had forgotten her fob and there was no one to let them in. Eliot was away and Nico would still be out with Theo. She had warned him that she would stay out late tonight and knew he was likely to do the same.

She bid Dieter goodnight, unlocked the pedestrian gate and walked up the gravel path, breathing in the night air. There was wisteria in it and she noted how different it was to Venice Beach where the air was twitchy with salt. She liked it here in Beverly Hills. Unlike Crushes, which sometimes felt desolate, this was cosy and pretty. She could be content here. Perhaps she would convert the loft into a study-cum-library and, there, she would write with a view. The thought filled her with warmth and she let herself revel in it as she walked into the hall. She dropped her bag on the sideboard, hung up her keys and kicked off her shoes. A glass of wine in the garden was the perfect way to end the evening. She walked down the hall and yelped in fright when she saw the figure in the living room.

'Jesus!' she cried in surprise. 'What are you doing here?'

The figure froze.

'At least have another glass before you run off,' said Nico as he walked into the room with two glasses of wine. That's when he spotted Lena in the doorway. He froze, his right arm still extended in the air. He was in a dressing gown and his wet hair matched his guest's. Lena looked from one to the other and time itself seemed to slow. Every sound in the house magnified: the shallow tick of the clock, the rustle of leaves on the window.

'Johanna?' said Lena dumbly.

Johanna was ashen, her eyes large and bug-like. A gummy sound rose in her throat and, then, she sprang into action. She snatched up her bag and slung it over her shoulder. 'My Uber's here,' she said and literally ran from the room. The front door slammed and her footsteps faded on the gravel.

Lena stared at Nico and the room swung around her, folding in on itself like Ariadne's Parisian street. 'Johanna?' Her voice was soft and hollow. '*Johanna?*'

'Lena—'

She launched across the room and barrelled into him, sending glass crashing into marble. The shards skittered everywhere, raining around her stockinged feet. She slapped him as hard as she could, losing grip on everything she valued: her empathy, her logic, her self-control. 'Johanna!' The word was in a register that Lena didn't recognise: long and shrill like a banshee's. She moved to strike him again and, this time, he caught her wrist.

'Lena, calm down.'

She tried to yank it free, then smacked her other hand into his shoulder, making him wince. He caught her free hand and in one deft move, twisted her around so that her back was against his chest. He wrapped his arms around her, pinning hers in place. She writhed wildly to free herself. 'Johanna!?' She thrashed against him, filled with rage and violence. When she failed to free herself, she leaned down and bit his arm. He swore and released her instinctively. She pelted away from him and snatched up a nearby lamp. She lobbed it to the floor and watched it smash to pieces. She wrenched open the sideboard and pulled out the china inside it, smashing it against the wall.

'Lena, stop!'

She darted out of the living room, onto the base of the stairs. She pulled a painting off the wall and threw it over the banister, watching the gilded frame crack open. Nico came after her and she ran up to the landing. That's when she saw it: a large silver elongated urn – the Formula One World Championship trophy. She snatched it up and held it like a weapon between them. Nico reached the landing and raised his palms in a bid to calm her.

'How long?' she demanded.

'Lena, I was in a state.'

'When!?'

'After you left me. After that night in Mazikeen. I was in

a state when you left. That's when I called Stephen Bay; told him to throw you off *The Liminal*. I called my lawyers to cut you off at the Aston. I must have called you a hundred times that day and never got through. That's when I came to your apartment. I was so *angry* at you for making me feel how I felt. I was losing control. I wanted to make you pay. I felt choked by it and I wanted to hurt you. To do the worst damage I could do – and she opened the door instead of you.'

Lena remembered her polite exchange with Johanna that day. To think that she and Nico were fucking soon after made her feel sick. 'How many times since?'

'Lena, I don't—'

She lifted the trophy in threat. 'How many?'

'Five. Maybe six.'

Lena was aghast. She remembered the yellow blazer that was so dear to Johanna – *it's Balmain darling*. Lena had known, she'd *known*, that it wasn't among the clothes that Johanna had let her borrow. Which meant that she had left it here. This wasn't Johanna's first time in their home. Lena folded against the banister. The trophy rolled gently to the floor and came to a rest against a marble column. Nico advanced towards her but Lena backed away.

'Don't you dare. Don't you *fucking* dare.' She gestured outwards. 'Of all the women in the world – *of all the women* – you chose her.'

'It wasn't about her. It was what she meant to you.'

Lena snarled with disbelief. 'Do you *think* that makes me feel better?'

'Lena, you don't understand. Everything maps back to

you and when you left, it scrambled my fucking mind. I was terrified that I'd lost you and the only way I could control that was to hurt you back.'

'And what about the five times you fucked her *after* that?' spat Lena.

Nico hung his head. 'It's like a poison, Lena. One I have to take to kill the greater danger inside me. I was trying to be a better man for you, but everything I tried to subdue – the anger, the ugliness, the violence – was still inside me. The pressure of the track made it worse and I needed a way to deal with it.'

'Why not *talk* to me?'

'Because you thought I was getting better and I didn't want you to see the truth.'

'So you lied to me. On the *proudest* night of my career – and for what? A cheap fuck?' Her voice broke. 'You will never change, Nico. You burn the things you care about and you will *never* change.'

'I will, Lena. I can.'

'How could you do it? How could you lie to me? Tonight of all nights?'

'I didn't lie. I was with Theo all evening but he got called away. I was on my way home when she texted to ask about her blazer. I told her she could pick it up and things escalated. It was just a release.'

'You have Sabine for that! What was it about Johanna that you had to have?'

Nico exhaled. 'It's because she wasn't allowed. It's not poison unless it has the power to harm.'

Lena felt bile in her throat. 'And that's something I can never give you,' she said, finally understanding. 'Despite what we have. Despite the fact that I love you and, god, I still believe that you love me too, I'll never be as thrilling as breaking the rules.'

Nico clenched his fist, his scar now taut and shiny. His entire body was tense with bridled energy – a racehorse under leash. 'Lena, I love you more than anything. Those weeks with you before I came back to the track – that was the happiest time of my life. It was more than I had ever hoped for myself; ever allowed myself to believe I deserved.' Nico's voice trembled. 'It showed me what was possible. I nearly destroyed it – I know that – but I want it back, Lena. I want you. I want *us*. Please don't give that up.'

She turned her gaze to the patch of sky outside the balcony doors. 'Gabe said something when he came to see me. He said, "My brother's not damaged. He's broken. Our father broke him." And I think he's right.' She looked back at Nico. 'You're broken and I can't fix you.'

His features creased with anguish. 'But we didn't have enough time, Lena.'

'I know.' She swallowed hard. 'And now we never will.'

'We will. We can. You just have to decide.'

'No, Nico. It was up to *you* to decide – and you did.'

'Don't do this, Lena. Please.' He clasped his hands together. *'Please.'* When he saw that she was unmoved, he dropped to his knees. 'Do you want me to beg? Then I beg you. I *beg* you, Lena. Please don't leave.'

She shook her head. 'It's over, Nico.' She deftly wiped her tears and began to back away.

'Lena, please.'

She turned and moved towards the stairs.

'Lena!' When she didn't stop, his voice turned hard in desperation. 'If you leave, I will burn everything to the ground, starting with this house.'

Lena was halfway down when she heard the crack. She spun and saw Nico on his feet, next to the marble column. Teeth bared, he punched it with all his might. Lena gasped, stunned into inaction. He punched it again and an ugly crack whipped through the air.

'I won't ever race again, Lena. If that's what will fix us, I'll make it so I can't.' He held out his bloodied hand like a piece of gory evidence. 'I'll destroy it all if it means that I can keep you.' He curled his hand back into a fist.

Lena twisted away, her eyes screwed shut in horror. She heard a wet sound as Nico's skin split further.

'I'll destroy it all,' he repeated, his voice dark with threat.

Lena waited for another crack, still hunched tight. When it didn't come, her senses sparked in alarm. She looked back at Nico and her blood turned to ice.

In his intact hand, he held the silver urn, the Formula One World Champion trophy. He raised it in the air as if testing its weight.

'Nico, don't,' Lena said in a whisper.

His eyes were cold and focused as he lifted the trophy backwards like a pitcher on a baseball field.

'Don't!'

There was a dreadful pause and then he hurled it across the landing. It shot over the banister and smashed into the opposite wall, coming apart on impact. Lena cried out as the pieces ricocheted off and crashed to the floor below with a sickening crunch. Over seventy years of history, gone. Nico had just destroyed the thing he had wanted most.

Lena's lungs closed with shock, making it hard to breathe. Desperate for air, she stumbled away from him and out onto the balcony. There was no reprieve, for Nico followed her out. He reached for her but she pulled away, backing into the balcony wall.

'Lena, please don't leave.'

She saw his scar, now streaked with blood, and started to weep openly. All the fight had left her and she was raw with heartbreak. He reached for her again and, this time, she caved into his chest, spineless with grief – for him, for her, for what they almost were.

'I need you, Lena.' He kissed her hair. 'I'm always going to need you. Not having you makes me crazy.' He wrapped his unhurt fist in her hair and gently tugged it back. He kissed her and she sensed the aggression moving through him. She tried to draw back but he held her in place. 'I need you.'

She pulled away but he held her wrist and dug his thumb into her flesh.

'I need you,' he repeated, kissing her neck. 'And you need me too.'

'Nico, stop it.' Lena tried to push him away, but he restrained her with ease.

He pinned her against the balcony wall and when he pressed against her, she felt that he was hard. She struggled to free her hands, but he held them fast and vicelike.

'Stop it, Nico.' She twisted in his grip to free herself. 'Stop it!' But Nico wasn't listening. He pulled at her dress. Lena freed a hand but her blows to his body were like skittles off a train. He yanked her dress down, exposing her breasts, and rubbed his thumb over her nipple. Lena felt her body respond and was disgusted by it. He closed his mouth on her and licked her nipple with his warm, wet tongue. Lena cried out, hot with fury that he could still make her feel like this. He traced a path down her chest, then dropped to his knees beneath her. He pulled aside her underwear and put his tongue there. He flicked her clit, making her press into him. He pushed his tongue inside her and she bucked with pleasure. As the last piece of resistance left her, she understood with a sharp and final clarity what she needed to do.

She tensed with resolve. And, then, she began to fight. She slapped him hard, catching the side of his head.

'Stop that,' he growled, but she slapped him again. He sprang to his feet and grabbed her wrists. 'Stop that,' he repeated. She tried to shove him, but he tightened his grip and easily held her in place. When she tried to fight, he thrust her up onto the balcony wall, just like the first time they met. He tilted her backwards and she grabbed at him, crying out in fear. 'Tell me you don't want it, Lena.' His breath was hot on her neck. 'Just say the word.' His breath was fast and shallow, on the cusp of losing control. 'Say the word,' he told her.

When she said nothing, he let himself go. He held her with one arm and unzipped himself with the other. He pulled up her dress and, knowing how much she loved this, rubbed his cock against her without pushing in. She moaned, loud and delirious, keying him up, turning him on, needing him at the right heat. She writhed against him, slick and wet, making that sound he loved so much. Quietly, she looked for it: the moment he bit his lower lip that signalled he was about to push his way in. She waited, waited, and, there, he sank his teeth into his lip. Lena arched backwards and locked eyes with him.

Then, firm and clear, she said, 'Red.'

Something flashed briefly across his face – confusion, a groping for meaning – but it gave way to sensation and he was lost in its grip. He pushed his way into her and as he thrust inside, Lena cried out – a strange, shrill sound that was a cry of victory but also a howl of horror for she was finally free of him, but at such a stark cost to her body.

Nico held her and fucked her until he came with a roar, folding into her body as the adrenaline left his own. When he let her go, Lena slid to the ground in a twisted reflection of the first time they met. Her tears were silent – despairing instead of angry – and she saw, she *saw*, the moment he realised. He understood what she had said and realised that he had carried on. His face was blank with shock and he dropped to his knees next to her. He shook his head no.

'Lena.' He reached out but didn't touch her, his hands moving from her hair to her cheek to her shoulder, too scared to make actual contact. 'Lena . . .' But nothing else came out because he knew what she had said, *knew* that she had looked him in the eye when she'd said it. 'No,' he said. '*No.*'

Lena's face crumpled, her sobs soft and weak.

'No.' Nico buried his face in his hands and, then, he broke

down. He wept and his whole body shook with disgust and grief. They both now understood that it had been theoretical: Nico pushing her beyond her limits under the illusion of control. When it mattered, it hadn't mattered at all. In that revelation, Lena was finally free.

For a long while, she listened to him cry. Then, she picked herself up. Gently, she stepped over him and left without a sound.

Chapter 19

The lone figure sat in the inky darkness on the concrete steps. A streetlamp cast a pool of light onto the neighbouring spot as if in wait of company. The writer in Lena noticed that it looked like the opening scene of a play. She approached tentatively.

'What are you doing here?' she said, noting how a mere two months had turned them into strangers.

Johanna shivered in the breeze, not built for February. She was thinner than usual, and ghostly. 'Can we talk?'

Lena squeezed the cold metal key in her hand. The sensible thing would be to step around Johanna and walk into the building that they had once shared. But Lena needed closure – something Johanna had denied her. After that fateful night, Lena had texted her and Johanna had responded by changing her number. Lena had felt rage, then disbelief, and finally a cynical insistence that she didn't care – but the truth was that she couldn't move on, couldn't understand how someone she had trusted so wholly could behave so callously. And now here she was, on Lena's doorstep, finally ready to talk.

Lena dropped onto the step beside her, lit by a halo of light. 'I texted you.'

'I know. I was a coward. I'm sorry.'

They sat in silence for a minute. 'Tell me how it happened, Jo.'

Johanna traced a rip in her jeans. 'It just happened. It was almost like autopilot. Like I couldn't help it. And I know that sounds weak. I'm to blame and I will never deny that, but it's like I lost my mind.'

'Tell me how it happened. That first time.'

'You don't want to hear it.'

'I don't want details. I just want to understand how it could have happened.'

Johanna dug her fingers into the rip. 'He came looking for you that day, after you had left for Paramount. He was convinced that you were home and that I wasn't letting him in to see you. He forced his way in and went to your bedroom. When he didn't find you, he went into mine. He was furious and I didn't understand why. You hadn't said anything, so I asked him what had happened. He told me that you'd left him and that he wasn't going to let you go. He was *so* angry. He punched the wall and when I tried to calm him, it was like . . . touching a livewire.'

Lena pictured the two of them together: all of Nico's energy focused on Johanna. Hurt seared inside her. 'You knew how much I liked him.' She pressed her lips together, determined not to give this yet more of her tears.

Johanna's own eyes were glassy. 'What I did was unforgivable. Despicable.' She swatted at her tears. 'And I want to say I'm sorry, Lena. I am so, so sorry.'

'How many times?'

'I don't know.'

'Then *count*.'

Johanna hung her head. 'Six. Mainly while you were broken up.'

'Oh, that makes it okay then,' Lena jibed. 'How many times in the house?'

'Twice.'

'The night I found you both. Were you really on a shoot?'

'Yes, I swear to god, Lena. I have the call sheet if you don't believe me. I needed my jacket and I didn't want to ask you in case you realised that I'd left it there. I texted Nico and he said I could pick it up. When I got there, he'd just got home. He was drunk and in a good mood and it just happened. I am so, so sorry.'

Lena hunched her shoulders against the breeze. 'Why are you here now? After all these weeks?'

Johanna ducked guiltily. 'I saw on Instagram that your play is opening tomorrow. I don't know why but I needed to see you.' She kneaded one hand with the other. 'I wondered if maybe it would be okay if I came to the opening.'

Lena shook her head mildly. 'No, Johanna, it would not.'

'We've been through so much together. Please, Lena, don't throw it all away.'

'I didn't do that, Johanna.' She didn't need to add the subtext. *You did*.

'Do you think you'll ever feel differently?'

Lena looked at the stars. 'I'm never going to forgive you. I don't want to carry this around for the rest of my life, but I think I'm going to.'

'Will you try? In time?'

'No. I don't think I will.' They sat in silence for another minute. Then, Lena stood up. 'Bye, Johanna.' She turned and headed into the warmth, letting the door slam shut behind her. She climbed the stairs to the flat that she shared with Kyle, the Venice Beach Channing Tatum. Her mind jangled with thoughts of Johanna and Nico. It was so typical of Johanna to screw with her mind the day before opening night. She couldn't let it rattle her. Tomorrow was the culmination of a year of work. *Please Understand* finally had a run at the Aston. In December, they had almost lost the theatre after Nico put it up for sale at auction. Thankfully, an unnamed arts patron beat Keller Stone to the sale and secured the Aston's future. Brianna had tried to find out the source. She suspected William McGregor, but the charity would neither confirm nor deny. Either way, it meant that they were free to finally put on a run of *Please Understand*. Apart from the auction, Lena had heard nothing of Nico. That's how she understood that he hadn't sold the Aston to punish her. He wasn't destroying what she loved. This was his way of letting her go. Of freeing her from the last vestige of his hold.

*

The air smelled of sawdust and bergamot, and as Lena breathed it in, she felt a sense of total peace. This stage, this place, is where her play was meant to be. Unlike her one-night show, which was mainly seen by friends and colleagues, there were actual critics in the Aston's audience. Word of mouth had spread and Lena was skittish with nerves. It was all in the hands of the actors now. Earlier, she had followed them to their dressing rooms and made last-minute changes until Brianna removed the script from her hands.

'That's enough now,' she said gently. Brianna had done this before and Lena had to trust that. Now, watching from the wings, she could feel the crackle of anticipation. The actors had practised and practised, for they were also aware that all it took was one scout, one producer, to spot you on stage and pluck you up for stardom. The script was solid, the rehearsals were thorough and Brianna was an old pro. It would all come together.

The curtains lifted and Hana spoke the first line. 'They're all going to blame me, Dad. But it's not my fault. It's yours.'

The audience watched as Hana expressed her frustration. Later, they laughed heartily as she taught her dad a TikTok dance. Then came the scene with the bailiffs. Lena watched the audience fall in love with Hana and – by proxy – herself, the writer. In the last scene, the dad came to rescue when Hana forgot her football boots. The two of them shared a fierce hug and ran off to the final.

When the curtains came down, the audience didn't make a sound. Lena was terrified that she had botched the ending; made it sentimental, far too saccharine. Panicked, she looked around the room. A woman in the front row swiped at her eyes. Next to her, her husband groped for tissue. Lena realised that people were reacting, only not yet audibly.

Then, the applause started. A couple in the front row stood and others followed suit. In groups of two and three, the audience rose to its feet and gave the actors a standing ovation. Lena choked back tears of relief. The actors bowed, but the applause didn't dissipate. Lena watched with a sense of joy that was rare and absolute. This is where she was meant to be. Ahmed appeared next to her and clung to her arm. They both laughed and cried at the same time. Gloria joined them too and they shared a jubilant hug.

'I should find Brianna!' said Lena over the applause. She went in search of their director. Outside in the corridor, people were discussing the play. Lena eavesdropped, collecting nuggets of praise and putting them in storage for difficult days.

The corridor filled with people and she had trouble steering through. As she squeezed past an older couple, she felt a tap on the shoulder. She turned and jolted with surprise.

'Oh my god, hi!'

'Hi,' said Davide, his smile on full beam.

Lena mirrored it instantly. It was impossible not to. 'I didn't know you were coming!'

'I snuck in last minute.' His smile dimmed. 'Lena, the play was . . .' He exhaled sharply, visibly emotional. 'My family is Italian and when we moved to Australia, I was basically that kid on stage; dealing with tax and housing and all of that shit.' He rubbed his stubble. 'It hit me hard, that did.'

'Oh, Davide, thank you.' She gave him a grateful hug.

He motioned over his shoulder. 'My mate's waiting so I've got to go, but I wanted to say hi. I'm so glad you got to show it here, Lena.'

'Thank you,' she said, beaming. But something in his

words struck her as odd. 'Wait, why are you glad I got to show it *here*?'

'Because I know it was in trouble.'

'How?'

'I don't know. I just heard.'

She frowned. 'Davide, you're not our anonymous patron, are you?'

He angled his head in askance. 'No,' he said, but it sounded like a question.

'You're sure?'

'Yeah, sorry. But now I kinda wish I was.'

She laughed. 'Okay, never mind.' She thanked him for coming and waved him off to his friend. Davide moved out of her field of vision and, with a stab of recognition, she saw the man behind him. She caught the look on his face and the pieces fell into place.

'You,' she said with awe. '*You* bought the Aston?'

Eliot nodded graciously.

'But how? Eliot, that was so much money.'

'Mr Laurent pays me handsomely.'

The mention of his name made something spark inside her. She searched the crowd and felt a sense of vertigo.

'It's okay,' said Eliot. 'He's not here.'

The drumbeat of her heart slowed. 'Does he know that you bought the theatre?'

'No.'

'But Eliot, why would you do this for us?'

He guided her to a quieter spot. 'I've seen your work, Lena. You're talented and you deserve this.'

Lena cleared the choke in her throat. 'Thank you, Eliot. For everything.' She paused, then quietly asked, 'How is he?'

Eliot's face was full of regret. 'He's . . . We're getting him some help.'

'Therapy?'

'Yes.'

'He'll be okay?'

Eliot considered this for a long moment. 'Yes. He will be.'

Lena laughed – a short, sharp sound that was less mirth than relief. 'Thank you, Eliot.' She threw her arms around him. At first, he was unyielding but then he closed his arms around her too.

'You take care, Ms Aden.'

'And you, Eliot. Of both of you.'

'I shall, Ms Aden. I promise you.'

They separated and Eliot smoothed his tie. He nodded once, then turned and walked out with the last of the audience. The cast and crew were backstage and she could hear the occasional shout or cheer rise from the celebrations. Lena wandered back inside the theatre, which hummed with the heat of recent activity. She walked onto the stage and looked out at the empty stalls. It didn't matter if she never got any press, or if the run didn't last. She had made a mark on the people who saw her work tonight and that meant something to her. She didn't need private jets, exclusive parties, or sparkling bottles of Dom Pérignon. The kernel of truth she saw here, the emotion and affection, that was enough for her. She sat on the edge of the stage and wept tears of joy.

Chapter 20

Lena zipped her laptop into its case and packed up for the day. It was Sunday afternoon and everyone else had left the theatre. She flicked off the lights and paused by a framed clipping hung by the door. It was the review of *Please Understand* that had run in the *New York Times* the week after opening night. 'A revelatory portrait of a young language broker', read the headline. Underneath, the sub-heading read, 'The season's most moving play deserves a place among the behemoths of Broadway'. In the three months since, the Aston had sold out every night. Lena had stopped worrying about paying her rent. Gloria had quit her job as a cleaner and Brianna and Ahmed had started a free class for underrepresented actors. They were small gains but profound in their own way. Lena had also got some press, most notably a half-page profile in April's *Vanity Fair*. It had amused her greatly to come upon a quote from her 'former mentor' Paula Gillard: 'I was fortunate enough to spot Lena's talent early and harness it at Paramount. I'm delighted that she has been able to use her experience here to achieve even greater success.'

Lena locked the theatre door and set off towards home.

Rare rain had washed the city clean. The street smelled of sun and sugar and Lena felt a sense of peace. As she passed the second-hand electronics store, its bank of TVs caught her eye. She paused for a moment to watch. Three men stood on a podium, their caps off in a sign of respect for the national anthem – Nico, Greg and Vossen. Lena studied Nico's face and all she saw was glory. He had just won the Miami Grand Prix. He shook a bottle of champagne and poured it over his fellow drivers. Lena smiled wistfully. She hoped that he was healthy. She hoped that Eliot and Gabe and Sabine were taking care of him. She hoped that, one day, he too would be at peace. She exhaled and turned towards home.

In her flat, boxes were lined up along one wall. Kyle, her housemate, was leaving LA and going back to Denver. She was in no hurry to replace him. Perhaps she would try living alone for a while. She tossed her keys on the kitchen counter and sorted through a pile of mail, plucking out two envelopes that were addressed to her. The first was from Paramount inviting her to the wrap party of *The Liminal*. She checked the RSVP and set it aside. The second envelope was heavy and cream, and the paper inside was thick with quality. There was no logo or letterhead, just a handwritten note.

Dear Ms Aden, I hope you will forgive this analogue message. I did try to email, but I fear that it got lost. I recently saw Please Understand and was incredibly moved by it. It struck a note that is so rare and difficult: poignant, kind and sensitive but never maudlin. In fact, it was weirdly *gritty. I'm in LA setting up a project that could use a writer like you. Could you drop me a line when you're free? My details are below. I hope we can work together, if not now then soon.*

Lena nearly choked when she saw the name at the bottom. Noah Baumbach. She studied the handwriting, thinking it a trick. Kyle knew how much she loved the director. Was this his idea of a parting joke? But, no, at the bottom of the letter was the watermark of Noah's production company. Lena was stunned. Her favourite director had come to see her play; had deigned to write her a letter when his email went astray. This was it. This was the letter she'd been waiting for, for six long years. She perched on the windowsill and read it again. It was Sunday, so she surely couldn't call him now? It's okay, she told herself. After so many years, what was one more day?

She drew her knees to her chest and looked out at the horizon. The sun was low now and inked the sky like wildfire. She felt a swell of affection for this crazy little town. *Home*, she thought wistfully. This crazy little town called home.

Acknowledgements

This book is dedicated to Jackie Collins, the grand dame of romance, because she changed a small but significant part of my life. Like Lena in this novel, I had a conservative upbringing which sought to instil in me a sense of shame around sex and desire. Jackie's novels dramatically changed my perspective. Her strong, sexy protagonists are different to mine but they taught me that female desire deserves to be indulged. For that, I owe her so much. Thank you for the good times, Jackie. Wherever you are, I hope you're giving them hell.

Thank you to my own trio of superwomen: Jessica Faust, Manpreet Grewal and Lisa Milton. Without you, I would not have a career. I am grateful for it, and you, every day. I know that *RUSH* was a curveball, but you caught it elegantly and played on. Thank you for believing in me and my work.

Thank you to everyone at HQ and HarperCollins who has helped make *RUSH* the best book it can be and who has worked so tirelessly to bring it to readers. So many of you work behind the scenes and I hope you know how much your authors appreciate you.

A special thank you to Peter Borcsok and the team at

HarperCollins Canada who have come out to bat for me. I hope to see you in Toronto soon.

Thank you, Fatema Akhund, Jawed Karim, Jerome Monnot and Peter Watson, for helping me with the details, be they letterboxes in LA buildings or the F1 circuit in Miami. There are some details I've made up, but I hope you will look beyond them and have fun with the story.

Thank you, Michael Schumacher, for some of the finest racing I have ever seen. Keep fighting.

Thank you, Lewis Hamilton, for changing the face of Formula One. I'll be #TeamLH for life.

Finally, thank you, dear reader, for picking up a copy of *RUSH*. If I can do for even one of you what Jackie did for me, then I will have succeeded. Go forth and have fun.